CODE OF SILENCE

By Doreen Martin

Co-author, Emma Dureski-Snyder

ISBN: 1467982393
ISBN-13: 978-1467982399

ACKNOWLEDGMENTS

Thank you to people who helped me a lot; I would like to mention:

Sandra, my daughter, for her continuous encouragement and help. To Bill her husband for getting Emma involved. Emma for being always cheerful and helpful. What a wonderful co-author, believing in my book, guiding and editing.

Wayne Martin dug out his best dictionary and never complained about the messy, littered kitchen table that served as my desk and our place of dining.

My brother Norman for his continuous help and belief I would succeed. He always had words of encouragement.

Thank you to Emily Stone for her beautiful cover art.

Thank you to Brenda Bender for her words of encouragement and to Jean, Gwen, Marjorie, Joan, Alice and Tilly. Many thanks for your encouragement.

Many thanks to my dearest friend Shirley who has passed on. Shirley gave me note books, always asking about my progress. Her frequent well remembered words: "Have you started?"

.

Dorie is a young girl growing up in a small town on the Canadian prairies. From childhood she faced struggles with friends and family, but with the love and the values that she was surrounded with, nothing was too hard to overcome. Whether it's the popular girl at school or her brother being injured in an accident, Dorie had the support and was surrounded by everything she needed to become a wonderful and successful woman.

The friends that she made and the perseverance she showed strengthened her skills in school and in life as she moved through grade school and directed her attention to her post secondary education regardless of what was happening around her.

As she grew, the values that she experienced as a young girl still stayed strong within her and she decided that she would like nothing more than to save up and take her biggest inspiration and role model on a trip. . . one that he could never have done without her help.

CHAPTER ONE

"Daddy, Daddy! They're coming! I see the horse and wagon!" A slight man with salt and pepper hair came and stood beside his tiny five year old daughter. Although the girl seemed pleased about this arrival, this would place another burden on his family's shoulders Paul was hard pressed to agree. Paul knew that the arrival of his father would affect each of his family in a different way.

Annie, his wife, would have lots of extra bedding to wash plus she would have to bed bath the man each day. Alex would have to help more in small ways like feeding grandpa and helping his mom hang clothes on the line. Alex and Garth had to give up their bedroom and bed. The boys now would have to sleep on mattresses on the living room floor. Dorie would continue to sleep on her cot in the living room. Dorie, dear Dorie would have to stay in the house during the day to watch Grandpa and her three year old brother, Garth. Dorie previously had helped her parents plant seeds and keep an eye on Garth.

It wasn't all bad. Paul was thankful that at least his dad was gentle, kind and would obey. He knew his father would listen to Dorie, but he also knew there was a possibility his father might sneak out of the house and run off into the woods. Dorie would have to keep a careful eye on Grandpa.

Annie had cleaned and reorganized the second small bedroom for the ninety year old man that was coming. Paul had attached a fold down guard to the old bed. The bed guard consisted of a wide wooden plank that was clamped to the bottom and top bedposts. Hopefully the old man wouldn't fall out of bed as he had been doing at the house he was coming from.

Besides preparing the room Annie had to get ready in other ways for this eventful day. Bedding, warm clothes, shoes and slippers were needed by the old gentleman. It was a hardship to buy these necessary items for her family let alone for another individual who had no wardrobe. Both Annie and Paul worried a great deal about all the new items they needed to buy for Paul's father.

The worry that had been building earlier that morning had been lifted a little when several of Annie's neighbors visited, carrying boxes of linen: sheets, pillows, pillowcases, towels, two soft woolen blankets, a robe and two flannel shirts. Also in a separate box was shampoo, several bars of soap, nail clippers and a pair of small, sharp scissors. Annie was speechless for a few seconds before bursting into tears. How wonderful and thoughtful her neighbors were! The golden door had opened, Annie's prayers were answered. People opened their hearts in a caring and loving way. Annie was very grateful and after a cup of tea and hugs for her neighbors, they departed also feeling a warm glow.

Grandpa, carrying a bible and wearing old clothes complete with a pair of socks full of holes was lead into the house by Paul. The three children stood to one side staring at the old man whom they had never met. This was their grandfather! Annie watched as Paul's dad was lead into the kitchen, turning her head to shed tears unnoticed. Here was an old unkempt man who needed lots of care and love. He was also nearly blind and fairly confused. Paul and Annie would let grandpa rest and give him some nourishment before they began to clean him up a bit.

After a long rest grandpa was gotten up, given a sandwich and tea while Paul visited with him. Once he was finished, they would wash and cut grandpa's hair. Rinsing the old man's hair would be a challenge. How could they rinse the hair properly? Grandpa's upper back and neck were stiff, he seemed in pain when his head was tilted to either side. Finally after some thought Paul said "I've got the answer! We'll place grandpa on the bed with his feet facing the headboard, after I remove the board off the bottom of the bed. Annie, I'll hold and support dad's head over the end of the mattress while you wash and rinse his hair. Do you have lots of warm water?"

His wife smiled at him, traces of her previous tears nowhere in sight. "Yes Paul, I have a large pail full and a big pitcher full that I will use for washing and rinsing his hair." Before placing his dad on the bed, Paul explained to his dad, in simple sentences what was to occur. Grandpa seemed to understand what was going on, which helped render this method a success.

After being brought back to a chair with a towel carefully wrapped around his head, Annie soaked grandpa's feet in warm, soapy water while she cut the old man's hair. It was much too long for a man his age. After she had finished, Paul cleaned and trimmed his dad's beard, then dried the old man's feet well before cutting the long nails with Annie's sewing scissors. Finally Paul applied butter to the cracked, crusty feet. The butter would keep the feet moist and soften the skin. Alex arrived in the room looking embarrassed, shuffling his feet, holding his favorite pair of soft blue woolen socks. After a small pause Alex said "I brought my socks to put on grandpa's feet."

Paul looked shocked. "Alex your socks will get grease stains on them from the butter!"

Alex nodded, continuing to hold them out. "That's OK dad." 'How wonderful of Alex to reach out and contribute to his grandfather's care.' Annie thought. It was unusual for Alex to reach out to anyone. Perhaps grandpa's coming to live with them would be good for the family.

It was time for supper. Grandpa smiled and looked happy. Alex fed his grandfather some soup, shepherds pie and a large piece of chocolate cake. Dorie had the family in laughter at the silly joke Rita had told her earlier that week. "What did one ear say to the other ear? We're on the same block!" Paul looked at his father who was now sound asleep. Alex helped his dad put grandpa to bed.

The morning arrived and Paul helped Annie give grandpa a bed bath and dress him in some of Alex's clothes, since the old man was small enough to wear them. Alex, although unhappy about it, agreed to let grandpa wear his slippers for two days. Annie knew she had to get slacks, shoes and slippers for the older man. She would have Paul take her into Purplehaven to purchase the necessary items Paul's dad needed. Grandpa didn't come with any clothes except for the ones that he had worn there.

A knock on the door was heard, and Dorie ran to answer. Their neighbor Jean appeared in the doorway with a large armful of clothes and a bag filled with two pairs of shoes, one pair of rain boots and one pair of slippers. Jean knew of Annie's plight and wanted to ease the stress and worry Annie faced. Dorie called for her mother when she saw who it was, and soon she arrived at the door as well. "Oh Jean! That's exactly what we need, shoes and slippers."

"Let's see if they fit grandpa's feet." Annie rushed toward Jean, giving her a huge hug saying "Thank you Jean, you're so thoughtful, your family has helped our family in so many ways lately. We are very grateful. Are you sure you can part with all those clothes and shoes?"

The woman smiled at the response of her friend, and nodded. "Annie, Harry's closet was jammed full and certainly needed cleaning. Otherwise he wouldn't be able to buy new clothes. My motto is, no room, no new things."

Paul led grandpa out to the kitchen, hoping to see who was at the door. After a questioning glance the two women explained "Let's try the shoes on grandpa."

After grandpa was seated and introduced to Jean he was asked if Annie could try a pair of shoes on his feet. The old man nodded and smiled, he seemed pleased, certainly happy about being the center of attention. As the shoes were tried on, the people in the room became very quiet. Would the shoes fit or would the shoes not fit? Then Annie was heard saying "The shoes fit. Harry's shoes fit." The tiny room erupted with cheers, even the old man clapped his hands.

Annie sat down thinking with all the help they received it wouldn't cost a lot to keep grandpa, and her view of the future brightened. Dorie and Garth climbed on grandpa's lap giving him hugs and kisses, they too were caught up in the joy that filled the tiny room.

After breakfast grandpa had his hands soaked in warm, soapy water. One basin was placed on each side of him. Dorie and Garth watched that Grandpa kept his hands in the water. Annie dried the hands after a lengthy soak and cut the long curved nails. Grandpa was very pleased about having his nails cut, every once and a while saying "Nice, nice." And rubbing his hands together.

Next day, Dorie stayed indoors with her Grandfather and Garth. At noon, Paul and Annie came home for lunch. After lunch, Paul took his father to the outdoor toilet, then placed Grandpa on his bed. Garth would have a nap on Dorie's cot. Dorie would watch and listen and when the clock showed two o'clock as her father had showed her, she would wake Garth and Grandpa. The time went by slowly, but Dorie stuck to it until finally the hands were where she had been shown.

After Grandpa was awake, Dorie would put his slippers on, let the guard rail down and lead Grandpa to a rocking chair. Dorie would then get Grandpa a glass of homemade juice.

One afternoon after Dorie had put Grandpa in his chair, Garth started to loudly cry, calling for his sister. "I have a stomach ache Dorie! It really hurts! Please get Mommy!"

Dorie went and sat beside Garth, rubbing his stomach and putting her other arm around Garth. While Dorie was busy quieting Garth, Grandpa quietly got out of his chair, walked to the kitchen, and came back into the living room carrying the old aluminum coffee pot. Grandpa hesitated a short while, then went in the direction of Annie's sewing machine. With a bizarre look on his face, he felt around the machine, finding and lifting the lid of it to reveal the machinery inside. Without a pause, the old man poured coffee and coffee grounds into the inner part of the machine. Dorie looked up at the sound and dashed across the room but was too late to stop the weird happening. "The fire is out now. You children are safe." Grandpa told Dorie with a smile.

Panic settled in while Dorie mopped up the liquid and cleaned most of the coffee grounds up with old rags. That was all she could do, and now she could only wait with fear in her heart.

"Oh please Dad, come home at the same time as Mom!" Dorie cried into her hands. Dorie cast another look at the sewing machine, sat down in front of it and cried. "Oh Mommy, please don't be very angry!"

There were footsteps but no voices. Only Annie was coming then. The door opened and she walked in. Dorie stood up, still crying and stuttering "Grandpa was in the chair Mom, I didn't see him get up, I, Mom, I, I..." Dorie's voice faded off. With tears rolling down her cheeks, Dorie took a few breaths and was finally able to continue her account of the strange happening. "Mom, Grandpa poured coffee into the sewing machine while I was looking after Garth. Grandpa got out of the chair by himself, went to the kitchen, came back with the coffee pot and poured the coffee into your sewing machine! Mom, Garth was crying, he had a stomach ache so I sat beside him and rubbed his tummy. When I looked up I saw grandpa pouring coffee into your machine, I ran across the room but was to late to stop him. I'm sorry mom."

There was a silence before Annie said "Come here Dorie." Dorie slowly made her way over, but when Annie suddenly turned and reached for Dorie, causing her to jump back with a startled look. Her mother's face gained a sadness to it as she spoke "Don't be frightened. Oh child you seem frightened, perhaps I expect too much and am too hard on you. You do so much for us at such a young age. I really don't know how we would manage without your help. I do appreciate what you do and feel I expect to much of you, Dorie, I think of you as older then you are." Annie moved toward her daughter then pulled Dorie into a hug.

There was a pause as Dorie's small arms returned the gesture saying "Mom is this the first hug you have ever given me?"

"I should be giving you more hugs. Please don't blame yourself for what happened. You must be watching and doing things properly as this is the first bad thing to happen since grandpa came to live in our home. You have done a wondrous job."

"Thank you Mom" Dorie whispered as she walked away. Her mother watched her turn away, and felt a sinking feeling hit the pit of her stomach. She was never able to bond as well with Dorie. Her heart ached and at times she felt great grief that she didn't, couldn't love Dorie as she loved her sons. She felt that her daughter was distant, secretive with an uncanny wisdom that was puzzling and frightening at times. At times Annie tried to form a closeness with Dorie but Dorie would falter, as if she didn't trust her mother.

It was mid summer and Annie had told Dorie she would start school this fall. That was not something she really wanted to do, so she would talk to her dad about school, perhaps he would let her stay home.

Annie had gone to pick a pail of beans which she would later can. Dorie and Garth had two pails of peas to shell for canning as well. Garth kept fooling around, but Dorie kept her anger hidden, shelling peas as quickly as she could.

Grandpa had become quieter, didn't walk around as much but he still ate a lot. He loved potatoes, gravy, and fish. Since grandpa had his fingernails cut he managed to feed himself with a spoon, if the food was soft and cut up. When Annie cooked fish, grandpa would have eaten all the fish if Paul didn't tell him the fish was all gone, just so the rest of the family could get some.

During the spring and summer Paul fished in the creek that ran through his land. He would leave early in the morning at times using a net to catch the suckers. After bringing the fish home he would place them in a pail of cold water that he hung part way down the well to keep them cool. Near supper time Paul and Dorie would quickly clean the fish so Annie could cook them.

That evening Dorie asked her father if she could please not go to school this year. Paul sat Dorie down, brushed his fingers through his greying hair and sighed. Dorie asked with curious eyes "Do I really have to go to school?"

The man sighed then spoke "Dorie you know about rules. Your mother and I have set certain rules to be followed by Alex, Garth and you."

"Yes dad I know those. We're not to leave messes behind for others to clean up, we're not to be rude or mean to others, we're to tell the truth, and we're to help you and Mom."

"Very good Dorie, you know *our* rules. The government has a rule for all families, that their children age six to sixteen must attend school. If a family disobeys the government, that family's school age children are removed and placed with family that *will* obey the government's rule. That is the main reason children attend school. You might not realize how fortunate you are to be able to go and learn, you can receive an education, then be able to get a good job, earn lots of money and not be poor and have to work long hours like your mom and dad." Dorie's dad sat in deep thought then said "Tell me Dorie what is troubling you about going to school?"

Dorie responded without hesitation "Dad I don't know anyone at school, I don't have any nice clothes, my shoes have holes in them and it's so far to walk."

"Dorie you certainly will get new shoes and socks. I'll talk to your mother about sewing you a dress, what color would you like?"

Dorie thought for a moment before responding. "Daddy, I'd like a pink flowered dress with a big bow in the back!"

The slight man hugged his daughter and told her "I bet you'll be the prettiest girl at school." He paused, returning to his previous train of thought. "Dorie this is a good chance to elevate yourself in life: live in a nice house with running water, have nice clothes and travel to other parts of the world. An education is priceless Dorie."

"Dad did you travel?"

"No Dorie there was never any extra money to travel and I didn't have the opportunity to finish school."

Dorie's face fell a little. "But dad you're so smart!"

Her comment earned her a warm chuckle from the older man. "I read a lot when time permits and have managed to teach myself over the years, but Dorie I could never get a good job because I'm not educated."

Dorie bit her lip, an idea slowly forming in her brain. "Dad I'll finish school, get a good job, save money and take you on a trip!" she exclaimed, clapping her hands and dancing about.

"Darling you're such a thoughtful person."

"Dad I'm very afraid but I'll go to school even though I don't have any friends."

"Listen Dorie I'll take you to school on your first day, I'll talk to your teacher, tell her you're shy, and don't know any of the other children very well."

"Oh Daddy thank you! That makes me very happy! I love you so much!"

Two weeks later while Mom and Dad were cutting grass for cattle feed during the winter Dorie was unable to wake Grandpa. She leaned down and spoke right into his ear "Wake up, wake up Grandpa." Grandpa didn't move, open his eyes or smile like he often did. The old man just lay quietly. Dorie's eyes widened and she scrambled backwards, rushing to Garth who she shook awake lightly. "Garth go watch Grandpa! Make sure he doesn't get up if he wakes up! I'll be right back!" With these instructions barely out of her mouth, Dorie started out the door, heading for the hayfield. She ran as fast as she could. Dorie's dad spotted her and stopped the horses, fear gripping him. He felt something terrible must have happened for Dorie to run out to the field leaving Garth and Grandpa behind. Dorie explained to her father that Grandpa wouldn't wake up and Garth was watching him. Dad tied the horses to a post and started home with Annie and Dorie. When they arrived home Annie asked Dorie to take Garth into the kitchen while they went to see Grandpa. Shortly Paul and Annie entered the kitchen with solemn looks. Dad took a deep breath and looked at the three faces staring at him.

"Garth, Dorie your Grandpa has died, the angels came down and took your grandpa's spirit to heaven."

"Daddy what is a spirit?" Garth asked.

Paul answered "the Spirit is life itself given by God to a baby before birth, when a person dies, an Angel takes the spirit to heaven leaving the dead body behind. The family then has a funeral, the bells toll, family and friends give speeches, some of the person's favorite hymns or songs are sung, then the body is buried in the ground. Dorie, Garth you were touched by the angels wings when they came down from heaven, that's the angel's way of telling you they will always watch over you."

Dad went to his special money box, got fifty cents which he gave to Dorie and asked her to run to Jean and Harry's. "Dorie give the fifty cents to Jean and please ask her to go to Purplehaven and have the undertaker come to our home." The words barely made sense to the girl, but she ran through the secret pathway which was hidden from view by shrubbery. Dorie dashed under and between the trees which shielded the pathway from onlookers, then down the hill through thick brush, under a fence and down the lane to Jean and Harry's house.

Rita answered the door. "I need to talk to your mom Rita." Dorie panted, without even offering a 'Hello'. When Jean appeared Dorie gave her the fifty cents which Jean looked at in a startled fashion. Dorie went on to explain "The fifty cents is for gas and could you please get the undertaker to come to our house? Grandpa has died."

The woman still looked startled, but she nodded. "Dorie, you tell your dad I will leave for Purplehaven shortly."

When the big black car had taken Grandpa away, Annie started cleaning the little bedroom so Alex and Garth could move back and sleep in their bed.

Moppet's parents; George and Alice gave everyone a ride to the Church the day Grandpa was buried. It was very crowded in the car, and it made Dorie understand suddenly what people meant when they said 'packed in like sardines'. The trip went quickly, it was so nice not having to go by wagon and horse. Harry, Rita's father, gave Paul a nice blue suit for grandpa to wear. He built a wooden coffin and Annie lined the coffin with light blue silky material. Moppets mom gave a small white pillow for grandpa's head to rest on. Grandpa looked handsome to Dorie, much nicer than he had when he had been alive. The funeral wasn't as scary as she thought it would be, it was peaceful. The hymns were joyful, Dorie knew why, grandpa was in heaven and everybody should be joyful.

After Grandpa was buried, there was a void in the Kinny household. The family missed his smile, the stories he told during his less confused states of mind, his gentleness with Garth and Dorie who would sit on his lap and cuddle with him. Dorie missed that Grandpa thought his rocking chair was a wagon and how he would quietly talk to his imaginary horses, coaxing them onward. At these times he was reliving part of his past.

In the morning Alex's dad noticed his son rushing off after completing his chores. Paul knew something was different with Alex but decided not to approach the matter until later.

At the evening meal Paul said to Alex "Son I noticed you rushing off early in the morning. Did you visit your friend David?" Although Alex knew he would be in trouble, he felt part of growing up was to be honest, especially with his parents, especially since the reason he had run off was to get a job.

Alex blurted out "I didn't go to David's, I walked to Purplehaven and got a job today." There was total silence at the table, the family was stunned.

Finally Paul said "Alex you're only fourteen, you need an education if you want to do well in life."

"Dad I hate school and farm work. I will not go back to school."

Dorie abruptly left the table and was outdoors before the family knew what was happening. She headed for her secret hideout, the place only known to Dorie and Rita. It was a special place they could go to grieve and mull over problems. Dorie and Rita had promised each other never to reveal the location of their secret not even to their families.

Dad had always told Dorie how important schooling was, now Alex was ruining his life. Dorie started to sob fearing for the brother she loved so much. Many questions raced through her mind. Would Alex be poor like Dad? Who would look after Alex, and where would he live? With Alex gone how would Dad manage all the farm work? He couldn't leave, she would miss him a lot! He protected her and showed her how to do things around the farm! Dorie sobbed until she fell asleep on the ground.

Awakened by a light shining in her eyes, Dorie jumped up, hearing Rita whisper "Dorie your family is worried about you, especially your dad. Your dad came to see my dad and mom to ask for help in finding you. Your family and my family are very worried, they're searching everywhere with lanterns, please Dorie go home."

"I fell asleep Rita, I will go right home, I don't want my family to worry and look for me. Thank you Rita for coming to tell me." She smiled weakly at the other.

"Good night Dorie." Rita replied with a smile of her own and a little chuckle.

Paul was angry, had been worried sick about his daughter. He grabbed Dorie, just wanting to shake her. He then looked down, saw Dorie's tear streaked face and his anger was swept away. Holding her close her father said "Dorie we love you so much, you had us worried, frantic we were. It's so good to have you home."

CHAPTER TWO

That night after Dorie was settled on her cot, Alex came to talk to Dorie. He sat down beside her and told her about his job, the home he would live in. He told her about the indoor toilet, water that came out of taps, the fact that the house was warm and he got good meals and a salary for the work he did. "Dorie you can visit me when you come to Purplehaven and I'll come home to visit you and Garth. I'll save enough money so you can buy a beautiful dress and matching hair ribbons for the school's Christmas concert."

Dorie sat up, threw her arms around Alex and whispered "That sounds wonderful! I'm so happy for you!"

In a gruff voice Alex replied "Now get to sleep brat."

Paul was very distressed about Alex quitting school and he tried to convince him to move back home and return to school. The only response Alex offered was "I hate school and hate working on the farm. If you make me go back to school, I'll run away." Paul knew it would be best to keep his son near by, not loose contact with him. If Alex ran away he knew the family might never see The boy again, or he could become involved with rough people or gangs.

Paul said with a heavy heart "Good luck with your job, we'll always be there for you, should you need us. We'll visit you, don't forget Dorie and Garth, those two adore you. If you visit occasionally then Dorie and Garth will see for themselves you're doing well and are happy."

His next trip to Purplehaven Paul visited Alex who was loading a truck. Alex was happy, saying "Dad the family I live with are kind and the meals are almost as good as Mom's. I'll be home shortly for a visit, give Dorie and Garth a hug from their big brother."

Paul nodded somberly, but managed a smile anyway. "Alex we'll all be looking forward to that visit. See you soon." The older man walked away with his shoulders stooped and head bent, knowing he had made the right decision to leave Alex to work but it weighted heavily on his heart that Alex wasn't going to return to school. It was his biggest hope that his children would complete school and attend college. Perhaps at a later date Alex would return to school after he got tired of lifting and loading.

After that, Dorie's dad would often take her hand and squeeze it several times saying, "Dorie I hope you hang in there and finish school."

"I'll try my hardest Daddy." She would whisper back.

Down the road from Dories' home an elderly couple owned land on which trees, bushes, and patches of wild raspberries grew. The raspberry branches were usually covered with ripe berries in the summer that fell to the ground. Occasionally, cattle would graze on the unkempt grass. Jean was driving by this space, owned by Mr. Crab when she glanced toward the trees. Noticing the numerous raspberry bushes covered with red berries ready to be picked, Jean stopped the car, got out, and eyed the berries. She was visualizing all the jars of raspberry jam and jelly that could be made. She knew that Annie had lots of empty jars her mother had given her. Jean turned the car around and headed for Mr. Crabs' home to get permission to pick the lovely berries. Everyone in town knew that Mr. Crab was mean, intolerant and arrogant. This being said, Jean was slightly uncomfortable and a bit frightened of visiting Mr. Crab, but the visions of jars and jars of jelly kept her moving forward to the Crab home. The children called Mr. Crab 'The Old Psycho'. All to soon Jean faced Mr. Crabs house door and before Jean lost heart she knocked. With an abruptness the door was opened and Jean was taken back by the angry, annoyed man standing before her. The woman timidly greeted Mr. Crab then proceeded to ask his permission to pick the raspberries that grew on his land. Mr. Crab immediately denied her of this before adding "It's my land, I don't allow people to trample my bushes down. If I catch anyone trespassing I will deal harshly with them." Jean hesitated for a moment before she drummed up enough courage, saying "We'll be careful, and share the berries with you. Or if you prefer we'll give you jam and jelly."

"Lady, are you deaf? I said no, and stay off my land period!" The grump snapped. Mr. Crab then slammed the door in Jean's face.

The woman was shocked. Children told stories of Mr. Crab being angry and dangerous yet Jean felt the children had exaggerated, but now she wondered. Next to Mr. Crab's land was a government fort that soldiers used many years ago when they fought the natives. Since the fort was near Mr. Crab's home the government had asked him to look after the fort. The children said Mr. Crab wouldn't allow children in the fort and that he threatened to hunt them down and shoot them if they came anywhere close. Jean would talk to her child, ask her to stay away from the fort and Mr. Crab's land, and she would also talk to Alice and Annie.

Both Annie and Alice felt it was safe to pick the berries on Mr. Crab's land if they were careful. Annie said to Jean "It's two miles from his home and he never gets up before noon, to busy watching for intruders most of the night. Let's pick the berries early in the morning, eight to eleven."

Jean nodded before adding "Mr. Crab was very nasty this morning and made a threat that we better stay off his land. He could be dangerous."

Alice shook her head, looking at her friend. "All the more reason. Let's get those berries tomorrow morning."

For the next hour a plan of action to pick the raspberries was developed. The ladies also decided to pick, clean and can the berries in Anne's house, then share equally, each women getting one third of the jam and jelly.

Next morning, the children, whistles in hand, followed Alice and Annie who had piled numerous empty containers into Jean's car. Jean drove to a place not far from the berries, hiding the car off the road and among some trees so it wouldn't be seen. The children had been forewarned to be quiet, not stomp about, laugh or talk, but stand on guard, be very watchful. If the children saw or heard someone approaching they would blow once on their whistle alerting their mothers of the danger, then quickly but quietly head for Jean's car. Dorie, Rita and Moppet meant to follow their mother's instructions closely, they knew Mr. Crab was mean and owned a gun. Garth would hide behind a bush near the road and Dorie would watch for people walking down the road. The ladies picked rapidly till eleven o'clock and filled numerous pails. Time to leave. Alice went to round up the children. After the group reached the car and were crammed inside with the berries, Jean started it and backed out to the road. In a loud voice Jean sang "We got every nice ripe berry Mr. Crab, no berries will go to waste this year! Lots of jam and jelly this winter! Hurrah!"

And suddenly everyone in the car joined in singing "Hurrah!"

Moppet was staying overnight with Dorie and would go home with Alice Sunday morning after the remainder of the berries had been preserved. That evening at supper Annie was telling Paul of their daytime adventures. After Annie had finished talking, Moppet piped up and added "Last summer Alex, my sister Spice, Alex's friends Jerry and Dave plus Dorie and I" - Moppet received a kick from Dorie, but ignored it to continue on with her story. All Dorie could do now was listen as Moppet spilled a secret she had been so careful to keep. "None of us had been inside the fort, we wanted to know what it looked like inside. Alex and Dave led us through the woods, down the bridge hill but when we where crossing the bridge, Alex noticed a thick rope strung across the bridge and tied on each side to a metal rail of the bridge. Alex told us to remember the rope, as we easily could trip if running. Finally we climbed the hill leading to the fort, and crawled inside. We made it without Mr. Crab seeing us! It was amazing! We climbed up the logs, looking through the holes that the soldiers had fired their bullets from. Alex whispered, 'we must leave, follow me and be very quiet.' Then he crept out of the fort. We all followed Alex when he climbed the hill on the other side of the bridge. We heard an ear piercing scream from Mr. Crab! 'Stop you brats, you aren't going to get away, I'll hunt you down like deer!' We all heard gunshots; Alex became very pale and upset, didn't he Dorie?" The Kinny family sat spellbound as Moppet continued on with the story. "Alex told us to keep low and crawl under Mr. Scott's fence and hide among the trees but stay close together. Alex whispered, 'Mr. Crab would think we were crossing through his land and exiting on to one of the three roads.' Mr. Crab came running up the hill with his rifle under his arm and crossed onto his land. Alex lead us across Mr. Scotts land, then we waited awhile before back tracking a short distance and coming onto an old side road. The road led us to Rita's farm. We were all very tired and glad to be safe."

Paul looked at Moppet and Dorie saying "I hope you two have learnt your lesson, one of you could easily have been shot."

Moppet said "That was a scary time, wasn't it Dorie?" Dorie's face was beet red and she sat quietly not replying to Moppet's question.

The local farmers would take turns going to the lakeside and buying white fish from the Natives in the late summer and through the winter. Tonight was Moppet's dad's and Dorie's dad's turn to visit the lake and buy fish. The natives had fishing rights but were only supposed to fish for themselves. They sold fish to the local farmers for twenty five cents a fish. Only two farmers went each night, visiting after midnight when police watch was low. It was important to keep traffic at a minimum so as not to draw police attention. Heavy fines were given to anyone caught buying fish from the natives plus the fish were seized.

Since buying the fish was illegal mom would sit up and worry till dad arrived home, once again having dodged a potentially bad situation with the law. Moppets mom had a large freezer thus after the fish were scaled and deboned they were stored with her.

On Monday Dorie would start school. Her pink dress was made, she had pink socks and new shoes, but the fear she felt never left her mind. Not even Alex would be there. Paul did promise to take her but dad would leave eventually and then she would be on her own.

Monday morning Dorie had to get up very early, do her chores, eat breakfast, get dressed for school and walk three miles to arrive before nine o'clock. She left for school accompanied by her father, with braided hair carrying an onion sandwich and a piece of cake in a brown bag. Dorie felt cold and shaky.

At school Dorie's father introduced her to the female teacher who assigned a desk to her near the front of the room. After her father left, Dorie couldn't help but feel lonely and frightened.

At recess Dorie left the classroom with the rest of her classmates. Once outside she stood against the wall. Further down the wall stood an older boy with a huge scar running across his forehead. Continuing to look about, eventually she turned to watch the other children running about, playing, and shouting to one another. A feeling of total, complete loneliness overcame her at this sight. Why couldn't she have friends at school? Before she even had time to dwell on this, she felt a hand grab hers. There stood a pretty red haired girl with big blue eyes asking her if she wanted to be friends. Dorie felt a strange feeling in her stomach and with tears in her eyes replied "I would like to be your friend, my name is Dorie."

The red haired girl said "I'm Matty". That meeting was the start of a friendship that Dorie was sure would last years.

Looking back to the boy against the wall, Dorie asked her new friend about him. "Why doesn't he play with the other children?"

Matty hesitated before explaining "His name is X-Cee. His family is very poor, one of his legs is much shorter so he walks with a big limp and the big scar across his forehead that came from being kicked in the head by a horse. X-Cee has difficulty learning and is often taunted by the other kids. No one wants him on their team, They think they'd be sure to lose." Matty paused, "Be careful, don't be too friendly with X-Cee or the other kids will tease and taunt you as well. X-Cee has a sister and brother that attend this school too but they're their at home, sick with the flu."

"How come you know so much about X-Cee if you're not his friend?" Dorie asked.

"My mom and dad know X-Cee's parents." Matty offered easily, with a shrug. "Last winter X-Cee had to wear his mother's old fur coat which almost touched his shoes. It was very sad, X-Cee was called the old bag lady and the hairy bear. The teasing never stopped. X-Cee would hide among the trees behind the barn." Matty kept her distance from X-Cee but Dorie, as time went on would answer his questions, smile at him, and always say hi. Most of the children that attended Elm School had lots of pretty clothes, took music lessons, swimming lessons and belonged to 4H clubs. Their parents drove cars. X-Cee's family was very poor like Dorie's family. X-Cee, his brother and sister wore drab, dirty clothes while Dorie wore clean drab clothes.

Dorie often thought of the hurt in X-Cee's soft brown eyes, his gentleness and desire to take part in activities. There wasn't anything Dorie could do to help X-Cee but be polite.

Early one morning Moppet's father came to visit. Paul answered the knock on the door to find the man with tears in his eyes. "Paul I can't come in I'll just give you the news." He told Paul of Moppet breaking her arm the day before when she fell off the slide at school. During the fall Moppet also landed on a dirty piece of glass puncturing the same arm. She was taken to the hospital and the doctors set the fracture, applying a cast but not noticing the cut from the glass. "We brought Moppet home," he concluded, wiping at his eyes. "Alice checked her fingers often till ten o'clock when Alice and I went to bed. Close to midnight Moppet woke up crying and calling out. Her fingers on the broken arm were swollen. The swelling was different not a firm type but when her fingers were touched the swelling made a rustling sound and swished about. We rushed Moppet to emergency. The doctor immediately removed the cast, found the angry looking puncture wound…" He broke off and tried to gather himself. "The doctor soon determined Moppet had gas gangrene. The hospital didn't have any serum to counter act it. The doctor contacted a large medical center who felt Moppet's arm had to be amputated right away. By the time Moppet was taken to the operating room it had moved to three inches above her elbow, so the doctors… had to remove Moppet's arm at her shoulder."

He paused again before getting to the main reason for his visit. "Paul could Annie go to the hospital and talk to Alice, see that she gets some nourishment and rest? Alice blames herself and is so depressed. Paul her hair turned pure white overnight from the shock! The doctor feels Alice needs rest or she will collapse. If Annie could come back with me to Purplehaven and talk to Alice. Paul, please. Alice has a lot of confidence in Annie. The hospital has an empty private room which Alice could use because they want to give her a sedative, but she's refusing. Your wife could talk mine into taking the sedative and spend time between Moppet and Alice."

"I'm sure Annie will accompany you, and help in anyway she can". Paul assured, leaving the man to check with Annie just to be sure. He returned soon enough to tell him what he had guessed before. "Annie will go to the hospital and help Moppet and Alice."

When Paul told Dorie about Moppet's injury and surgery, she wanted to visit and stay with her friend. Dad told Dorie she was too young to visit and during this traumatic time in Moppets life she needed her parents and sister. "When Moppet comes home you can visit and stay overnight if her mother consents."

Dorie was overcome with sorrow, crying out, "I wish I had lost my arm instead of Moppet because she needs two arms to play the piano and ride her horse! Now she can't be a doctor, a doctor needs two arms!" With tears rolling down her cheeks Dorie said to her father "Dad I need to be alone and cry, I can't… I'm so… I'm so sad for Moppet!" With these words Dorie ran off to her secret hideout.

After having a cry Dorie came up with a plan. The plan was to help Moppet, tell her she was loved, and help her do things, be there for her when she needed help. Dorie returned to the house.

Dorie had been noticing her classmates running and jumping into sand pits, jumping over a stick placed between two bars, throwing and catching a ball. The children that were catching a ball wore a huge mitt on their hand that had a big dip in the center. She loved watching these activities and an idea formed in her mind. She would practice at home and when she became good at running and jumping she could compete with her classmates.

That evening Dorie asked her father for help in making sand pits and a jumping stand. Her father replied "Dorie I would love to help you. We'll soon start work on this new project." Rita had a softball so she could help Dorie practice catching the ball. All these new ideas happened so fast. The girl was filled with joy about her new plans. She could focus on these new activities, and become good at track and field.

The fall sped by, and Dorie had to miss several days of school to help harvest the vegetables. The teacher didn't put on a Christmas concert much to the dismay of the children and their parents.

Finally the snowy winter months passed and brought warm melting weather. The snow quickly disappeared causing the rivers and creeks to overflow, flooding some roads and yards. All livestock were moved back to their corrals where they would be safe. All the children were instructed not to go near any running water.

One afternoon a neighbor came rushing up to Paul, telling him that the main bridge had washed out. It was the gateway to all the main roads. The structure was extremely important to people that shopped in larger centers and drove cars.

Dorie's dad couldn't imagine the bridge being washed away so he said to his daughter "Get your mother and Garth, we're going to see the unbelievable, one of the largest bridges in our province has apparently been washed away! Hurry!"

Horse and wagon travel was slow through the mud and water, but a car wouldn't have been able to travel on the roads either. On arrival at the bridge site the whole Kinny family stood back and watched in wonder at what remained of the bridge swaying, rocking and groaning against the force of the gray water with white peaks. Nobody moved. They just sat in the wagon, captivated by the violence of the water.

Dorie noticed a horse trying to swim ashore, four men running along the creek bank beside it. One man had a lasso in his hand. At this point a log floating down the creek at a great speed knocked the horse into the corner of the bridge giving the man with the rope an opportunity to lasso the creature. Paul and Annie ran to help the four men pull the horse out of the raging water. Dorie had hidden her head in Garth's lap. The younger boy patted her head, watching the scene unfold. "The horse is out of the creek, look, look Dorie!" He told her after a short silence. The beautiful roan horse tried to stand but collapsed, laying quietly on the ground, totally exhausted. One of the men that rescued it checked the horse for fractures and other injuries but the roan seemed fine, except for being tired. A crash was heard, drawing everyone's attention. The remaining corner of the bridge had washed away.

When Dorie's father and mother returned to the wagon, Dorie smiled, not being able to stop her joyous laughter. She hugged her dad crying over and over "The horse is safe!"

One of the days that Paul took to go visit Alex, he ran into an old friend of his who operated a shoe repair shop. He offered to buy Paul a cup of coffee in the new restaurant owned and operated by three Chinese men, Tom, Molly, and George. He introduced his friend to the three restaurant owners and told Molly, a short stout gentleman, that Paul lived on a farm and did mixed farming. Molly and Tom suddenly became very excited, and asked dad if he would raise some special Chinese ducks for them, and if he would please shoot a skunk for them as they used skunk parts in making herbal medicine. Paul replied yes to both questions but told Molly and Tom the only time he saw skunks was when they came around the hen house. Occasionally at night or early morning a skunk would enter the chicken coop which would cause the hens to fly about shrieking. If he woke to the hens, he would grab his rifle and shoes and make a dash to the hen house. If he was lucky enough to shoot one dead, he would bring it in.

The three restaurant owners asked dad to bring his family in for Chinese food. Paul thanked these three nice men and on his next trip to Purplehaven took Annie, Dorie and Garth along to meet his new friends.

Dorie and Garth especially liked Tom and Molly. George was friendly but quiet, usually out running errands and buying supplies. This day George left out the back door and soon returned carrying a crate with two strange looking ducks inside quacking madly. George said to Paul "Macon ducks are very rare, the meat is delicious and we use the meat for birthdays and special occasions. We would travel great distances to taste Macon. It gives us great pleasure that you can raise these for us. We will purchase the special food the ducks eat." Paul nodded in agreement and replied "It would be our pleasure to raise them. They will have lots of space to run about and they'll be in the open air".

The Chinese food was delicious, but the ice cream cone was what was enjoyed the most by Dorie and Garth. After this meeting with Tom and Molly, tasting a new food and getting treats like ice cream, watermelon and pop Paul found it difficult to keep Dorie and Garth home when he traveled to Purplehaven on Saturdays.

When the wagon came to a stop behind the restaurant, Dorie jumped out then helped Garth down. The two would run for the back entrance of the restaurant. Tom, George, and Molly enjoyed Dorie and Garth's visits, always welcoming their two guests with big smiles, saying "Sit down, sit down, what would you like to eat?" Dorie and Garth were asked by their dad not to make a lot of requests for food and goodies.

This visit Dorie noticed a round orange fruit in the fruit bowl. She had never seen this type of fruit before and it made her curious. Pointing to the orange fruit in the bowl, Dorie asked Molly "What kind of fruit is that?"

"An orange." Molly replied. "Would you like to taste it?"

"Yes Molly please!" responded Dorie. Molly washed the orange and cut it into small pieces, then handing the pieces to Dorie explaining that she must eat the inside only, leaving the peel. Dorie felt spellbound, never had she tasted anything so sweet and unusual, Dorie enjoyed every bit of that orange. No other fruit could compare to it. Dorie thought oranges must be made in heaven.

The first part of summer dad asked the three Chinese men to visit the farm to see their four baby ducklings which were growing at a fast pace.

One Sunday evening Tom had two of his friends look after the restaurant while George drove Tom and Molly out to Paul's farm. All three men were delighted about the ducks. Molly kept looking at the ducks and laughing. "Soon we will have delicious roast duck with plum sauce!" Tom said. George wondered around the yard with Dorie following.

Once in awhile George would stop, look about and occasionally ask Dorie a question. "Does your father have a car?" George asked.

"No," Dorie replied. "we travel by wagon pulled by horses. We don't have enough money to buy a car."

Next George stopped by a small herd of cows and pointed to a brown cow, asking "Do brown cows give chocolate milk?"

Dorie with a twinkle in her eyes replied "No."

Then George walked up to a cow, lifting up its tail asked Dorie "Is that where milk comes from?" Dorie was unsure if George was teasing or didn't know much about cows. She decided to stay quiet.

Paul then took his visitors, Dorie, and Garth inside the house for refreshments. Tea and chocolate cake were served. George was interested, puzzled by the inside of the Kinny Home. George couldn't see water taps, a bathroom or electrical outlets. George kept looking around wondering how Paul heated that house and what he used to light the house when night came.

George thought the conditions his friends lived in were very poor and this greatly saddened him. He didn't see any toys or bikes that Dorie or Garth could play with. Suddenly he needed to leave, he felt tired, depressed and hopeless. This wonderful, poor family working so hard and barely surviving made him feel so helpless. With an unexpectedness George leapt out of his chair saying "Tom, Molly we must get back to the restaurant." and rushed out to the car. Paul shook hands with Tom and Molly and Dorie gave each gentleman a hug.

That visit changed the restaurant owner's feelings toward Paul and his family in a big way. Tom, Molly and George wanted to reach out to this poor family, help them in whatever way they could without touching the family's dignity. Molly thought everyone needs self respect and a feeling they can manage. Paul had a lot of pride, so they would start by helping in a small way, by brightening the lives of Dorie and Garth.

A big surprise awaited the two children on their next visit to the restaurant in Purplehaven. As usual as soon as the wagon stopped Dorie and Garth left the wagon running toward Tom and Molly's back door, Dorie visualizing an orange and Garth seeing an ice cream in his mind. As soon as the two children entered the restaurant, they could feel a sense of excitement. Molly said "Sit down, sit down, close your eyes."

Finally Dorie and Garth were asked to open their eyes. On opening their eyes they saw Molly and Tom grinning then as Molly and Tom stepped aside Dorie and Garth saw two new shiny bikes, a smaller boy's blue bike and a larger girl's green bike. Not thinking the bike was hers Dorie went over and lovingly touched the leather seat, the handlebars with bell and the big tires. There was a large ache in her heart, Dorie thought won't it be wonderful to own such a beautiful bike, she was mesmerized, unable to speak. Molly came up to Dorie asking "Do you like the bike Dorie?"

"Molly the bike is gorgeous, your daughter will be very happy, I'm glad we were able to see the bikes." A sad hopelessness surrounded Dorie but she knew a bike wasn't that important but an education was.

Molly put an arm around the girl's shoulders saying "The bikes are for you and Garth. We have no children only lots of friends. We would like the two of you to look upon us as family."

Understanding finally came to Dorie, she jumped up, eyes a brilliant blue, danced about, and ran over to Molly and Tom to give them hugs. Garth, still not sure one of the bikes was his was caught up in the happy mood, hugging everyone, including the delivery man. Paul knew the moment he walked in and saw the bikes and the happiness on his children's faces a dream he wasn't able to fulfill for his children had been satisfied. When Paul looked about he only saw joy. There was no way he could quash that feeling, he must accept these big gifts, and push his pride back for now. Paul would try harder to shoot the skunk these dear friends wanted. In a gracious way Paul sat down to have some Chinese food with a good cup of coffee. Dorie had her orange and Garth his ice cream. Then Paul thanked Molly, George and Tom for the bikes, they said their good byes and left.

Paul found it very hard not to scold Dorie and Garth about their laughing and noisiness. It wasn't their fault they received the bikes, it was his pride he knew, if only he had been able to put that joy and happiness on Dorie and Garth's face. Dorie's bike was even her favorite color!

Dorie was still having trouble understanding she owned a bike. She owned a bike. Dorie could see herself riding the new green contraption to school like other children. Dorie remembered her first day at school last fall. The girls had worn colorful dresses with lace and frills, some girls even wore necklaces, and they all owned a bike, even Matty! This fall Dorie would have a bike!

The children from poor families received a different type of treatment from the rest of the classmates, they were teased more about clothes and lunches, called names and often excluded from activities at school. Dorie's parents told her that the onion and lard sandwiches she usually had for lunch were healthy, but Dorie would sneak out of the classroom at noon eating her sandwich behind the school. At times Dorie would wake up at night and hear her classmates taunting 'Hey Dorie you forgot to take your breath freshener mints! Onions again? Don't you have anything else to eat?'

That summer, Dorie's learning to ride her bike ended up in numerous falls causing bruises, scrapes and cuts. Dorie persevered with bull dog courage, refusing help, ignoring the injuries and pain. One bright sunny day after Dorie had completed her chores she got on her bike and rode like a pro even surprising herself and her father who watched. Paul watched with happiness filling his heart, all the falls and accidents Dorie had with her bike while learning to ride never brought tears to her eyes. She wouldn't give up, her courage was amazing. There was one purpose in mind, to ride her bike well, and in the fall ride her bike to school, place it in the bike rack, then walk away as if she had been riding a bike for years. By fall Dorie was riding masterfully, down hills, around curves and coming to a graceful stop. Her father was astonished at her bike riding ability and gave his daughter permission to ride her bike to school in September.

CHAPTER THREE

When Dorie visited Moppet for a few hours each Saturday afternoon she found Moppet sad and unwilling to play. Dorie returned home full of woe, very unhappy and she felt this great pain in her heart for Moppet. One evening Dorie went to sit on her dad's lap saying "Dad, how can we bring the old Moppet back? The one that was fun and full of good ideas?" I still love Moppet, but I'm so upset that she's so unhappy."

"Dorie talk to Moppet about her arm, tell her she's still a wonderful, important person, tell her you would like to play."

Next visit to Moppet, Dorie asked her why she was so disinterested in playing. Moppet looked at her shoulder with no arm attached saying "I can still feel my arm being there, but its gone, Dorie do you think of me as a misfit?"

"Oh Moppet. You're like a shining star, you have nice long hair, a beautiful face, you're very smart and you can still do everything other children do except play the piano and ride your horse."

"I can still ride Sweet Pea, I rode her around the yard while mom watched, then I took sweet pea for a long ride on my own. I can still play the piano, mom has bought some sheet music that one arm people use... Oh Dorie I don't ever want to play the piano again! I don't want to do anything! The kids are going to tease me when we get back to school, I just know it!"

"They won't tease you Moppet, not you, that I'm sure."

"Your classmates respect you, you'll never loose that respect, they love your new ideas, the fun you can be and your smartness. Don't worry Moppet you're classmates will be waiting for you. Your arm is healed, can you come and practice track and field at my house? Please come, I need your help. " Alice overheard that conversation between Moppet and Dorie and later hugged Dorie, whispering in her ear "Thank you for saying those kind words to Moppet and for encouraging her to practice track and field. It's a start, and I shall bring her over for practice tomorrow." That was the start of Moppet slowly coming back to life.

Monday was the start of school, Dorie wasn't happy about starting back but having a new bike made it seem less painful. With a captivating smile Dorie rode her bike into the school yard, parked it in the bike rack and proceed to the school house. Before Dorie reached the school house a group of children unexpectedly surrounded her. Jody, the belle of the school, said "I love your bike! The color is nice. Lets have a race after school!" The other children near Dorie showed their approval of her new bike. Dorie beamed and replied "Thanks for liking my bike, its so much fun riding instead of walking to school and I *will* race you after school." Dorie thought what fun it would be to have a bike race.

After school the children gathered around to watch Jody and Dorie race on their bikes. Most of the children cheered for Jody but Dorie won the race easily by a wide margin, and Jody congratulated Dorie in a pleasant way, having no hard feelings over losing.

Dorie's small thin legs ached as she rode into her families yard, she could hardly wait to tell her family she'd won a bicycle race. Dorie's family was delighted on hearing the news. Dorie had a new teacher, a male, a huge man who wore glasses. "Dad because I'm the only child in grade two Mr. Joma makes me go over my lessons at his desk near the blackboard." She reported.

Dorie had more chores to do since Alex left home. She must bring the cows home, help milk, gather eggs, feed the chickens and ducks, turn the cream separator, make butter from cream which could be done later in the evening and after supper help with the dishes. She didn't mind the chores, as long as she had time to practice jumping or running. Dad had made a large sand pit and a soft sandy spot on one side of the high jump that she could fall into after completing her jump. Paul also promised Dorie on their next trip to Purplehaven he would take her to the library to choose a book to read during her spare time. But Dorie used her spare time to run and jump, also throwing the ball against the shed door, practicing to throw the ball rapidly, striking the middle of the door where her father had placed a large red circle. Next May Dorie wanted to win numerous points for her school.

Once a month Dorie spent a weekend with Moppet. After starting back to school Moppet realized how kind and accepting her classmates were. She was still admired and soon was the same old Moppet she had been before her accident. The two friends now played games, rode Sweet Pea, went for walks in the woods with Alice, learning about birds, flowers, trees and plants. Occasionally they would see a movie at the library and they always practiced running.

Next Saturday Dorie and Garth would visit Molly and Tom, it was several weeks since their last visit to the restaurant. On arrival at the restaurant all was forgotten when Tom and Molly brought out a new satiny green parka for Dorie and a new blue parka for Garth. The parkas fit well and Paul was grateful but felt the gifts were to costly. Molly and Tom assured Paul it was no hardship for them, they enjoyed giving gifts to Dorie and Garth and loved them like their own children. Paul consented half heartedly, he was a proud man and felt he wasn't providing adequately for his family. It was difficult as Paul had this inner war fighting inside of him, he felt he should be bringing the joy to his children and yet he was grateful to these wonderful friends for giving items to his children he couldn't afford.

For many days Paul argued with himself but one day he awoke and realized a huge weight had been removed from his heart. He knew instinctively that he had let pride interfere with Molly and Tom's love for his children. They just wanted his children to have a few nice clothes and toys like other children. Dorie's bike made it easier to get to school. Dorie and Garth didn't love their father less and they understood their father always gave them as much as he could afford. They were good kids, and understanding. Their father mustn't deny them the wonderful gifts his friends gave them. Coming to this conclusion it felt good being rid of the gnawing envy that had started destroying his good nature.

Rita would be starting school next week. Rita was Dorie's best friend, she was beautiful, had big brown eyes, shiny long brown hair and a smile that warmed people's heart.

When it was snowing, rainy or cold Rita's mom would drive her daughter to school and Dorie was welcome to join them. When the weather was nice the two girls took their bikes. The younger girl grew to like Matty but liked Bess more. Bess was X-Cee's sister, dressed just as poorly and had no friends. Rita went up to Bess and said "You can play with us, we'll be your friends" The smile Bess gave, the happiness that radiated from the girl's eyes made Dorie happy but ashamed she hadn't asked her last year to play with Matty and her. Rita was a perfect person, she always did what was right.

On returning home from school, strong winds started to blow, followed by loud thunder and much lightning. The school children had barely made it home when the heavy rain started, lasting throughout the night. Garth and Dorie were instructed not to go out to the outdoor toilet. Annie would provide them with the toilet pail they used during the winter nights.

"The lightning is severe and seems to be close. You never know where it will strike. Dorie," her mom said, "this evening is not a time to run out in the rain which I know you love to do." The girl was a little disappointed, but would obey.

Morning came with a clear sky telling Paul it would be a sunny day but wet and muddy. Rita's mom drove Dorie and Rita to school and would pick them up afterwards. On arriving home from school Dorie found her dad looking for two horses, he had checked the field, creek area, yard and now was going into the bush. After walking into the shrubs a great distance Paul and Dorie came across the two horses. Mag was lying near the fence and Daisy was standing quietly nearby. The man turned to his daughter with a sad look. "Mag was struck by lightning. Dorie, can you see the burn mark running from her head to her hind foot?" Tears rolled down Dorie's cheek as she asked if Mag had felt pain and if she could touch Mag and say goodbye. "Dorie Mag didn't feel pain and yes you can give her a good-by pet and don't forget Daisy who has stood guard over Mag for hours. If you want to, you can help me dig a grave on top of the hill near the trees".

That evening the grave was dug. The earth was soft and easy to move. Mag was buried and Dorie nailed together two pieces of wood to make a cross which she then stuck into the ground covering Mag. Daisy cried out and stood beside her friend's grave for days. Paul was worried about his horse, and eventually took a pail of water and oats to Daisy, which she did drink and eat but refused to move.

A week had gone by when one morning Dorie went to visit Daisy and talk softly to this beautiful white horse. She petted the horse's face and said "We need your help on the farm, the other horses miss you. You can always visit Mag's grave, come and follow me back to the yard, your home." As Dorie turned to leave, the white creature lifted her head high and loudly neighed before she looked down at the grave, turned, and followed Dorie. When her father heard this, he cried out "Thank you, Dorie! What ever you did sure worked! It's good to have my horse back."

In the morning Rita and Dorie took their bikes to school. Rita was a very loyal friend at school. If the other classmates asked Rita to join their activities she refused unless Dorie, Bess and Matty were included as well.

Dorie had difficulty with reading and spelling but loved math and science. Today as usual Dorie did her lessons at Mr. Joma's desk and he concentrated on the subjects Dorie liked, math science and history. The teacher took great delight in Dorie's learning ability and love for her three favorite subjects. Language, grammar and spelling were the forgotten subjects. He didn't seem to want to teach her things she didn't do well in, or didn't like. Today near the end of her lesson time Mr. Joma decided to give Dorie a spelling test for report card grading. She was sent to the blackboard standing with her back to the class. The poor girl didn't realize the class was watching until the test was completed and the children erupted into laughter. Later she realized the class was laughing at her as they watched her spell one word correctly out of twenty. Even after the poor results in spelling Mr. Joma didn't change his method of teaching.

Dorie felt humiliated and after school rushed to her bike. "Wait Dorie!" Rita called. Her friend rushed to her, hugging her and saying "You're smart in the other subjects and very good at sports, and wise like my mother. Please don't feel ashamed. I didn't laugh and neither did a bunch of the other kids."

"I felt so stupid, as if I was on a stage and forgot my lines. My classmates must think I'm dumb, oh Rita I'll never get over this!"

"Dorie stop being so silly, Ray got 5% on a math test, I got 48% on my math test, Jody got 10% on a science test. You're just good at different things. I would always choose you first out of all those school kids to be my best friend."

Dorie smiled thinking 'My wonderful friend who loves to sing hymns, play with dolls, walk in the woods and talk'. Rita was very different, full of kindness, never teased in a hurtful way or laughed at others, she seemed to have a light inside of her that shone outward making the world look peaceful. Angels must be like Rita. All at once failing the spelling test wasn't so important. Dorie would tell her dad about failing, she knew he would still love her even if she wasn't able to finish school. She would try her hardest to finish school and take her dad on a trip and make his life easier though, that was her goal. Rita would help her with her spelling, and she would spend less time on track and field.

After supper Dorie decided to make a little playhouse. She headed for a group of trees, carrying thick cardboard, a hammer and nails. Paul had given her the hammer and nails trusting his daughter to be careful. After nailing several pieces of cardboard to the trees, Garth came running down the hill, angry he hadn't been asked to help. Her brother tore the cardboard she had nailed to a tree and threw the pieces into the air. Dorie, not being in a good mood, became very angry and shouted at Garth "Grandpa is coming down from heaven, he'll pick you up, carry you off and maybe drop you in hell! Oh look Garth I see Grandpa coming in that cloud!" Garth looked around and became hysterical screaming at the top of his lungs for his mother. Annie came dashing down to Garth's side, pulling him into her arms, talking softly, cooing "There there baby, Mom is here." Dorie tried to leave, but her mother cried out "Don't you leave! What terrible thing did you do to Garth!?"

"Mom, Garth was wrecking my playhouse, he tore the cardboard off I had nailed to the tree!" Annie replied "That didn't give you a right to hit your brother!"

"Mom," Garth spoke up. "Dorie didn't hit me. She called grandpa from heaven. Grandpa was in a cloud coming down to pick me up and throw me into hell. Mommy I'm so scared!"

Annie had a shocked look on her face, she was speechless for a moment then said "How could you tell him such a dreadful, frightening thing!? Think of the panic Garth must have felt!"

Dorie said "I'm sorry Garth, Grandpa can't come out of heaven."

Annie confirmed "Dorie is right people can't come out of heaven so you need not worry Garth." Annie then said to her daughter "I am so upset with you for frightening Garth like this. As punishment your bike will be locked up for a week." Dorie left her mother and Garth, she was going to practice spelling in her secret hideout.

Dorie's one great love was practicing for track and field, she could now run behind a wagon pulled by trotting horses for a mile and she could throw a very fast spinning softball across home plate. Dorie practiced high jump some evenings until darkness descended. Her father, using Rita's soft ball played catch with his daughter. Dorie's classmates knew she was a good ball player, she caught the ball like a pro. Still she was not asked to play on the school team, not even as an outfielder. Being snubbed by her classmates did not dampen Dorie's enthusiasm, in fact it propelled her drive to do well at the track meet.

Each May seven schools met at a central point and students from each school competed. Teachers and students wanted their school to win the trophy, it was a great honor for a school to receive the utmost sports trophy. Dorie hoped to win a lot of points for her small school and to win the respect and attention of her classmates.

One evening after school Dorie heard her father calling for her. She quickly ran to fin her father who was putting water into the animal's water troughs. Paul smiled upon his daughter saying, "Dorie would you help me with hay cutting by riding one of the horses?"

"Yes dad I will, it sounds like fun."

"Thanks Dorie, that will free your mother so she can do more canning and the horse will have less weight to carry." Dorie looked at her dad and giggled, her father joining in with his own chuckle. Dorie's giggle was contagious.

When the laughter finally faded Dorie asked "What do I do?"

"You sit on the horse, steer the horse in a straight line while I sit on the mower being pulled by the horses, and work the levers. First, Dorie, you must get used to being on a work horse, riding about the yard, getting used to steering and stopping the horse. Would you like to practice riding this evening?"

"Yes dad I'll practice but will the horse run off?"

"No Dorie I will lead the horse and be with you at all times. Now run off and change out of your shorts into a pair of worn slacks."

When first placed atop the horse Dorie had a feeling of fear and strangeness, she was a long way off the ground. The horse was so tall and Dorie's short legs barley reached over the sides of the wide animal but she liked the feel of the movement once the horse started to walk and after several walks around the yard using the reins to direct the horse, the young girl felt confident, very much at ease when steering the horse. Her father felt that Dorie should practice a couple more evenings before they started to hay.

Early Saturday morning Paul took Dorie and the horses to the hay field, they would cut hay for forty five minutes before he would allow Dorie to get off the horse and walk about for ten minutes, hoping Dorie wouldn't become too sore. Paul and Dorie saw more then half the hayfield cut by the end of Saturday. If Dorie stayed home Monday from school, they would complete the mowing, Paul relaxed at this thought.

Sunday morning Dorie got up to do her chores, leaving the house Dorie noticed a nicer, stronger high jump stand with a cross bar she could keep moving up small amounts at a time. The running broad jump sand pit had also been increased in length. Oh, how Dorie loved her dad, her love for him could travel up the side of the highest mountain and all the way back down. Dorie hoped she could get more points this year for her school. Last May, Elm school hadn't done well and Dorie felt she had let her school down.

These days spelling was forgotten, a thing of the past as Dorie felt consumed, driven to make the softball team and make lots of points at the meet. Moppet now took a great interest in track and field, she was used to being number one thus became competitive with Dorie who was very good in all categories for her age. The rivalry became intense but there was a good natured understanding between the two girls, that the winner deserved to win.

Dorie was weak in batting so her father had made a crude bat out of wood. Rita would pitch the ball so Dorie could get batting practice.

Next morning when Rita and Dorie arrived at school, the school children were buzzing with excitement and Matty with eyes the size of saucers came running up to Rita and Dorie. When Matty reached the girls, with shortness of breath said, "Ray was looking for his dog when he came across a dead man, leaning against a tree, with no eyes. The dead man's missing one arm, his hand, and most of a cheek. Ray took a group of the older boys to see the dead man last evening and after school, when Mr. Joma leaves, he'll take whoever wants to go."

Raymond and the older boys warned all the other students standing around that no one must tell the teacher or their parents about the dead man. After Mr. Joma had left Ray led a large group of students including Matty, Rita, and Dorie to the scene he had discovered last evening. Matty had repeated Ray's description of the dead man to Rita and Dorie that morning. The scene and smell Dorie encountered caused her to feel sick to her stomach and gave her an anguished feeling, that could be someone's dad, he could be missed and needed! Rita looked at the dead man briefly then full of anxiety, ran off with Dorie following closely behind.

Dorie knew they must respect the code of silence, regardless of what they had witnessed. Rita's lips were also sealed but she wept most of the way home.

That night Dorie had a horrid dream. She saw the eyeless dead man looking down at her and asking her to locate his family so they would know he hadn't deserted them and to tell them he loved them. She woke screaming, bringing her parents in. Paul hugged his daughter and asked "What was wrong? Did you have a nightmare?"

"Mom, Dad I just had a bad dream. I'm fine." The girl finally got out.

Her mom went back to bed but her dad stayed to talk. "You can tell me what the dream was about." her dad commented kindly.

"Dad I can't because of the code of silence. The dream was something real I saw in the woods after school. In my dream the dead man asked me for help, help to find his family. The dead man has no eyes or arm, oh Dad I can't talk about what I saw!"

"Dorie you must talk about what's on your mind, you might keep having nightmares, become afraid to go out in the woods, or start sleeping poorly. Dorie it's a good idea to talk about what scared you."

"But Dad! If I told, no one would talk to me anymore! Ratting them out would make the school kids angry and they might try to teach me a lesson! Then I'd never be able to go to school again!"

"Dorie you can't keep this inside of you. Whatever happened at school frightened you badly, please tell me exactly what happened with this dead man, I won't go talking about the experience without your permission."

Slowly Dorie started her story and her father listened with a solemn expression. After she told her dad about the dead man in the woods and all about her scary dream, her father said "I know exactly what to do and your name will never come up." Dorie's father held and rocked her 'till she fell asleep.

Next day Dorie's father went to Purplehaven to visit his friend on the police force to ask for advice and report about the dead man in the woods. Paul spoke to Corporal Price for a long time. Corporal Price finally said after sitting in silence "This code of silence in schools is difficult to deal with, as no one knows how far some students will go to protect the code. The code is much stronger in some schools then others. I believe the code is strong in your daughter's school, we have had a few parents come in and talk to us in private, they did this being very concerned for their children.

"I'll send an undercover policeman, no lights, uniform or police car. He can pull off the highway and enter the woods when school is in session. The undercover man will take photos and get a general description and compare his information with a photo of a missing Montreal man who was to visit his brother who lives near Elm school. This will be a difficult task, but height, approximate weight, hair color, clothes he has on, rings will give us a general idea about the dead man. Then we'll send a couple of policemen to six or seven schools, then no student can be blamed for breaking the code of silence as we'll make it look as if we have been searching for him for some time. We'll ask for the students help, if anyone should see this man, have your parents report the sighting to the police. This missing man has family who miss him, we would like to help ease their worries. Students your help is appreciated…" he faded off, making the explanation sound like he was talking to the students, just to try and drive the point home. Paul seemed satisfied.

The next day two policemen each with their search dog went to a different school. The policeman spoke to the children about the man in the photo then searched the school yard and around the area. The police rushed through these phony searches and arrived at Elm school mid afternoon. Since the police knew where the body was they found it within minutes. The Elm school children were told not to go near the dead man as it now was considered a crime scene. A week later the police visited all the schools telling them the missing man was found dead, and a medical examiner determined the dead man died of a heart attack. The man was from Montreal on his way to visit a brother who lived near Elm school. No one would ever know why the man entered the woods instead of staying on the main road. Dorie was delighted the way the police handled the case of the man, it allowed her to finally relax.

It was the weekend. Dorie's father was letting her stay at Moppets both Friday and Saturday night which was longer than usual. This weekend was special, Moppet was performing in the talent show. Dorie would be going with Moppets parents to the show.

Once a year talent scouts would hold talent contests in a large center surrounded by many small communities. Children, teens and adults could compete but must be pre screened for talent ability. The top ten were chosen out of a hundred or more hopeful contestants. Later a date was set and the top ten competed for the top three prizes.

Moppet had played the piano beautifully but after losing her arm, lost interest in playing the piano for months. Only recently Moppets love for music resurfaced and she decided to perform in the talent contest winning one of the ten spots much to Moppets parents, friends and classmates happiness. The community was planning to give Moppet lots of support by attending the talent show. She ended up winning second prize, two adult sheep. Dorie was very happy for Moppet. It was really good to see her friend beaming with joy.

Moppet's mom and dad had two new horses, a mare and her colt, waiting in the barn for Moppet to see. The horses were a gift to Moppet for doing so well in school and the talent show. When Moppets family and Dorie arrived home, Moppet was led by lantern light to the barn. On hearing the two new horses belonged to her Moppet was overcome with joy, ecstatic saying "Are they really my horses!? What a beautiful gift! There isn't anything nicer than horses!" Moppet would shut her eyes then open them saying "The horses are still here! I'll name the mare Bell and the colt Pepper. My, oh my, Dorie, I'll have to break Pepper, make him rideable!" Dancing about Moppet said "Thank you Mom and Dad, you couldn't have given me a nicer gift!" A dream had come true for Moppet. She could now ride in fair competitions. In the night Moppet woke Dorie, asking was it really true she had two new horses. It was difficult to fathom for her, having such lovely horses. Moppet thought of breaking and training Pepper, make Pepper realize she was his master, but a master who loved him a lot.

The next evening Moppet and Dorie were with the horses when Alice called the girls for supper. Moppet said "We better hurry and get washed up." After the girls washed up they took their seat at the table. Alice sat down, said grace and started to pass the food around. When Dorie saw what was being served she felt ill. The main dish was kidney pie. Dorie's family never ate kidneys. Dorie passed the pie to Moppet and reached for the salad. Alice noticed Dorie passing the kidney pie on and said "Have some pie Dorie, you've had a long busy day."

Dorie replied "No thank you, salad is all I feel like eating, I don't feel well."

"Nonsense Dorie" Alice said. "Salad isn't sufficient nourishment to see you through the night." With a sudden movement Alice placed a large spoonful of kidney pie on Dorie's dish. Dorie didn't want to be rude so she took a small spoonful of pie, popping it quickly into her mouth, swallowing the food and taking a big drink of water to wash the taste away. Dorie couldn't stop thinking she had kidney in her stomach.

Dorie went to stand up and race for the washroom but the food and water rushed out of her mouth before she could leave the table. Dorie cried out "I've painted everywhere! I'm sorry!" then rushed outside heaving and vomiting some more. Alice found Dorie sitting on the grass weeping. The woman took Dorie in her arms saying "Dorie, I'm sorry, I should have listened to you, hush, hush my little darling. When your tummy settles let me know and I'll make you a toasted tomato sandwich, give you a large glass of milk and an orange."

Dorie abruptly sat up straighter saying "An orange? A real orange!? That's my favorite fruit!"

Alice replied "Yes Dorie, Moppet told me."

Next morning Moppet's mom sent the girls to take coffee out to the railway repairmen. She made coffee each morning for the railmen who rode their railcar up and down the rails checking if repairs were needed. The railway ran next to the highway and Moppets family lived across the highway, close to the main road. Moppet's mom owned and operated a gas station, selling gas, oil, pop and other treats. The railway men would stop each morning across from Moppet's home, blare a horn and Alice would run a big thermos of coffee out to the men and bring an empty thermos back. This morning when the horn sounded Dorie grabbed the thermos and she and Moppet headed for the railway across the highway. Usually two men rode in the car and on occasion four men rode in the car. After taking the thermos one of the men asked Moppet and Dorie "Would you girls like a ride for a short distance then walk back?" "Yes please," replied the girls, jumping into the car. As the car sped off, Dorie thought what fun this ride is, a convertible ride must feel like this. The girls each blew the horn twice but all to soon the ride was over.

On the walk home Dorie spotted a bottle with some whiskey in it. Dorie said "When we find other bottles with a little whiskey or beer in them we can pour it into this bottle and when its full sell the bottle to the older boys at your school!" Dorie removed the cap from the whiskey bottle, smelled the contents then passed it to Moppet to smell before replacing the cap.

Moppet thought for a moment then said "It's the real stuff Dorie." Dorie asked Moppet if she thought they could sell a full bottle for one dollar and fifty cents." Moppet replied "Sounds like a good price. Should we hide the bottle of whiskey under the hay in our barn? Before we start out on Bell, we can put the bottle of whiskey in a jacket pocket or a canvas bag." Moppet continued. "I have a small canvas bag with handles."

Dorie said "That sounds good, we take the bottle when we leave the barn and on our return we ride Bell to the barn and quickly hide the bottle under the hay." Moppet confirmed

Moppet asked "Dorie what will you buy with your half of the money?"

Dorie replied "I'll buy a comb, have my own comb to take wherever I go! And a green ribbon for my hair and some oranges. What will you buy?"

"I will buy a small bottle of perfume and a new curry comb for Bell and Pepper. When the whiskey bottle is full, I'll take it to school and sell it to Norman who always has money and hangs out with a rough group of boys that attend high school."

Dorie's dad was always busy, if he had some extra time he would cut down trees to sell as logs, cut up logs to be sold as fire wood, caught and skinned wild rabbits to sell to the meat market, raised an extra cow to sell and this fall would be helping a man build a garage. Paul was hoping he could earn enough extra money to buy another property that was nearer Elm school. He hoped to move his family someday to this new property because besides being closer to school, the property bordered on a main road that was snow plowed after snow storms. Mr. Kinny looked forward to the day he didn't have to shovel snow off a mile long road. It took Paul and Harry a week of hard shoveling after a snow storm with a high wind causing much drifting. Harry was thinking of moving back to his father's farm near Purplehaven. Rita and Dorie often missed school during winter if the road was blocked with deep snow. Paul kept thinking if Harry moved it would take him two weeks to clear a heavy snow fall off the road and thought he needed to invest in a small snowplow that could be pulled by horses.

Dorie thought her dad looked tired and asked her father if she could help with the extra jobs he was doing. He responded by saying, "Dorie if you have extra time I'd love some help." He showed his daughter how to skin rabbits and help him saw logs into fire wood length. Paul felt he would be able to purchase the new property soon. Dorie's dad had a dream of buying a new log house, that he could move on his new property, but he would have to settle for an older home. A farmer ten miles distant was building a new home and told Paul he could have his old house at no cost. Moving the house would be the only cost Dorie's dad faced.

Paul's friend William said he knew a house mover with the proper equipment. William would ask the house mover the expense of the ten mile move. The next time Paul ran into William, Paul was quoted a price of fifty dollars to move the house. The new house sounded exciting but it still wouldn't have running water. Garth and Dorie would each have their own bedroom. Dorie would still continue to sleep on her cot and use cardboard boxes to store her possessions but what Dorie liked was that she would get her very own room with a door!

CHAPTER FOUR

Dorie's Aunt Martha came with her two young sons. Dorie was practicing jumping when she arrived. Dorie said "What a surprise! Dad didn't tell me you were coming." Aunt Martha was very upset and crying a lot, when Paul finished his chores he took Aunt Martha into the kitchen for a long talk while Dorie and Garth with their two cousins played outside. Dorie and Garth taught their cousins 'Mother May I' and 'Tag'. After awhile Paul came outside to say aunt Martha would be staying two weeks. Garth would sleep on a mattress beside Dorie's cot and Garth's bedroom would be shared between Auntie and her two sons.

The next morning while milking cows Paul told his daughter about Aunt Martha's life. Aunt Martha's husband was very abusive with her and their children. Auntie and the boys were often beaten. The boys were frightened, jumped at noises as their father would quietly come up behind them and slap the sons on the side of their heads or pick them up and throw them around the room, laughing when they fell to the floor. If Aunt Martha took the two younger sons and left for awhile, uncle was nicer to them on their return but as time passed he returned to his nasty behavior.

While Auntie stayed she helped mom can, cook, clean and sew needed clothes. She was an excellent seamstress, and Annie enjoyed the help. Dorie and Garth treated their cousins in a very kind way, letting the boys win games and giving up treats. Dorie was teaching her older cousin how to ride a bike which he enjoyed immensely and had almost conquered, he was able to ride short distances by himself. Dorie asked her father if they could take the boys to visit Tom and Molly on Saturday when he travelled to Purplehaven.

Dorie's father talked to Martha about taking her son's to Purplehaven without her. Would Dorie's cousins become fearful and unmanageable without Martha being present? Martha smiled and said "Paul my sons will be fine with you and this will be a great adventure for my two lambs." Suddenly a sadness came over Martha and she seemed to talk to herself, looking off into space stated "If only my two lambs could find peace at night. Paul you must see the change in the boys, they're not as scared, they now go outside without me, they play with Dorie and Garth and of course you know about their appetites," said Martha. "All these good effects have happened in a week's time Paul." Martha said. A feeling of hopelessness overcame Martha as she pondered the thought of returning to her husband.

Paul went and sat beside Martha, taking her hand and telling her "Martha I will be visiting a friend of ours who we call Aunt Jane. Aunt Jane is elderly, needs help and lives in a huge house near Purplehaven. If she is willing to open her doors to you and your sons Martha, would you be willing to move?"

Quickly Martha replied "Oh yes Paul, I'd rather not return home, I see behavioral problems developing in my two younger sons and I feel Willie can't be helped. Willie is very angry, flies into rages with the younger ones, breaks items and wanders around at night, I hear him pacing in his room or leaving the house only returning when the sun rises."

"I'll visit Aunt Jane on Saturday while Dorie, Garth and your sons stay with Tom and Molly. Perhaps you won't have to return to your husband. We'll have Willie live with us, perhaps it's not to late for him. Over time Willie might change with love, kindness and gentleness." said Paul.

Saturday morning on arrival behind Tom and Molly's Dorie helped Garth and her two cousins out of the wagon, then guided the group into the restaurant. Paul had gone to visit Aunt Jane. Neither of Dorie's cousins had eaten Chinese cuisine before but both boys enjoyed the Chinese food immensely and asked for an extra helping much to Molly and Tom's delight. Dorie had never seen her cousins' smile but when the ice cream cones were brought out their faces lit completely, smiles included.

Dorie's father returned from Aunt Jane's with good news! Aunt Jane was happy to have Martha and her sons move into her home. Having children around would cheer up, brighten and make her surroundings more lively. What Aunt Jane looked forward to , were home cooked meals and help with the house cleaning plus it would nice to have company. Martha and her sons would move to Aunt Jane's on Monday.

Martha's sixteen year old son would live with Paul and Annie till he became more emotionally stable and was able to deal with life issues in a normal way. Everyone hoped that eventually Willie would move in with his mother.

Paul alerted Garth that he would have to move out of his bedroom and sleep on a mattress in the living room. Paul also talked to his children about some of Willie's emotional problems. Dorie and Garth were instructed not to tease Willie, never laugh at him and to leave him alone. Dorie asked her father "Does Willie have to come to our home?"

"Yes Dorie Willie lives in an unpleasant environment, he needs help now. Paul went on to say "Willie becomes angry easily, is edgy, stubborn and likes to be alone your Aunt Martha was telling me. Let's love Willie, be kind to him, help him realize the world can be a good place to live. We will erase his hurt, or certainly try. The man paused. While they were talking about helping friends, he had something to tell his daughter.

"Doris, you were telling me about Bess and X-Cee's family being poorer then us. I've talked to Tom, Molly and George about this family and their nine children. Molly said a box of clothes would be ready Saturday. Tomorrow ask X-Cee to check with his mom and dad, if they would mind us bringing a box of clothes over, if X-Cee's parents don't mind ask when it would be convenient to bring the clothes."

Next morning Dorie gave X-Cee the message from her father and the following day X-Cee told Dorie "Our parents would be happy to get the clothes and would they please come Sunday afternoon?"

Saturday Paul picked up two huge boxes of children's and adults clothes. George had bought some clothes, and picked up clothes and shoes from Molly and Tom's relatives and friends. William also had contributed a pile of clothes. Annie was taking jam and canned fruit. Jean was baking several loaves of bread and rolls. Moppet's mom was sending head cheese and bacon to the poor family.

Sunday afternoon when they arrived at X-Cee's family farm, X-Cee's dad came out and helped Dorie's father with the horses, led the horses into a corral with full water pails and fresh cut grass. Paul and X-Cee carried the clothes and food into the house.

The children were excitedly pulling out clothes and trying them on. Dorie beamed when X-Cee found a new dark blue parka that fit him. A proud look changing to a look of pleasure passed over X-Cee's face, no longer would he have to wear his mother's fur coat. X-Cee also found a nice blue dress shirt and several t-shirts plus some next to new jeans that fit. Bess also found dresses and jeans that fit.

One of the children pulled out a toy car from near the bottom of the box and screamed "A toy!" alerting all the other children. The clothes brought delight but the toys brought triple cheer. Dolls, games, books, puzzles, yoyos, a basketball, a bat, a ball and two kites. X-Cee's brothers and sisters had a great time choosing toys. X-Cee chose the ball, bat and a book, Dorie loved to see the warmth and happiness on X-Cee's face. Dorie and Garth didn't have many toys but neither child was envious.

Next Dorie's and X-Cee's families went out to play ball. It was a slow fun game, everyone had a chance to bat the ball and to catch the ball. All too soon it was time to go home after everyone had a drink of cold water. Before leaving, Paul gave Dorie's ball that she had found in a ditch to X-Cee.

Dorie was cross and expressed her feelings to her dad on the way home. "Dad how could you give my ball away, now I don't have a ball!"

Dorie's father replied "That family has nine children. They have never played ball and you got along without a ball before you found the ball in the ditch a week ago."

"Dad you're right, but it still hurts."

"Rita will let you use her softball." Her father told her. Dorie thought 'When it is warm I could always leave early for school on my bike and practice pitching the school ball over home base.' Behind home base was a tough netting that would stop the throws. Dorie needed lots of practice throwing the ball rapid and with a spin.

Mr. Joma was upset with the class not doing well on their examinations and he said to the students "No talking, writing notes or getting out of your desks without permission from me. Sassing the teacher will earn a strapping" he said, as he pulled a short, wide leather strap out of his top drawer.

Mr. Joma had become very strict with the students, if they talked he threw small pieces of chalk at them or used a long ruler he carried around with him and gave the guilty students strong taps on their head, shoulder or hand. Mr. Joma also said "No recesses and no Christmas concert if exam marks aren't up by mid November." The students soon got the message to work harder at their lessons and to study. The majority of the students wanted a concert.

Mr. Joma said if the students marks improved he would hand out play parts after exams in November and the students would have short practices starting in December. The older students would decorate the tree. Maxi would play Christmas carols on the old piano. This year all students would receive a bag of treats after the concert.

On this lovely warm October day X-Cee wanted to try riding a bike, he kept asking students only to be refused each time he made the request. X-Cee approached Dorie and asked her to get Rays permission to let him ride Rays bike. Dorie felt X-Cee was becoming too friendly with her and was very unhappy but she didn't want to hurt his feelings so Dorie timidly approached Ray and made the request on X-Cee's behalf. Ray shouted at Dorie "No brat, I don't want my bike all smelly." A couple of older boys over heard Dorie's request to Raymond and approached Ray at recess.

"Ray come on let X-Cee ride your bike a short distance, then he'll quit bugging every student about riding their bike. Maybe X-Cee won't ever be able to ride a bike because of this short leg."

Ray replied "Alright don't nag, X-Cee can ride my bike under the conditions I set.

During afternoon recess Ray approached X-Cee and told him he could ride his bike a short distance up the road and then turn and go over the ditch bridge. The bike was placed in X-Cee's hands by Ray.

Fairly close to the road was a creek, about four feet deep. A wooden bridge with no guard rails spanned the creek. This bridge was used by students as a short cut into the school yard, otherwise the students had to go up the road half a mile and enter the school yard through the main gate. Jody and Ray's fathers had built the bridge after they had discussions with the school board.

Excitement was building among the students who lined the road. Then up the road came X-Cee riding Ray's bike, wobbling from side to side, X-Cee looked like he might fall any minute. The school children chorused "faster, faster X-Cee!"

Then Raymond shouted "X-Cee turn and go over the bridge!" X-Cee turned, went down the ditch incline, losing control veered off the bridge into the water, fell with the bike landing on top of him. The students didn't make a sound, they didn't move, they stood and stared at X-Cee. A strange look, a fearful look appeared on X-Cee's face.

Dorie turned to Rita saying "Rita, oh Rita he might drown we have to get Mr. Joma!" Rita simply nodded.

Rita and Dorie ran toward the school screaming loudly "Mr. Joma, Mr. Joma X-Cee is going to die! Help!" Mr. Joma came running out of the school door, raced over to the scene, waded into the water, grabbed X-Cee by the collar of his shirt and pulled him to safety. X-Cee sank to his knees, blue in his face, coughing out water and shaking like a leaf in the wind. Mr. Joma removed his sweater placed it around X-Cee's shoulders, then stood X-Cee up and half carried him into the schoolroom. Lying X-Cee on a bench, Mr. Joma rushed outside to his car pulling a blanket off the front seat and grabbing a couple of towels from the back seat.

He locked the school door, ushered X-Cee into the cloak room, telling X-Cee to quickly remove his clothes, dry himself, then wrap the blanket around himself and lie back down on the bench in the school room. In the meantime Mr. Joma phoned Ray's father who lived very close to the school, asking him to bring warm clothes and a couple of blankets as one of the children had fallen into the water. Ray's mother also sent a hot honey lemon drink in a thermos. After X-Cee dressed himself in warm clothes, wrapped himself in a blanket and lay down on the bench, he fell asleep. Ray's dad returned again with some dry slacks and socks for Mr. Joma. Mr. Joma was very grateful for the help given by Ray's parents.

After school Mr. Joma drove X-Cee home worried he might have aspirated some dirty water and would get pneumonia. Mr. Joma explained what happened to X-Cee's mother, asked her to keep X-Cee warm and indoors for two or three days and to put mustard packs to his chest before bed and in the morning. "Should X-Cee get feverish cough a lot, or have trouble breathing, send a note to school with Bess. I will drive you and your son to the doctor and pay for the expense."

After supper Moppet and her mother visited. Moppet was upset and said she needed to talk to Dorie. The girls went outside and sat on the steps. Tears came to Moppets eyes. "Dorie I took the full bottle of whiskey to school and sold the whiskey to Norman for one dollar and fifty cents. After school Norman and that rough gang of boys he associates with drank most of the whiskey getting very drunk. Norman was running around the yard singing, 'My mom has forty girdles, blue, pink, white and even a purple girdle. Boys, there's girdles everywhere. Mom loves girdles, she wears them everyday maybe even to bed!' Some of Norman's friends climbed trees and hung upside down, one friend was rolling around on the ground. Dorie, Norman's dad talked to my dad telling him it was a terrible scene. Norman's mother heard the singing had her husband go out and check. There was some whiskey left in the bottle so Normans dad poured it out on the ground and their dog lapped it up. After awhile the dog ran around in circles howling. Norms mom stayed in the house, was too embarrassed to go out. Finally Norman's dad got the boys in his car and drove them home. The parents are very angry especially Norman's mom who said she will leave no stone unturned to find the guilty person and have them thrown into jail. Norman's mom is upset to think one of the boys might have badly injured themselves and embarrassed, as it's apparently true she has many girdles. Dorie, what if one of the boys tells who sold the whiskey to Norman?"

"Moppet they won't tell, can you imagine what the kids would think if an older boy broke the code of silence? No one but the two of us know how it was collected, although I wish we hadn't collected and sold that whiskey! We were very wrong, our fathers would be very upset to think we would harm another person."

"Yes Dorie we hurt the older boys and their parents, never again will I sell bad things like that.

"Yes, it's evil, and I thought of the idea. Do you think I'm bad or becoming a really bad person?"

"No! You're kind and thoughtful, we didn't think ahead, we thought of collecting the whiskey and the money from the sale but not what could happen if the older boys got drunk, how they then might injure themselves or others. Please don't blame yourself entirely, this idea of selling the whiskey was not only your fault, it was equally my fault because I went along with the idea. Just because we made a mistake doesn't make us bad but we did learn a precious lesson." Moppet and Dorie sat on the steps in silence feeling great emotional pain.

Finally Dorie spoke, changing the subject. "A stray dog came to our house yesterday, he's inside with Garth. He wants to call him Tony and I agreed. Dad said we could keep Tony and feed him table scraps, he likes the idea of having a dog around as a dog will alert him and the rest of the family when company comes or a stranger lurks around. I love Tony, he loves to cuddle and be petted."

There was still silence, so Dorie changed the topic again. "Moppet will you come Saturday afternoon, we can practice running and high jump?"

"No, Dorie I can't as I have an extra piano lesson in the afternoon but perhaps I can come Sunday afternoon."

Tony was with the family two weeks when their loud uncle came to visit. Uncle was an unpopular man in the neighborhood. After years of scams and conning money out of his neighbors Uncle was shunned by the people living in his community.

After Uncle stopped his car in front of the house, opened the car door and proceed to get out, Tony came running at uncle snarling, his lip pulled back from his upper teeth. Uncle quickly climbed back into the car, slamming the door shut. Tony went ballistic, jumping up on the car and growling. Tony seemed frantic.

Dorie ran into the house to get her father as Tony wouldn't obey her. Then Paul came out and took control of the dog, leading Tony to the barn to lock him inside. When Paul returned to Uncle's car, he found the man angry and red in the face. Uncle said "Paul I'm surprised you would keep an attack dog around two young children." He made no reply. Uncle then asked if he could borrow the other's hammer. Dorie's father replied "No I'm helping build a garage and need the hammer." Upon hearing Paul's refusal Uncle drove off in an angry mood.

Three days later Tony was missing. Dorie went through the woods, down by the creek, checked the sheds and barn calling for Tony he didn't answer her call by appearing. Each morning when Dorie got up she looked for Tony. Her father tried his best to reassure Dorie. He said, "Dorie remember, Tony came to us as a stray, perhaps he's living in another home being loved."

"No Daddy Tony would never leave us forever, Tony loved us, dad something has happened to Tony. Do you think Tony was hit by a car?"

"Dorie it's only been three days since Tony's been gone, if he loves you as you feel, he'll be back."

"Dad I know something bad has happened to Tony."

Next morning dad went to Purplehaven when he returned he had an orange, a real orange to be shared between Garth and Dorie. Dorie whooped it up, dancing about for joy. Suddenly it dawned on Dorie, something was wrong, dad looked hurt, sad, staring out the window. "Dad I'm sorry, I really got carried away!"

"No Dorie I know how you love oranges and to get excited is okay. Dorie, Garth come and sit down, I have some news for you." When Dorie and Garth were seated, Paul placed his arm around his children saying "I'm sorry about what I must tell you, I'm not sure how to start." Dorie and Garth looking up at their father waiting to hear what he must say, what was the news? Paul finally started to speak in a low sad voice. "As I was driving along the highway on my way home I noticed the body of a dog in the ditch. I stopped the horses and went to check on the dog."

Dorie became stiff, tears forming in her eyes, then she cried out "Daddy, oh Daddy it was Tony, wasn't it?"

"I'm sorry Dorie, it was Tony." Quietly Paul spoke. "I picked Tony up, placed him in a box and brought him home. Dorie this was his home where he was loved and where he'll be buried." Sobbing Dorie threw herself into her father's arms. Paul whispered in Dorie's ear "I'll build a cross and paint it yellow like the sunshine. We'll get a blanket from your mom. Garth and I will dig a grave on top of the hill where Tony liked to chase rabbits. You can say the grave side words. Should we ask Rita and Jean to come?"

"Yes Daddy."

Sunday afternoon Jean and Rita came to the funeral. Jean was carrying a box like package for Dorie and a smaller package for Garth. The packages Jean said were to be opened later. Rita had picked a handful of wild roses which she gave to Dorie, to place on the grave. After Tony was buried the cross was put in place by Garth, then Dorie placed the wild roses on the grave while Rita sang her favorite hymn, 'You Are My Sunshine'. Everyone standing around the grave had tears in their eyes. Rita pulled Dorie into her arms saying, "Tony was lucky to have had you as a friend Dorie."

Dorie opened her package to find a softball and Garth found a fire truck in his package. Both Garth and Dorie were delighted with their gifts but the gifts could only attempt to lessen the painful memory of Tony being gone.

Later Dorie confided in Rita that Tony had been shot. "Rita, I think uncle shot our dog." said Dorie. She went on to explain "Uncle was very angry when he came to visit and Tony wouldn't let him out of the car."

Rita replied "How sad that a person could kill an animal out of meanness."

"Rita I have to tell you a strange story about Jetta my cousin who is four years old. Last Tuesday my uncle Trey was to be residing over a funeral service in the afternoon. The relatives of the dead man asked Uncle Trey if they could bring the body in the casket Tuesday morning to the Church. Tuesday morning Uncle unlocked the Church. Mid morning the relatives arrived with the casket in the back of the truck. The casket was unloaded, and the family left the Church door unlocked when they left. Jetta then entered the Church, pulled a chair over to the casket; Jetta heaved and pulled until she finally managed to open the casket. Looking at the dead man, Jetta said, 'wake up, hurry wake up, open your eyes silly man or you'll be stuck in the ground!' Jetta didn't receive any response so Jetta left the Church then returned carrying a pail. As Jetta climbed back on the stool with the pail, her nine year old brother Brian appeared in the doorway saying 'Jetta what are you doing?'

Jetta tipped a pail full of sand in the dead mans face before Brian could reach the coffin. Jetta then said 'there now wake up.'

"The seriousness struck Uncle and Auntie as they rushed off for equipment to clean up the mess."

An oil company had started doing seismograph near the new property Dorie's dad purchased, and the land Dories family lived on was only one mile away. Paul had mineral rights on his property and he hoped the seismograph crew would end up with positive findings. One month later Dories father noticed new equipment was being delivered by huge trucks and an oil derrick was starting to be assembled. Dories father would walk the mile each evening to check on the progress being made by the workers. Dreaming and hoping the final outcome of this project would be much oil being pumped out of the ground. Soon the oil derrick was operational, drilling deeper and deeper.

Occasionally Paul would take Dorie and Garth. The sight was beautiful at night, lights all over the work area and derrick except it was really rather noisy. There was a derrick man who adjusted and put pipes in their proper place. Dorie thought these derrick men were so brave, what if they fell. Would they land in the dark deep pool of water near the derrick? Dorie shivered to see the daring man climb up so high.

As the days passed the workers didn't feel hopeful they would find oil. One evening as Paul, Dorie and Garth approached the derrick, they noticed a new bright light, a burning fire at the end of a pipe. The workmen told dad they had struck a small amount of gas and were burning this gas off. The workmen called this gas fire a flare.

That evening the foreman told Dorie's dad they had been instructed to stop drilling by the oil company. The gas pool was to small and deep so they would cap the well.

Dorie knew her father had a feeling of heaviness of heart, for days he didn't speak much. Dorie wished her father's happy spirit would return, Dorie knew her father was disappointed no oil had been found in the oil well, Dorie's father wanted to give his family a good life like most of the families in the community.

Garth was putting together a wooden platform and small crude derrick. Garth's dad gave him some old wood and would help Garth do some of the building.

The harvest was completed. It was getting colder in the evenings and was dark by five. Dorie needed to study, especially spelling and she had started reading books. Mr. Joma told Dorie, reading was an important tool in education, it would increase her general knowledge. Dorie's parents retired early putting out the coal oil and kerosene lamps before they went to bed. Dorie often would lie awake after the lights were put out wishing she could read. On weekends as soon as the light filtered through the window, Dorie would wrap a blanket around herself and sit by a window and read till it was time to do chores.

Dorie dreamt a lot of making the softball team in the spring, she was fast, a good catcher, strong ball thrower, good pitcher but she still had to work on her batting skills. But during the winter she would work on her lessons, especially spelling. Come spring Dorie knew she would make the softball team. Her heart told her this would be the year that she would become a player on the softball team.

One morning at school a girl named Wanda said to Dorie "Did you hear what Betty did yesterday after school?"

"No I haven't heard." Dorie replied.

"Betty went to play with Irene but instead of going the long way around by following the road, Betty crossed through Mr. Ames field and the mad bull was out. Mom screamed and screamed, she couldn't seem to move, then she fainted just as Dad ran into the room to see what all the noise was about. Dad checked mom, picked her up and put her on the sofa. Then he came to the window, when he looked out the window he turned white, grasped the window sill and cried out, 'Betty how could you go into that field?!' The bull was coming closer and closer to Betty and just as the bull was ready to connect with her, she quickly stepped aside and hit the bull on the nose with a small stick. The bull went running off across the field while Betty continued on her way to Irene's. We all let out a sigh of relief. She got a spanking on her bottom and had to go to bed without supper, that's how mad mom was, she seldom gets angry and has never spanked any of us. Anyway, I thought it was funny. Also, I wish you could have made the ball team. You're a really good ball player. I know I came over here for something else… Oh right! Dorie will you be able to come to my birthday party?"

"I must check with my Dad, I'll let you know tomorrow." Dorie walked away thinking her classmates were nicer, kinder, less taunting and name calling, she was now being included in her classmates activities. Dorie felt like a rose opening in the spring, instead of releasing a scent she released happiness and joy bringing her to a new elevation with her practicing track and field. Dorie could now run graceful like a gazelle for two miles without stopping and little shortness of breath. She was beginning to leave her mark, hopefully next May she would earn many points for her school. Dorie received below average grades in spelling and grammar but she excelled in sports, driven by her need to be acknowledged and accepted by her peer group.

Paul continued to instruct Dorie how to throw a fast ball with a spin, he also spent much time aiding her to improve her batting ability. Moppet continued to visit and practice jumping and running with Dorie. Her life was full of practice.

Dorie was continuing to practice high jump while her father was working near by on the root cellar. Garth was playing with his boyish built oil rig and flare line. Their parents did not realize Garth intended to make his flare line authentic. He had built up an imagery in his mind, seeing a large leaping flame flowing out of his pipe line, this fire fancy became a fixation and a reality as Dorie and her dad turned in answer to the uncanny high pitched screams for help. Garth had caught on fire. Dorie called loudly "Mommy, Mommy come quickly!" as Paul raced past Dorie, removing his coat as he ran, grabbing Garth, wrapping his coat around his burning son, throwing Garth to the ground and rolling him. With the flames out, dad removed his burned coat from Garth, turned away from his son, his body shaking, tears flowing down his face,, Paul finally managed to say, "Dorie move, get your mother, have her bring clean sheets then run quickly to Jeans and ask her to drive Garth to the hospital." Dorie stood rooted to the ground in a state of shock, tears flowing down her cheeks as she watched Garth moaning and crying in pain. A complete feeling of hopelessness invaded her body. Paul shouted once again, "Dorie, move! Do as you are told, get Mom and go to Jeans for help!" The blank look in Dorie's eyes finally disappeared. She looked at Garth and realized the great tragedy that had just occurred, with super speed ran to find her mother. As asked Annie grabbed clean sheets and raced out of the house while Dorie sped to find Jean.

When Jean and Dorie drove into the yard they beheld a strange scene. Jean thought 'What a calamity!' Annie was lying over Garth's chest while Paul was trying to shift Annie's body off Garth. Paul was saying "Annie help me wrap the sheets around Garth, perhaps if the air doesn't get at the burns, Garth will have less pain plus we want to keep the dirt and dust off the burns."

Jean jumped out of the car and rushed over to Annie saying gently, "Annie stand up so we can cover Garth and take him to the hospital."

In a stupor like fashion Annie rose, standing stiffly, muttering "My Garth, my dear Garth." After Paul and Jean placed Garth on the back seat, Jean led Annie to the car.

Jean then turned to Dorie saying "Go visit Rita darling, your dad will come to the hospital to give your mother emotional support and help make decisions about Garth."

Dorie waited until she saw the car leave for Purplehaven, then she wandered slowly in a dazed fashion to Rita's home. On arriving at Rita's home Dorie threw herself on the front lawn sobbing visualizing Garth's burned off shoes and slacks leaving legs looking all black but what hurt most was Garth whimpering interspersed with weak cries of it hurts that Dorie couldn't forget. Rita on hearing Dories sobs went to comfort her grieving friend. Rita took Dorie in her arms, sobbing with Dorie and feeling her great sadness. When Harry arrived home from doing his field work he found Rita and Dorie with tear streaked faces sleeping on the lawn. Harry roused the girls leading them into the warm house.

CHAPTER FIVE

Jean brought Paul home then returned to Purplehaven with a bag of personal items for Annie who would stay in town with Mrs. Salt, a close friend. Annie would spend most of her time at the hospital sitting beside Garth. Paul asked "Jean, could Dorie spend the night with Rita?"

Jean replied "Dorie is welcome to stay" and Jean asked if Paul wanted to come for supper. He declined the invitation as he needed time alone to gain his composure. Paul, with tears in his eyes kept repeating to himself 'The fire was my fault.' He felt he should have watched Garth more carefully, he shouldn't have allowed Garth to build the flare line and most importantly he should have hidden his smoke matches. Paul had a long sleepless night of reflection on his guilt and sorrow. By morning he realized he needed to be strong and composed to guide his family through this ordeal. Annie, Garth and Dorie needed his support and strength. Paul knew he must push back the regrettable, sorrowful time of Garth's accident and forge ahead with life. The man's body relaxed as the tenseness left him and placing his head against the back of the chair, fell asleep.

Dorie woke early, got dressed and quietly left Rita's home, anxious to see if her dad was okay and how Garth was doing. When Dorie last saw her dad, he was a strange color, very white and had tears in his eyes, looking lost and hopeless. When Dorie thought of the sadness she saw in her dad, she felt strong anger toward Garth for lighting the fire but then felt great sympathy for his suffering. Dorie's emotions were mixed, she loved her dad but at the same time she loved Garth, his kindness , gentleness, his sense of humor and how her brother would hug her and say 'Dorie I love you, I'm glad you're my sister.'

Dorie entered her home through the back entrance surprised to see her dad sleeping in a chair at the kitchen table. The girl stood still but as her dad's eyes slowly opened, she ran to her father, throwing her skinny arms around her father's neck. Paul lifted his daughter on his lap placing a kiss on Dorie's forehead, wrapping his arms tightly around her saying "You're home to help me with the chores are you?"

"Yes dad we'll work together doing the chores and we'll help Garth and Mom. We'll be like a team of horses working and pulling together."

"Yes Dorie we'll be there for one another always."

"When can I see Garth? How did he make the big fire? Will he be okay Dad?"

"Dorie stop. One question at a time. No you won't be able to see Garth yet and he will be in the hospital for a long time but you can write him letters, make little drawings and let him know you miss him and hope he'll be home soon. Your mother is staying at Garth's bedside as he's in a lot of pain. As to your second question, Garth took some of your mom's washing machine gas and helped himself to some of my smoke matches lying on top of the dresser." Paul paused before adding "Should have kept the matches out of sight, and talked more to Garth about his flare intentions, perhaps I would have clued in to Garth's plans to having a real burning flame."

"Oh Daddy, don't blame yourself, you and mom taught us not to play with matches! You won't even let us light the lamps which burn gas, you're afraid there might be an explosion!"

"Dorie we have learned lessons from this tragedy, let us now forge ahead, put all blame, the fire and hindsight behind us. We must look ahead and plan for the future." Grabbing his daughter he hugged her, telling her "We must help and support your mom and Garth and work at becoming a happy family once again." Paul continued "Never blame Garth. What has happened is now the past. Garth is suffering, is very ill, the accident that occurred and the pain he has and will endure will always be solidly dug into his memory. We should pretend we're taking our eraser, removing all blame, replacing the blame with love, help and guidance. You can make drawings, write fun notes to your mom and Garth. I'll cut extra fire wood for sale so mom has extra money to spend on herself and help bring comfort and happiness to Garth's life. Now little lady lets pick rose hips before doing chores. When Garth comes home I'll have lots of rose hip jam for Garth to eat, to help build up his immune system."

Suddenly Paul said "Dorie before we pick those rose hips lets kneel and say a prayer for Garth." Father and daughter, alone, full of grief bent their knees to the cold ground, praying that Garth would come home soon. Praying that when Garth came home he would be healthy and his legs would be healed. Then in silence they continued to kneel until finally father and daughter arose to pick the hips and go about their daily chores.

After school Dorie did her chores then was told by her dad that Jean had asked them for supper and Dorie could spend the night with Rita. Dorie liked the idea of spending the night at Rita's since she always made Dorie feel peaceful, surrounding her with happiness and goodness. Rita was all goodness, her large brown eyes shone, when Rita walked she seemed to float. Yes, Dorie thought Rita was an angel.

After supper Rita took Dorie's hand and said "Lets go to my bedroom." Dorie thanked Jean for supper, ran and gave her father a huge hug before following her friend. On entering the bedroom Rita said, "Dorie would you like to talk, listen to music, play grain or careers or just lie quietly on the bed? You can choose. I know how your heart aches."

Dorie said "Rita lets talk, you're so wise." Talk they did, way past bedtime, and they even fell asleep fully dressed. As Jean did her final check before retiring a smile curved her lips as she looked down upon the fully clothed girls with arms around each other, looking so at peace. Jean threw a warm blanket over the girls and left the room thinking of her teen brother being burnt to death in a neighbors house fire years ago. Paul had told Jean on his visit to the hospital that afternoon, Garth was in severe shock and the doctors were giving Garth blood and pain medicine through a vein. Annie looked tired and fretted a lot, spending most of her time at Garth's bedside. Annie's friend, Mrs. Salt packed nourishing brown bag lunches for Annie to eat during the day.

Next morning Dorie left Jeans early to do her chores at home before leaving for school. There would be extra chores for Dorie to do after school. She would now change the beds once a week, wash clothes and keep the house clean. Paul would cook and do the ironing. His daughter was encouraged to pack her lunch in the evening but often Jean packed a lunch for her instead. Jean told Paul it was just as easy to pack lunch for two as for one. Dorie loved Jean's lunches of ham, chicken, beef or peanut butter and grape jelly sandwiches. A cookie or cake plus an apple or banana were always included in the lunch.

Moppet's mom felt sorry for Paul and Dorie and would bring over a small pot of stew or a pot of vegetable soup twice a week. Jean would bring over casseroles, fresh baked bread and once a week a roasted chicken. Dad often cooked fish, made potato pancakes or stewed a rabbit in cream sauce. Dorie would get a jar of canned vegetable from the root cellar which also became part of their meal. Dad was a good cook despite what he said and thought.

Friday, Dorie rushed home from school planning to wash the clothes that evening so she could go to Purplehaven next morning with her father. She would rub and cleanse the clothes on a scrub board using hot soapy water then leave the clothes to soak in basins full of soapy water till after she had done her chores. Later Dorie would quickly rinse the clothes twice in clear water, and wring most of the water out by hand, while her father hung the clothes on the line by lantern light. The young girl, while her father was doing this, emptied the basins of water by carrying a half a pail of water outside several times. After cleaning up the supper dishes, she felt very tired, going to bed and instantly falling asleep.

Next morning Paul and Dorie left for Purplehaven, Dorie was looking forward to seeing Alex, Tom, Molly and George. Dorie knew she wouldn't be allowed to visit Garth but Dorie had printed a 'hope you can come home soon' love note with lots of 'I miss you Garth'. This note was accompanied by several drawings of Garth petting the horses, feeding the chickens and running after the mean rooster. While Paul went to visit Annie and Garth Dorie stayed in the waiting room looking around. She noticed how busy the hospital was, people dressed in white and green rushing about, people coming and going and the fact that the hospital had a strange odor. Quietly she sat and waited, wishing her mother would come and say hello. She hadn't seen her mother in over a month, but Dorie knew her mom was tired and the extra walking for her would be difficult.

After the hospital visit dad and Dorie visited Alex. Alex had a huge smile on his face as he greeted Dorie. "Remember I promised you a dress for Christmas, brat? It's stored in the office and you can take it home today."

Dorie jumped up and down calling out "It's green isn't it Alex!?" Then running over to Alex she wrapped her thin arms around his waist. Hugging him tightly she was saying over and over 'Thank you Alex!" Pausing, she added "Is there a green hair ribbon?"

"Yes brat and a pair green socks."

Dorie looked at her father saying "Daddy aren't I lucky to get such pretty clothes?" Paul turned away, nodding his head unable to speak. Paul thought he and Annie were truly blessed to have such a caring, unmaterialistic child whose only desire was acceptance. Paul still hurt that Annie hadn't visited Dorie for a few minutes in the hospital waiting room. He had asked his wife to visit their daughter and say hello but Annie had stood her ground, justifying it by saying she would be home for part of Christmas day. Annie was still feeling a great deal of guilt and felt she couldn't face Dorie at this time. After Garth was burned, Annie would lie in bed wondering why Dorie hadn't been burned instead of Garth. She knew it was wrong, very wrong to have wanted to see her daughter hurt. She was responsible, helpful, put others before herself, a model child. How could Annie be so uncaring toward Dorie? Annie knew she couldn't see her child today. Dorie's wisdom might see through Annie's feelings. The secretive inner wisdom that Dorie had frightened Annie. Who could she talk to about this?

Instantaneously Annie had her answer and she went searching for the head nurse. When Annie found the head nurse, Mrs. Fayor, Annie asked when Dr. Meisner, Garth's skin surgeon, would next visit. Mrs. Fayor turned to her desk calendar and replied "Dr. Meisner will see Garth at ten tomorrow morning." Annie thanked Mrs. Fayor and turned with a sigh of relief thinking perhaps there was an answer to the problem she had with Dorie.

After seeing Alex, Paul and Dorie visited Tom, Molly and George. George had been up to see Annie and Garth at the hospital several times but George was shocked when he looked at Paul's tired drawn look and Dorie's thinness, paleness and aura of sadness surrounding her usual energetic self. The middle Kinny was so young yet wise and grown up beyond her age many times. George was happy he had gone shopping for warm fashionable clothes for her. If you asked him, she needed to be pampered a bit. The Asian man gave Dorie a new parka, stylish hat, scarf, two pairs of mitts, lined winter boots and ski slacks. She felt she was living in a dream world, these clothes weren't real, she thought she would wake up and the clothes would be gone. Every time she opened her eyes the clothes were still there. With lightening speed Dorie ran to George, hugging him around the waist, then to Molly and Tom hugging them and expressing her thanks with tears rolling down her cheeks. Then she danced about saying "The clothes are beautiful, warm treasures."

Dr. Meisner arrived as scheduled, he examined Garth and decided to do skin grafting in a months time, in the mean time he would arrange to have the family tested for skin compatibility with Garth. When Dr. Meisner had finished discussing future medical care for Garth he turned to leave. Annie timidly called, "Dr. Meisner could I talk to you about a personal family matter?"

Dr. Meisner hesitated before he replied "Yes. Let's step into the interviewing room." After listening half an hour to Annie, Dr. Meisner took Annie's hand and said "I have some questions. If someone's dog is about to have puppies, does Dorie predict how many puppies will be born? Does she know the sex of a child before birth? Does she make predictions?" Annie answered no to all the questions Dr. Meisner asked. The doctor then looked at Annie for a moment before speaking again. "I know you said Dorie does poorly in school, this doesn't mean she isn't intelligent. I think she is intelligent, wise beyond her age and very responsible. She knows you and Paul need help and she is there for your family. Because Dorie has grown into a small adult wise beyond her years doesn't mean Dorie knows what you're thinking or what you're feeling in your heart. From what you've told me I think Dorie fears you, feels your distance and perhaps even feels unwanted by you. She needs your love and acceptance, Annie. She probably knows how much you love the boys, that in itself tells me a great deal about your daughter, she isn't jealous of Garth as she plays with him, protects and helps him. Alex and Garth love and respect Dorie. I think you have a precious family, don't let Dorie's emotional needs go unattended, don't let her slip away. To build a relationship with your daughter you must start slowly. Start with smiles, little compliments to her, when friends are around and your daughter is within hearing distance tell your friends what a wonderful, helpful child Dorie is. Occasionally bake her favorite cookies. Once in awhile put a surprise in her lunch. As her trust in you returns, hug her before she leaves for school, give her a good night kiss and teach her crafts - a mother daughter activity. You'll know how to reach Dorie's soul and in the end you'll find what a wonderful individual she really is. I wish you the best of luck and on my visits to Garth perhaps you can give me progress reports."

Dorie didn't have much opportunity to study for her exams and nor did she tell her father about the upcoming ones. Dorie knew her father would help do her chores to give her more opportunity to study. He already looked tired and when awake never stopped working. He would get sick if he did more work. Dorie helped her father more when she could. Her exam marks surprised Dorie; she only failed two subjects, spelling and English.

The Elm school children had done well in their exams so the Christmas concert would take place. Mr. Joma gave the students their play parts for memorization. One of the main plays was about fairies, a fairy mother and her helpers. Matty would be the fairy mother, wear a long white dress, a tiara and carry a wand. The five helpers would wear colorful dresses and carry a star on a wand. At the end of the play the fairies would sing 'Over the Rainbow'. Jean was sewing the dresses and told Dorie she would sew her a forest green costume while Rita's would be pink.

Dorie loved to sing, but she knew that it wasn't her strong suit. She knew her strong suit was running and jumping. Singing definitely wasn't one of Dorie's talents but it still hurt when Mr. Joma asked Dorie to sing quietly.

All too soon it was concert night. The excitement was building, Jean hovered over Rita and Dorie making the girls look prim and proper. When the students entered the school they went backstage behind the huge curtain that hung across the back third of the school room.

The concert was a huge success with parents and students. After the concert the students received a brown bag of goodies, they even gave Dorie a bag to give to Garth. Dorie received an extra easy peel orange. X-Cee came over to Dorie, looking embarrassed he handed her his orange saying "I want you to have my orange." X-Cee turned and disappeared into the crowd. A fourth orange made its way into her possession when she traded Rita her chocolate bar.

'It will be nice to have two weeks of holidays' Dorie thought as they climbed into Harry and Jean's car. On arrival at home dad told Dorie she could have Garth's orange, nuts and apple as Garth could only eat very soft food.

Christmas Eve Paul chopped a small evergreen tree down and placed it in the living room. Dorie and her father decorated the tree with ribbons, colored string, and school drawings. Christmas Eve Dr. Meisner visited Garth and talked to Annie a bit more about the skin grafting surgery he would perform on Garth. Then Doctor Meisner asked to speak to Annie in private. As Doctor Meisner and Annie entered the interviewing room, Doctor Meisner retrieved a large bag from behind the door. It was full of wrapped gifts. After the doctor placed the bag which was full of gifts on a desk, he removed a small brown box and opened it for Annie to see, saying "This is a gift for Dorie from you and Paul." Annie gazed down at the golden heart and chain thinking how dainty and feminine and how it gleaned in the light. It was ideal for her daughter.

Annie looked up at Doctor Meisner with a glow on her face, saying "Its lovely, so dainty and elegant. Dorie loves beauty and color, she will treasure this beautiful piece of jewelry."

Doctor Meisner said "I'm glad Dorie will like the necklace and in this bag are several gifts for Garth and Alex. Sam, my wife, wanted to choose the gifts for the boys, the gifts are unusual and charming." Sam and I had a four year old boy who was struck by a car and killed two years ago.

"Each Christmas Sam and I go caroling with a fun group and make up special hampers and give them to less fortunate families who have difficulty scratching out a living. This year we had the added fun and joy of choosing for your children."

"Dr. Meisner, Thank you for your kindness. Medically you have done a great deal for Garth plus we have commenced the healing process you advised to bring our family closer together and remove some of the old scars."

"Thank you Annie, its wonderful to see families work out their problems. Merry Christmas."

Christmas morning Moppet and her mom dropped off stuffed peppers, cut up yams and Christmas pudding. Jean brought cake, bread and buns. Later Dorie found three oranges in a bag placed on the table.

At noon, her parents returned. Dorie heard the horses arrive and dashed out to see her mother. Annie gave her daughter a small hug, then with a smile on her face told Dorie "You should be wearing a coat."

On entering the house Dorie said "Mom I peeled the potatoes and also peeled two carrots for the turkey dressing."

Dorie's mom gave Dorie a big smile saying "How thoughtful of you, would you like to help me bake cookies later?"

"Oh yes mom!" Dorie replied.

Dorie had moved into the small bedroom since Garth's hospitalization. She now retreated into the bedroom to be alone instead of her secret hiding place. That afternoon Dorie heard a knock on the bedroom door and when she opened it she faced her dad who had a gleam in his eyes and a big smile. Then mom appeared smiling and looking happy. "Dorie there is a surprise for us at the back of the Christmas tree. Quickly let's go." She said. Dorie ran ahead to see the gifts, shouting with joy when she saw the beautifully wrapped presents.

"Dad, Mom can we open the gifts now!?"

Annie replied "Yes Dorie, bring the gifts out and you can open the ones that have your name written on the little tag." Dorie opened her gifts finding a pair of skates, a comb and brush, several colored ribbons for her hair, a big doll, a bottle of perfume, a pair of white runners and as Dorie looked down at her beautiful gifts, belongings she never dreamt she would have at this time in her life, she heard her mother's voice which seemed so far away. Then the girl felt a warm hand on her shoulder, bringing her to a conscious level, reality set in. Her mother was handing her a gift. In a dazed fashion she turned and received the green wrapped box from her mother, which Dorie immediately opened finding a brown case. On opening the case her eyes fell upon a heart necklace that shone in the light. The heart looked so beautiful, a movie star would wear that kind of jewelry. The girl touched the heart, removed it from the case lying the heart against her cheek, then against her heart, finally raising the heart to her lips and gently kissing this gorgeous gift from her mom. Finally Dorie said "Mom, you never gave us a Christmas gift."

"I talked to your dad and he said we could give each child some gifts this year, you all needed to have some extra joy brought into your lives." Annie responded with a warm smile.

Looking at her mother, Dorie noticed tears in her mom's eyes, something was wrong, her mother never cried. Suddenly Dorie ran to Annie, threw herself into her mother's arms asking if her brother was okay. At that moment, Annie knew her daughter couldn't read her mind. The doctor had been right.

"Garth is fine, Dorie." Her mother assured her. Stroking her daughter's short hair, she noticed how lovely this sensation was, just how wonderful it felt to hug the girl close. It was a feeling she hadn't gotten with any of her other children. Relaxing her grip a little, she found that Dorie had fallen asleep, holding tightly to the beautiful necklace.

On entering the living room, Paul was overcome with emotion, a smile curved his lips, his eyes shone with joy, the golden door had opened, his hope that Annie would bond with Dorie was starting to become a reality. What a wonderful Christmas present.

After Dorie woke from her nap, the family headed to the kitchen to finish cooking Christmas dinner. The turkey was delicious. Dorie felt sad that Alex had to work but he would be home in the morning to open his presents. All the gifts were from George, Molly and Tom except the gifts Paul and Annie had given.

Annie took Garth's bag of presents, some cookies, and pudding when she returned to Purplehaven, driven by Jean.

On entering Garth's room with the gifts and food Annie learned from the nurse that Alex's skin was the most compatible with Garth's skin. Annie would talk to Paul on his next visit then Paul and Annie would talk to Alex, see how he felt about sharing some of his skin with his brother.

On Paul's next visit to Purplehaven, Paul took Annie to visit Alex, so they could explain that his skin was the closest match to Garth's skin and how would he feel about donating skin to his brother? The Skin grafts would be put on the larger, deeper burns, enabling them to fill in and heal faster. Paul also explained to Alex that he would have to miss about five days of work. Alex without hesitation agreed. "Dad will you join me when I request time off from work?"

Paul nodded. "Shall we see your boss now?" Alex's boss agreed to give Alex five days off with pay, saying that Alex was one of his best employees, and requested that if possible if they could give him three days notice before Alex went to hospital.

Soon Alex was called to hospital and the skin grafting procedure took place. Then the medical staff, Paul, Annie and Alex eagerly awaited news of the surgery being successful.

Annie started placing two chairs by the window, a chair for Garth to sit on and a chair for Garth to rest his legs on. Garth's legs were badly contracted remaining in a stationary position, not being able to flex or straighten his legs. Garth loved sitting by the window, it seemed to ease his boredom.

This morning Annie would play some board games with Garth while they waited for Garth's dressings to be changed. Today would be the day that Annie, Paul and Garth had waited for. Did the skin grafts take?

As the doctor entered with a dressing change tray, Annie knew the Kinny family would soon have an answer to the question, was the graft surgery successful?

Most of the skin graft had taken and looked nice and pink. A few grafts didn't take, and there were a few open areas that drained yellow discharge but the doctor in charge of the medical staff and bed availability decided Garth should be discharged and return twice a week for dressing changes. Doctor Meisner could do further grafting at a later date. He wasn't happy about Garth being discharged from the hospital and spoke at length to Paul and Annie about good technique. "Annie and Paul should carefully wash their hands before working with Garth, to keep dirty linen or clothes away from Garth's bed, don't allow Garth to touch animals and never put Garth on the floor." He lectured. Dr. Meisner also encouraged Annie to cook food that was high in protein, and give Garth vegetables twice a day if possible.

Moppet's mom brought Garth home. Dorie and Garth hugged and cried with happiness when they saw one another. Garth would use Dorie's cot which was situated near most of the family activity. Also the cot's height made it easier to care for Garth, plus it was easy to roll about. Dorie would stay in the small bedroom till Willie came.

After supper and with the chores done, Paul pulled a chair up to Garth's cot to talk with him about his plan to straighten the boy's legs. "If my plan works to have your knees flex and extend you will have a more normal life, be able to walk and ride your bike. If my plan doesn't work, you will be no worse off.

"The procedure I will use will cause some pain and discomfort while I work on your legs and perhaps you will feel some pain after I finish working on them. I hope that never at anytime will I cause great pain. If I do, it should be tolerable and not last long. If you have severe pain at any time you must let me know." Paul paused, regarding his son. "Are you willing to try my procedure?"

"Yes Dad, yes lets try, I want to walk."

"Hurrah for you Garth!" shouted Dorie. "Dad will fix your legs!"

Paul went to Purplehaven that afternoon to buy some dressings, a big box of salt and some material to make splints and on the way home Paul would stop at Alice's. He knew Alice worked in an operating room before she had her children thus Paul felt Alice could give him tips on how to change dressings properly.

Alice said she would come in the morning, bring the equipment needed and teach Paul how to change Garth's dressing.

After supper Paul worked on Garth's legs a short while. First he held Garth's legs slightly apart for a short while then gently rubbed Garth's thighs, beneath his knees and finally his feet. Lastly dad put warm moist face cloths under each knee held in place by a large towel, when the cloths cooled dad rubbed in the special herbal paste he made each summer. Dad then had Dorie get Garth a piece of bread covered with rose hip jam each day. The boy would be given rose hip jam to eat to help heal his legs. Their father said it had lots of vitamin C.

Dad had mom scrub a chair well. The clean chair was near Garth's cot and would only be used for dressing changes.

Alice arrived next morning with equipment to be used in changing the dressings of Garth. Alice took a small pot full of water, placed tweezers, small tongs and scissors into the pot of water, then boiled the tools for ten minutes. Annie had boiled a kettle of water which she placed outside to cool.

As Annie and Alice worked getting items ready for the dressing change the two ladies chatted. Annie told Alice Mr. Joma was going to order correspondence lessons for Garth. Mr. Joma said that Annie and Dorie would have to help Garth with his school lessons and Mr. Joma would come once a week and help with difficulties encountered in the lessons and spend some time teaching Garth.

Annie told Alice she was worried about Paul building up Garth's hope that he would walk normally some day and she didn't want Garth to suffer anymore. Alice was bewildered at Annie's thinking and asked in a soft tone "What type of life will Garth have lying in bed the rest of his life? Paul is an intelligent, caring person with extremely creative ideas, Annie surely you're aware how smart Paul is and he never seems to take risky chances. Paul needs your help and support, he is thinking long term, he needs your assistance."

"Alice I know you're right and I know Paul is right," Annie said. "Alice I admit, I am afraid Garth will suffer and then remain bedridden and he has suffered pain and discomfort now for months. I think of the probability that he won't walk and the emotional distress this will cause him."

"Annie life is all about taking chances. Garth can handle the outcome, he's a strong little fellow, and he's willing to try."

"Yes he is a strong child, the likelihood that he will walk is fair, why should I take away a dream that might become a reality? I know I must support them." She finally determined.

Annie went to retrieve the water which she placed outside to cool to a warm temperature, then she would pour the water from the kettle into two small bowls that had been boiled before Alice would add salt to them and carry the bowls in a special way to the washed up chair.

Alice placed clean folded bath towels under Garth's legs, washed her hands again, opened a glove package, moved the gloves aside with tongs and removed dressings from a package with the tongs, placed the dressings on the open glove package. Next, using the tongs, she dipped some of the dressings in the saline water then placed these wet gauzes on the yellow discolored areas on the leg dressings, then placed the tongs aside. As Paul watched, Alice then removed the outer leg dressings, taking the inner dressings off with a pair of tweezers and discarding the dressings in a small plastic bag. Then, laying the tweezers aside, asked Paul to wash his hands really well and when Paul returned she told him how to put the sterile gloves on in a special way. Paul was to take the second pair of tweezers while Alice went to get the second boiled bowl full of saline water which she had placed aside. Paul then washed the open areas with salt water dressings using tweezers then dried the sores with dressings and tweezers. Finally using the same procedure Paul cleansed the rest of the legs and dried them. Paul then had Annie bring the healing paste he made last summer from two wild plants growing in the woods. The paste was placed into and around the open areas by using dressings and the tweezers. Alice knew the paste worked, she had seen many times the rapid healing after the paste was used.

As the weeks passed and spring approached little by little the amount that Garth was able to stretch his knees increased. The open areas were healed, the leg skin was soft and smooth and Paul was using leg splints during the day. Annie was overcome with joy that Garth's legs were straightening.

In the evenings Dorie was to help Garth with his school lessons. She was to stay by the cot while he worked and to listen to Garth read, then one day, play checkers or chess with him to bring fun into his life. Mom asked Dorie not to win all the games but let Garth win some checker games. Dorie couldn't understand her mom these days, she was kinder actually showed her how to bake a cake and cookies and made little surprises for her. Much to Dorie's surprise her mother took her side in an argument that Dorie had with Garth. She was so surprised at her mother's reaction that she stood rooted to the floor, feeling she had heard wrong. The girl continued to stand and wait for punishment to befall, would Dorie be spanked or given more chores? She was so afraid as she waited for her mom's reaction. There seemed to be nothing, but eventually she felt a hand lay on her shoulder. Dorie stiffened and began to shake, at once her mother wrapped her arms around the girl, telling her "It isn't your fault, even if Garth isn't able to be up he knows right from wrong. Garth was wrong this time and he won't get cake for supper." Dorie looked at her mother, turned and ran into the small bedroom. Dorie threw herself on the bed thinking 'What is wrong with Mom? She is actually being nice!' Annie knew she must be patient, it would take time to bond with her daughter.

CHAPTER SIX

At times Garth didn't want to do school work and wouldn't listen to Dorie when he needed help. At times she would ask her mom to talk to Garth. Annie scolded her son, telling him "If you want to be twelve years old and still be in grade two don't let Dorie help you." That little scolding encouraged him to work on his lessons and inspired Garth to work harder for awhile but fairly quietly Garth said to his sister, "You're a rat, you broke the code of silence." Dad coming up behind said "I heard that statement Garth and I wish to inform you the code of silence isn't used in our home and young man you're getting very sassy, Dorie is giving up play time as well as study time to help you so you'll be able to meet grade two requirements when you go back to school in the fall. Perhaps you should share some of your candies your grandmother gave you yesterday and you have hidden under your pillow." The word 'grandmother' had Dorie turn and enter her bedroom.

Grandmother always brought candy or a toy to Garth, even before the fire. Alex and Dorie especially had to listen to Grandmother's cynical words such as 'You're so short Dorie.' and 'You don't have a pretty face.' or 'Are you still failing in school?' If Dorie saw her grandmother coming she would leave the house and go to her secret hide-away. Paul called Dorie and when she came out Garth was holding a handful of candies. "Dorie these chocolate candies are yours. I'm giving you half." Running to Garth, Dorie hugged and kissed her brother while he whispered in her ear "Grandma is a mean lady."

Paul told his son he was a good son and very brave the way he let them work on his knees, but regardless of this, he still needed to do his lessons. Dad gave Garth a loving tap on his shoulders while mom stood nearby smiling.

The middle of March they had a heavy snow fall with howling strong winds. This storm lasted five days.

At the start of the storm Paul locked the horses and cows in the barn with hay and water, and the poultry in the shed with food and water. The pigs had their own pen and shelter, but they needed water. Every so often Paul would open the door and push off the snow from the steps with a shovel so they wouldn't be blocked in the house by the drifting snow. Before going out each morning he would encircle his waist with a tied knot then tie the other end of the rope to the door knob. This method kept him from losing his way in the blowing snow as visibility was poor. Paul would make sure the livestock had water and food, then bring in wood from the woodpile. He would sleep in the afternoon, then milk the cows and gather the eggs. During the night Mr. Kinny stayed up all night to keep the fire burning in the pot bellied stove and watch for fire around the chimney. Paul had two pails of water near his chair just in case something bad happened.

Towards evening on the fifth day of the storm the snow stopped falling and the wind became silent. This eerie quiet surrounded the family, and Paul opened the door. All anyone could see were huge banks of snow, everything was covered with a white blanket. Paul went and got Garth so he could see what the snow storm had done. The cold still was intense the next morning but the sky was a beautiful blue with the sun rays making colorful dancing sparkles on the snow.

Paul told the girls to stay in while he shoveled pathways to the barn, shed, pig sty, and water well. He wouldn't lead the live stock into the field or yard till the drifts went down. In all that snow he had milked the cows, collected the eggs, fed and watered all the animals plus bringing canned food from the cellar and keeping the family supplied with water. Now the hard part came, shoveling the road. Five men shoveled for two days and hadn't even uncovered half the road. All the men including Paul complained of sore backs and shoulders but knew they had to continue. The government didn't clear side roads. The next morning the men were shoveling snow with all their aches and pains when they heard a strange sound, like a tractor. Looking yonder they spied a huge caterpillar with a huge snow plow blade in front. The men quickly scattered to safety from the machine and the mountain of snow it was throwing into the fields and ditch. Harry whistled. "It looks like a monster out of a science fiction movie." The machine went to the end of the road, turned and returned cleaning the other half of the road. Everyone was very pleased with the government's help, even the government realized that after this severe storm families living on side roads would have difficulty clearing the snow. After eight days of captivity the people were free to travel once again.

Dorie was getting anxious to practice her running and jumping. She kept thinking 'If only the snow would disappear.'

Grandma and Grandpa moved their old trailer upon the other piece of land dad had bought. Paul wasn't keen on letting his in-laws move on the land he had bought. He told her "I don't like your stepfather, he's mean and I feel he's unbalanced to the point of being dangerous."

Dorie piped up "Dad, how is grandpa unbalanced? He seemed to walk okay."

"Darling, unbalanced can also refer to the mind meaning he doesn't always think in a normal way like most people."

Annie approached Paul one day telling him what a wonderful job he was doing with Garth's legs. "Paul, Garth will walk, you're a remarkable man! I only thought of the present, not the future. Have you seen the change in Garth's personality? He's happier, full of joy, making plans for going back to school in the fall and having bike races with Dorie. Can you forgive me for doubting your intentions?" Annie walked over to her husband, throwing her arms around his neck and kissed him saying "Paul you have such mental strength, you're kind and caring, oh, Paul I'm so happy you found and married me."

"Annie you're also a very pretty lady with a great spirit, a truly amazing woman. I love you a lot my fiery soul mate. You rarely complained or longed for things we couldn't afford, you truly are a wonderful wife and I pray someday I can give you a better life." Then Paul and Annie walked off hand in hand, to search for Dorie.

Paul was thinking how wonderful it was to be married to such a compatible woman and have such nice children. Marriage really was about loving, caring and sharing. Annie was thinking how lucky she was to have married Paul. Paul was caring and very supportive, he never complained once all the while she stayed with Garth in Purplehaven. Paul did extra chores, watched Dorie, cooked and faithfully visited Annie and Garth several times a week for short periods, always asking if she needed anything. Not once did Paul complain.

Lately the excitement in the Kinny's household was building. Garth's legs were straight, Paul exercised his son's legs twice a day and told him to bend and straighten his legs several times a day stimulating the blood flow and strengthening his legs. Garth worked hard extending and flexing his legs, he wanted to walk and play outdoors.

Dorie, on the other hand was puzzled by her mother's attitude toward her. Her mother seemed nicer, kinder, but the girl supposed it was her imagination because she wanted if not a loving, a kinder caring relationship between her mother and herself. Dorie felt her mother didn't care for her, this feeling caused her a lot of pain. Suddenly she heard her mother call for her.

Dorie found her mother putting on Garth the thigh length flannel stockings she had made to protect the tender skin on his legs. Annie was afraid if the new skin was bumped the skin might split open. She asked her daughter to get the thick blue blanket and line the children's wagon with the it, a gift from Tom, Molly and George. "Mom, where are you going?" asked Dorie with fear in her heart.

"We are going to visit your grandmother."

"Mom can I please stay home?"

"No Dorie I need help pulling the wagon." Her mother denied her. "We'll take turns." Dorie knew if she refused there would be a storm of words and she'd end up going anyway. The girl thought she would go quietly, do as she was asked.

When the three of them reached grandma's trailer, Annie went inside leaving her children outside. Dorie peeked through the living room window then let out a gasp, turned away, looked again, just to make sure it wasn't her imagination. She did see two oranges and an apple on the living room table. Before Dorie knew what she was doing she was at the side door ready to sneak into the living room to grab an orange. But she stopped just as she was reaching for the door knob, it was wrong to steal even from a mean person. Suddenly the girl had a better idea, she ran to her brother whispering in his ear "Garth ask grandma for an orange and we'll share when we get home. Give her an extra big smile."

After awhile the two women came out. Grandma went to see Garth, giving him a hug and asking him how his legs felt. Annie headed for the tool shed and came back with a ladder that she placed against the trailer. She called to Dorie. "Put this hammer and some nails in your coat pocket, then climb the ladder and nail the loose shingle down. You'll know which shingle; it's the one flapping in the wind."

"No Mom, I won't do it for Grandma. Grandpa can nail the shingle down." Annie's face took on a look of disbelief and helplessness. What if Dorie wouldn't do the shingle task? Annie was afraid of heights.

Grandma turned and said "I told you a long time ago that Dorie was lazy and rebellious."

Dorie took one look at her mother's face and said "Mom I'll nail the shingle down." Rushing up the ladder she completed the nailing down chore. When she climbed down the ladder she saw an orange in Garth's hand. 'Good for Garth!' Thought Dorie. 'Grandma doesn't know that half of that orange is mine!'

Dorie said "Mom I'll go and wait for you and Garth by the main road."

Suddenly Grandma spoke. "Dorie I have a gift for you." She entered the house returning shortly. Walking over to Dorie she handed her a folded up brown scarf. The girl unfolded the scarf and found many small holes in the cloth, this was very clearly a rag. Without thinking Dorie threw the scarf at grandma's feet. Grandma sneered. "Annie you have a very ungrateful child, she is rude, has no manners, is ugly and isn't very cleaver." Dorie's face turned white and with an abrupt movement she headed for the main road.

Unexpectedly Annie realized how many times her mother had belittled Alex and Dorie in front of Annie and Garth. Alex left home early, Dorie was still distant and although a closeness was slowly growing between mother and daughter, Annie didn't want to see the small progress destroyed between them. Surprising herself Annie turned to her mother and firmly said "Mom I care for you, respect you and should you need help at anytime I will be there for you. But mom I love my children and love you but I can't tolerate you belittling Alex and Dorie. Did you see how hurt Dorie was? If you don't apologize to Dorie you're not welcome to visit us."

Grandma turned toward her house while Annie picked up the wagon handle and started for the main road. Garth was thinking he must tell Dorie later about mom telling grandma off like that. It was the first time ever.

Next morning Paul had left for Purplehaven, Dorie was in school and Garth had gone back to sleep. Annie sat in a chair, a vision of Dorie's pale, sad and frightful face as Grandma said those nasty words to her. Not wanting to wake Garth, Annie went outside sitting on the house step sobbing uncontrollably and reflecting in a jumbled way how unjust and unfair she had been with Dorie. When it came to giving her children love, attention, care and even gifts Dorie was always put on the bottom of her list. What Dorie wanted was never a priority with Annie. She must feel her mother's biased feelings thus shying away and turning to her father. Annie wondered how a mother could treat their daughter so shamefully. Why hadn't she paid attention to her mother's poor and wrong attitude towards Dorie and Alex before? Annie had seen the way her mother never spoke to Dorie and how her mother ignored them and often made unbefitting remarks to her two older children. 'I was so wrong, how could I have been so disrespectful to Alex and Dorie?' Annie knew Dorie was having academic problems in English and spelling since she started school, Annie even wondered if Paul was aware of Dorie's problems since she was the one who received the report card, signed it and returned it. No one helped Dorie with her school work or took an interest. Paul probably thought she was doing okay since he hadn't heard otherwise.

Since Annie was focusing on trying to build a relationship with Dorie, she had started to notice her daughter's excellent memory, her quickness to learn to bake, her love for reading, how she sensed when others needed help and her overall eagerness to learn new things. At long last Annie thought she was beginning to understand Dorie's fanatic attitude toward running, jumping and playing ball. These activities her daughter could accomplish on her own power, also being good in these activities swayed her classmates attitude toward her as a peer member in a positive way. Even with Dorie's zealous love for track and field she put her chores, helping Garth and doing extra things for the family as number one in her life. The girl obviously loved and cared for her family. Annie smiled sadly as she recalled how her daughter watched grandpa and Garth when she was barely five, Dorie asked for so little yet gave so much willingly. Annie had been so blind, not understanding her children, she had been on the way to becoming a complete stranger to her only daughter. What a blessing she had talked to Dr. Meisner. The woman continued to reflect in a jumbled way about her past attitude to Dorie all the while sobbing. Unexpectedly the door behind her opened and Garth stood there.

"Mom are you hurt or in pain?" Startled, Annie turned finding it hard to comprehend but knowing Garth had walked from the cot to the door. Garth began swaying. "Mom catch me before I fall."

Those first steps Garth took to check on his mother soon turned into normal walks about the house. The family was overcome with joy. Dorie whispered in Garth's ear "Garth you should do something special for Dad, if it wasn't for him, you would still be lying in bed with bent knees. He worked very hard to get you to walk."

"I want to do something special for Dad. Can you help me?

"Dad likes chocolate cake, have Mom bake a cake and we'll decorate the cake. You make a drawing of a boy lying in bed then point with an arrow to a boy up walking and I'll help you make up a nice note that you can print, a love and thank you note. I can write the name of Dad's favorite pipe tobacco down and have George buy a package. Do you have money? I have a dollar fifty that I've had a long time and if you could get a dollar from Mom and Alex? Don't mention the cake to Mom 'till we get everything organized.

On Dorie and Garth's next trip to visit Tom and Molly Dorie approached George about buying pipe tobacco for her father and gave him two dollars and fifty cents. Alex had given Garth a dollar, but Mom didn't have any money. George came back with four packages of tobacco and a new corn pipe. To hide the package George took a box, placed Paul's package in the bottom and covered it with fruit.

"Dorie, lets give Dad the surprises after supper tomorrow!"

"No Garth you must give everything to dad at once, it will show him how grateful and happy you are for what he did for you."

Dorie was to stay at Moppets overnight but Alice came to say that Moppet had the flu and was in bed. When Matty heard next day that Dorie wouldn't be going to Moppets for a stay over, she asked Dorie to stay over night Friday and accompany her family to Red River park for fun and a picnic on Saturday.

"Matty will your mom mind if I come?"

"Mom said I could bring a friend and she likes you, so no."

"Okay! I'll ask Dad tonight… What do you do on a picnic?"

"Each family packs a good lunch. Several Churches are providing entertainment. Before lunch adults and children can play games and after lunch there will be a sing-a-long, followed by races and contests for children. Later the children can play on the beach till supper. The day closes with a marshmallow roast."

"Oh! I hope I can go! Do the Churches give prizes away to the winners of the races?"

"Yes! The Church committee gives money to race winners and prizes to contest and game winners."

"I must get home, see you tomorrow." Dorie commented abruptly, taking off.

As Dorie was riding home she noticed an old woman dressed in her usual raggedy clothes outside near the fence and as Dorie drew closer, the old woman beckoned with her crooked fingers. As Dorie came nearer, she said "Come here child." Dorie wasn't sure she should stop, the children said she was a witch and might roast you in her oven. She looked at the sad thin woman and thought 'I have my bike thus can easily get away. I just mustn't get too near.'

The girl braked her bike, got off and asked "Are you okay?"

The old woman came closer, beckoning. "I'm hungry, if I give you a bowl would you fill it with milk from one of those cows in the field?"

Dorie replied "Those cows belong to someone else, I can't milk cows that belong to a neighbor and give the milk away, that's stealing!"

"Please child I am so hungry, I haven't eaten for two days." Dorie's heart skipped a beat as she thought that the old woman hadn't eaten for two days.

"Give me the bowl" Dorie said. "I'll milk a cow." The old woman turned and limped toward her shack in a very slow fashion as if she had pain. Finally when the old woman limped back with a painful stride, Dorie met her at the fence to get the bowl. As she approached the cows she wished they wouldn't run off or that the cow she milked wouldn't kick.

When Dorie had milked a cow and was returning the bowl full of milk to the old woman, she said "I'll carry the milk into the house for you." When she entered the house it was cold, dirty and she could see mice scurrying around. There was a mattress on the floor and the odor in the house was strong. Dorie looked at the woman who had dull eyes, a very wrinkled face, and a very thin body. Compassion cut to the heart of Dorie's soul. She wanted to cry and without further thought ran to the old woman, hugging her and saying "I'll find food for you, you'll be fine. My dad will help you!"

A smile formed on the ladies lips as she enfolded Dorie with her swollen gnarled hands. "Please bring me bread. Have your mother cut a loaf of bread in half and bring both halves. Thank you child. I'll heat milk and place sugar and bread in the milk."

Dorie nodded. "I'll be back soon" and with that she turned and left for home.

Mom was anxious as Dorie was late returning from school. Dorie peddled into her yard, dropped her bike and ran into the house shouting "Mom! Oh Mom, you have to help that dirty, hungry old woman!"

"What are you talking about Dorie, sit down and tell me what happened." Annie called Paul. Both Paul and Annie listened to their daughter relate her story, astonished that a woman lived there. They only knew of a middle aged man that stayed there occasionally.

"Annie could you prepare some soft food for our new friend while I try and find dads' slippers, robe, a couple of sweaters and one of the thick blankets? They are packed in a box under Dorie's bed. She can help me find them." The man of the house dictated.

Annie quickly put some beef vegetable soup in a jar, cheese, slices of bread, a little jar of canned blueberries into a basket before she made an onion omelet.

Paul asked Dorie if he could use her bike and back pack, to which Dorie replied "Yes Dad."

Soon the clothes, blanket and food were packed. Mr. Kinny also took some foil to cover the food at night, a bit of protection against the mice.

The man said to his wife "I'm sure she's an elderly woman who wandered away from her home."

When Paul arrived on the doorstep the woman had the door open. "Hello, how are you?" Paul said. The woman made no reply. "I have brought you some food and warm clothes" Paul said. Then added, "Don't you find it cold in your home?" The woman nodded. Paul entered further into the shack, took the food from the back pack and placed it on a small table. Then he loosened the jar lids so they would be easy to remove. Dorie's father sensed movement behind him, the woman was moving toward the table. She had spied the omelet. Grasping the omelet in her deformed fingers the old woman began to hungrily devour the food.

Leaving some bread and the soup the woman turned to Paul. "Thank you for the food and clothes, bless you and your daughter!"

Before Paul left, he asked the woman what her name was and where she had lived. The woman answered, "I'm Liz Keef, Bill brought me here after he was unable to make payments to the family I lived with. Bill is my son, he has been gone for several days. I'm worried about his well being, he looks after me."

When Mr. Kinny arrived home, Annie quickly served the thick hot soup and fresh buns, followed by vanilla pudding. Everyone wanted to know what Paul thought of the old woman and her shack. Dorie also wanted to know how the woman felt about the food and clothes. He explained about the woman's hunger, gratitude, who she was and why she lived in the shack. He continued on to say he would visit Harry and Jean, perhaps they had some news.

Jean had heard Bill Keef had died a week ago as he was helping a farmer stop a runaway team of horses. As Bill reached to grab part of the horses harness, Bill fell and was run over by the wagon. Jean was surprised Bill's mother lived there. Harry said, "Jean and I will visit social services in the morning so they can find a clean loving home for this poor woman. Sounds like she could use some arthritis medicine as well. They will have to tell Mrs. Keef of Bill's death and help her sell the land." stated Paul. "Mrs. Keef is lucid, very clear about her life and seems knowledgeable." He added.

The following evening Annie answered a knock on the door and to her surprise found a policeman standing on the step. The policeman introduced himself and told Annie he was checking for Doctor Penny on how Garth Kinny was doing . Apparently Garth's file had fallen off and behind Dr. Penny's desk last fall and the cleaner found the file yesterday when she moved the desk. Doctor Penny noticed Garth was to go to the hospital for dressing changes twice a week but when Dr. Penny checked with the hospital he was told Garth had never returned. The medical staff wondered what had happened.

Annie called Garth to come and show the policeman his healed legs. Garth came to the door, pulled up his slack pants to expose the pink uneven surfaces that looked freshly healed. The young policeman looked embarrassed and said, "Garth looks like he's done great, sorry for the inconvenience madam."

When the policeman reported back to Dr. Penny, the doctor couldn't and wouldn't believe what he was hearing. Doctor Penny jumped out of his chair, yelling at the policeman and saying "You must have gone to the wrong house! Garth's legs were extremely contracted, he would not be walking!"

The policeman responded irately "I was at the right place, the woman's name was Annie, the boy's name was Garth, Garth pulled up his pant legs, the legs had been badly burned but there were no open areas and he walked."

After Corporal Price read the young policeman's report, the corporal said "I know this family well, had there been infections Paul couldn't deal with or other problems Paul would have taken Garth to the hospital." The corporal turned to Ben and said "Did you say Garth can walk?"

"Yes, Corporal Price, Garth can walk very well."

"Ben when I last saw Garth, he was in hospital and his legs were badly contracted with huge dressings covering them." Corporal Price continued "That Paul is a miracle worker, very poor but a loving, caring, hard working man. The whole family is wonderful, makes you wonder how a file can be lost for months, nobody remembers to ask about this child that's been in hospital for months, that's what you call faith, gave Paul his opportunity to do his own kind of healing."

Next visit to Purplehaven Paul took Garth in to visit Dr. Penny. Dr. Penny was thunderstruck, and kept saying "remarkable, remarkable."

"Paul tell me how did you straighten Garth's legs?"

Paul replied, "I used a little of this, a little of that, I'm not sure which ingredient played the greatest role. Love and hard work were the main factors and Garth's unbending faith he would walk someday. Bye Doctor Penny, we must be on our way." Paul said, turning to the door. He didn't give the doctor an opportunity to reply.

Next evening Garth had his surprise party for his father at suppertime. Paul was overjoyed and his beautiful blue eyes lit on Garth several times when the chocolate cake with 'Thank you Dad for straightening my legs!' written in pink icing was placed in front of him. He went around the table to hug Garth saying "I'm so glad my idea and all your hard work paid off."

Annie was as surprised at Paul when Garth handed the pipe tobacco and pipe to his father.

"How did you manage to buy the tobacco?"

Dorie gave Garth a warning kick under the table before Garth could say a word. Garth finally said "Dad that's a secret." Paul, not wanting to ruin the thank you party thought he would at a later time follow up on how his two youngest arranged to purchase the tobacco and pipe, and where did they get the money for the buy? Paul felt that George had helped his children.

Shortly after Dorie finished supper, Matty's mother picked the girl up for the stay over and picnic. Dorie loved going to Matty's home as the atmosphere was full of happiness, there was cheerful talk, telling cute jokes and playing board games. Matty's mother was tall, thin and full of energy. Mattie's father was a semi invalid, who had been in a tuberculosis sanitarium for several years, he was kind, funny and helped as much in the house as he was able to and also played the piano beautifully. Dorie was never asked to sing quietly by Matty's father when the family had a sing along.

Matty's mother, with the help of her three girls did all the farm work, they built fences, raised cows, grew and harvested grain plus planted a large garden. Matty's mother was probably stick thin because she worked so hard.

Matty's family had two hallway closets, one large and one small. The large closet was used for outdoor wear, the small closet was called the quick clean up closet. Matty's family lived a mile off the main road, and the view to the main road was very good from the kitchen and living room windows. When a car was noticed coming up the long drive way, whoever saw the car shouted action then whoever was in Matty's house picked up any items lying about and threw them into the small closet. People marveled how Matty's mom could keep her house so tidy.

Early next morning Matty's family and Dorie jammed into the car with towels, play items, and a huge picnic basket and headed for Red River Park. The day was packed full of fun. Dorie won a couple of games receiving hair clips and a pair of socks as prizes but she also won two dollars and twenty cents in the track and field events. Dorie also won a flashlight for being winner of the major category called 'Most Points'. The flashlight would be her fathers. Paul had always wanted a flashlight in the house to keep near his bed.

All too soon it was time to leave. Dorie dozed in the back seat thinking of the prizes and money she had won plus the delicious picnic lunch of roast chicken, potato salad, cheese, buns, watermelon, and apple pie. "Today was a magic day, a really fun day, one I'll never forget. Thank you!" Dorie said to Matty's mother as the car entered the Kinny's yard.

On entering the house Dorie headed for her room flopping down on her bed fully dressed, instantly falling asleep. Annie covered Dorie with a warm blanket, tip toeing out of the bedroom.

Next morning Dorie woke fully dressed clinging on to the flashlight she had won. After washing up and changing clothes she went out to start chores till her mother called her for breakfast. After that she did some indoor chores and was prepared to join her parents' planting seeds in the field. As she turned from closing the door she found herself face to face with Rita's cousin Mark. Mark wanted Dorie's softball as he had lost Rita's. Dorie said to Mark "Why don't you come back later and practice catch with me?"

"You're joking. That will be the day, I practice with a girl. Now give me the ball!"

"No Mark." Dorie said. "You can't have my ball, you may lose it." At this point Mark picked up an old axe and ran at Dorie. She quickly retreated and Mark knew he couldn't catch her so he threw the axe. The girl heard a swishing sound come at her, she ducked and sidestepped as the axe sailed near and overtop her head. As Dorie jumped aside she stepped on a piece of broken glass cutting the bottom of her shoeless foot. The gash was about three inches long on the side of Dorie's foot, and bled strongly. Dorie hopped to the house not wanting to go inside and spread blood all over the floor. Dorie hopped to the gong, beating hard several times on the metal. After Grandpa died Paul had put up the gong so if there was another emergency it could be put to good use.

Sitting down on the step Dorie pressed hard on the open cut to help stop the bleeding as her father had once taught her. He had said 'Put pressure on the bleeding area if you cut yourself Dorie.' Her foot felt strange but she kept pressing on the cut with her hand. Suddenly her dad was there, out of breath. He had ran into the house , returning to his daughter with a basin of water and towel. He told her "Your foot is dirty from running about without shoes, the glass you stepped on was dirty, and the hand that you applied the pressure to your foot wasn't clean either so we'll clean your foot well, apply a flour paste dressing for now then at a later time this morning I'll apply the special paste I make and put a dressing on top."

"Dorie, what happened? How did you cut your foot? Why weren't you wearing shoes?

"I accidentally stepped on some glass while running." Then Dorie's eyes filled with tears as she said "My shoes pinch my feet, the shoes hurt a lot at times."

"Dorie you should have told me about your shoes being to small sooner!" Her father commented. "When you outgrow your shoes let mom or me know so we can buy you new ones."

Next morning Dorie's foot was swollen and to painful to walk on making her hop if she wanted to move about. Paul told her she would have to stay home from school for several days and wear Alex's old shoes. He would soak her foot in saline twice a day and apply the home made paste and a dressing. For the first two days the foot was swollen, painful with a small amount of yellow discharge but the fourth day brought good news, the edema had receded, very little pain was felt and the wound looked nice and pink, bringing a look of happiness to Dorie's face. By Saturday morning Paul thought his daughter could be fitted for new shoes but Dorie would have to wear Alex's old shoes to Purplehaven and to the shoe shop. Dorie asked if she could visit Tom, Molly and George for a short while, to which dad replied "Yes." Paul said. "I have to buy some nails from the hardware store then I'll pick you up to go shoe shopping."

On entering the back of the restaurant Tom spied Dorie's big shoes, asking her "What's the matter? Sit, sit, why are you wearing big shoes?"

Dorie explained her old shoes were to small, she was barefoot and had stepped on glass gashing her foot, and now that the sore was healed her father would take Dorie shoe shopping. In a wink of an eye Dorie was surrounded by activity, Tom demanded "Dorie take your shoes off!" Then Molly stuck a piece of paper under Dorie's foot, drawing around it with a pen. Next Molly ran off with the foot paper in his hand, calling back to Tom "Give Paul some food and coffee!" "Tell him to wait for me, I would like to talk to him."

When Paul arrived at the restaurant, Tom excitedly told Paul to sit and eat. He declined the invitation saying "I must take Dorie shopping for new shoes and then she and I must leave for home as lots of spring farm work needs to be started."

"Paul wait Molly will be back soon." At that moment the back door opened and Molly rushed in with a box in his hand, darting over to Dorie saying, "Dorie take off your shoes and try these new shoes on!" Paul sat with mouth agape while Dorie looked at her dad trying to tell her dad with her eyes that she didn't know.

Paul looked heart broken saying, "Molly I can buy shoes for my children. How much did those ones cost?"

Molly replied "The shoes are a gift, you bring us pails of strawberries, you shot a skunk that we could use to make herbal medicine, think of all the ducks you have raised for us. Your family is wonderful and we don't have children, let us spoil your children." Molly said, placing his hand gently on Paul's shoulder. "We love to buy presents for your family, let us spoil your children a little, please don't deny us this joy, Paul. Have the presents we gave your children harmed them in any way?" Molly asked.

Paul said "No Molly the presents have only brought Garth and Dorie happiness, they haven't spoiled the children. Molly, Tom, George, I have trouble dealing with my pride, I would love to give my wife and children the lovely gifts you folks give them, it hurts me a great deal not being able to give beautiful presents, instead I can give my family only the bare essentials" George who had been standing in the back by the stove came forward saying, "Paul consider us your family, you know families help one another, let your children and wife benefit a bit from our wealth, please don't push us aside, you never ask for material items, you're humble and grateful. Don't let pride eat away at your soul, pride can be a nasty people destroyer if left unchecked. You're a good, kind, strong, caring person, don't change and may we continue to give gifts to the children?"

"Yes George, Tom, and Molly I appreciate your thoughtfulness and caring, you can continue to give presents and I will continue to work at overcoming my pride. Just as I feel I've conquered this sin it returns, give me time George, I'll triumph" Paul said. Before leaving Dorie tried on her beautiful soft black leather tie shoes which fit perfectly. Before leaving with her dad she thanked and hugged her three friends.

The girl felt she needed to ask her dad a question and she wasn't sure how to phase the query that was troubling her. Her love for her father was what counted, soft leather shoes didn't matter, only her dad's love was important. After traveling in silence for several miles she said "Dad I have a question for you."

"Fire away Dorie."

"Dad would you want to return the shoes Molly bought at the shoe store, give the money back to Molly and buy me a pair of shoes with your money? Dad it would be okay with me." Dorie said.

"Dorie, my darling elf you can keep your new shoes. This morning I learned a hard lesson. Our three Chinese friends really feel they are part of our family and they want to treat you children like the children they don't have. Perhaps they give you and Garth nice clothes and toys other children your age have so you will feel more like your classmates Dorie." Paul concluded "They truly are wonderful, sensitive people."

Next morning Paul received news that Aunt Jane and Martha would have Willie stay with them now. Willie might easily adjust to the peaceful, loving environment that his mother, Martha would attempt to provide then going to Paul's where he knew nobody. Aunt Jane had also found Willie a job working in a grocery store. Aunt Jane had told the manager, a friend of hers, to guide, praise, assist and overlook small mistakes Willie made, give this poor abused half child, half adult a chance in this life. The grocery store manager told Aunt Jane he would do his best with Willie.

While Paul was digesting the news about Willie, Dorie left for school. When she arrived she found all Elm school students standing around, as Mr. Joma hadn't arrived yet. He was late. The older boys said "Everyone in the barn, hurry!"

Elm school had a horse barn that was occasionally used by a few students during the early spring when the snow melted quickly leaving some roads muddy with ruts full of water. The parents of the horse riding students kept the barn clean, storing hay and a pail in the corner of the barn. When the horse riders rode their horses to school they would fill the water trough with water from the school water pump using the pail stored in the corner of the barn. The barn hadn't been used for months. The snow melt had been gradual this spring, not bringing flooding and muddy roads.

Once the students were in the barn the older boys said "No talking, not even whispering." Raymond stationed himself by a crack between two logs, giving him a good view of the school. Another older boy took up a position by the door and looked through a small crack in the door.

Raymond quietly said "If we keep quiet and wait long enough we'll have a holiday from school today." Soon Mr. Joma arrived at school, got out of his car looking around not able to see any students. Mr. Joma wondered where the students had gone, he knew he was late but if the students had returned home he thought he should have met several students returning home on the west bound road. The teacher was deeply puzzled but he felt since he was at school he would make up some new tasks, work on assignments for the students and correct tests.

The more Mr. Joma thought about the students the more edgy he became, what if the students were kidnapped en masse? Something has happened to the students he knew! Mr. Joma decided to phone Raymond's father and check if he had seen any children on their way to school or playing in the school ground.

After some thought Raymond's dad said "Yes I did see children on their way to school and playing about in the school yard." Then in a worried tone of voice said to Mr. Joma, "I'll be at the school shortly."

When Raymond saw his over protective dad drive into the school yard, he knew the student's lark was over. Raymond even thought his father might go to the police. He very quietly said to the students "We'll sneak out the barn, go to the school and tell Mr. Joma that when he was late we decided to go on a treasure hunt and we just got back." Mr. Joma and Ray's father doubted the student's story but were overjoyed to see the students safe.

After the students filed into the school, Mr. Joma said to Raymond's father "Would you object if I make the students stay one hour after school tomorrow and the following day to make up for the school time they missed? I strongly feel they shouldn't have gone roving around or hiding."

"Mr. Joma you have my support, the students need to be taught a lesson, the older students made a rash decision by taking their youngest classmates along."

Mr. Joma told the students they would make up the class time they missed by staying an hour after school for two days, tomorrow and the following day and would they please tell their parents.

After school Dorie was helping her dad seed carrots when the sudden peace was shattered by an ear piercing noise, then squealing and banging was heard followed by an eerie quiet. Paul looked startled saying, "I wonder if that was a train crash."

CHAPTER SEVEN

A short distance from where Dorie and her father worked was a long gradual slope that lead to a valley through which the rail line ran. Paul said to Dorie "Lets go and see what happened, perhaps we can help." The two of them headed across the field, half way down the slope the train derailment could be seen. The engine, coal car and two freight cars were off the rail track pitched on their sides. Dorie could see a few chickens running about, lettuce, and apples lying around and then her eyes fell on a booted foot sticking out from under the front of the engine. She felt sick to her stomach, her heart started to pound, a feeling of panic started to build then escalate as she looked at her fathers face, pale, grave and solemn as he viewed the boot. Suddenly Paul ran toward the engine. Kneeling he unlaced the shoe pulling it and sock off in one yank, quickly feeling for a pulse. There was none to be found so he turned to his daughter saying "Quickly go to Jean and tell her to contact the authorities." As she ran off he looked at the white, cold, pulse-less foot then replaced the sock and shoe. Climbing the slope Paul looked back with a heavy heart. The men lying under all that heavy steel couldn't be alive, they were probably married with families, this thought stabbed into Mr. Kinny's soul, deeply into his mind leaving a wound that needed time to heal.

The Kinny family learned next day an item had been placed on the railroad causing the derailment. Four men died in the accident. Dorie woke up several times during the night, seeing cold white feet dancing above her bed, her father had told her the train derailment was sabotage, a person or persons had meant to cause the train destruction and cripple the rail line.

A tired girl woke the next morning, doing her chores and leaving for school. On arrival she found Mr. Joma in the school yard helping students practice for the track meet that was to be held in a few days time. Dorie needed a hair cut.

The girl wanted her hair cut in a cute style and asked her mom if Alice would cut her hair before track and field day. Annie said "Yes Dorie, I'll ask Alice when she visits in the morning."

Next evening Alice came to cut Dorie's hair. It was a very close cut making her look elfish and appear as if she was wearing a cute brown cap. Moppet exclaimed "You look darling!" When Dorie looked in the mirror she had to admit the hair cut made her look hip and different, not as childish. A very happy Dorie went to bed that evening. When she woke, there was a lovely surprise. Hanging on the bottom of the bed was a moss green pullover sweater and green socks with lace around the top. The girl thought her mom bought those clothes for her, that her mom was actually becoming like the mom she had always wished she had. With a big smile Dorie said to herself 'Mom I love you. Maybe someday I'll be able to say those words to you.'

Paul told his daughter that her mother had used the cream money to buy the special clothes for her. Annie had been saving the cream money to buy herself shoes, but she thought her shoes could wait, this was her daughter's special day, she had worked really hard and deserved to look special today. Dorie thought it really was wonderful to have something new and different. When Dorie's mother saw her all dressed she said "Dorie you look pretty."

The girl ran to her mom, hugging and squeezing her saying "Oh thank you mom for the new clothes!" The woman thought she and her daughter were communicating more and a warm hearted feeling seemed to pass between the two when they hugged or held one another.

The surprises never seemed to end this morning as Dorie sat down for breakfast she was served a large bowl of porridge and an egg. Her father said "You've a busy day ahead of you, a good nourishing breakfast is essential."

Sitting beside Rita on the way to school Dorie was thinking how nice it would be for Elm school to win the sports trophy. The teacher of the school and the student that won the most points for the winning school were asked on stage, while the other athletes surrounded the stage cheering. She thought how wonderful it would be to stand on stage next to Mr. Joma while he received the highest sports honor of the seven schools represented at the track and field sports day.

A jab in Dorie's side pulled her out of her day dream as she heard Rita say, "Are you okay Dorie? I was just saying that you look so pretty today, I feel jealous"

"No you don't Rita, you have such wondrous big, soft brown eyes and thick wavy brown hair that dances when you run." stated Dorie. "You'll marry someone rich and handsome and live in a big mansion. If I'm poor Rita will you still be my friend and ask me to spend time with you?" Dorie asked.

"Yes of course! You're my best friend and always will be!" Rita responded, surprised as she leaned towards Dorie and hugged her friend tightly.

Several students from the other schools noticed Dorie's hair cut and wanted to know the name of the hair salon she had gone to. Moppet who had joined her friend would interject saying "Alice's Salon but she's so busy she can't take any new clients." Two girls actually left their names and phone numbers so they could be contacted if Alice's salon was taking new clients. The two friends giggled and giggled.

An announcement blared alerting the students that standing and running board jump would commence in five minutes behind the school . In Moppet and Dorie's age group the two won all the first and second prizes, Dorie won most of the first prizes in high jump, broad jump and racing. Usually the two won equal amounts of first prize ribbons but this year Dorie was driven and better practiced. Near the end of the day the teachers had fun races like three legged, the crawl and wheelbarrow races for the students. The winners of the fun races were given tickets for the food stand. With the tickets you could choose ice creams, hot dogs, chocolate bars, or pop. What fun Dorie and Moppet had as they didn't lack partners for the unusual races.

Halfway through a hot dog Dorie was approached by Mr. Joma who whispered "Dorie our school won the trophy and you are to stand on the platform next to me when the trophy is presented to our school." Dorie's heart hammered, she seemed unable to think, felt faint, she had hoped this moment would come, but actually didn't believe Elm school would win the trophy. The girl had heard on the radio that occasionally soldiers got shell shocked and don't know what to do, well at present Dorie felt like that. She couldn't seem to move or think.

Finally she roused when Moppet kept shaking her and yelling in her ear "Dorie you're to join Mr. Joma on the stage!" Next Mr. Joma was there pulling on Dorie's arm, urging her to get up and join him on stage.

Elm school had won by only three points, but it was a double honor to win as it had the smallest enrollment. Mr. Joma and Dorie beamed with happiness as they climbed on to the stage amid the loud cheers and clapping. Mentally Dorie was thinking 'Daddy I can be good at life things, Daddy you wait we will go on that trip one day!'

Mr. Joma was congratulated and praised for his school's accomplishment and for being a great motivator, for being able to make his students learn and focus on academics as well as sports.

Dorie was given an instant photo that she was allowed to keep. The photo showed Dorie holding the trophy, while Mr. Joma stood nearby smiling widely. Then Mr. Joma gave a bit of an acceptance speech and as he spoke he laid his hand on Dorie's head and said "Winning this trophy came about due to the students' hard work and the pride they have in their school. They worked together and practiced on their own, determined to bring the trophy home to Elm School." The teacher patted his student's head and continued "It was students like this that made our school 's dream come true."

Rita's mom dropped Dorie off in her yard then left. Her parents were smiling, hugging their daughter and hopping about with joy. Paul thought it was Dorie's determination and hard work that helped win the points. If only Dorie would be decisive in a quest for a high school diploma! He smiled to himself when he looked at his wife and daughter, seeing the mother daughter relationship slowly growing filled his heart with joy.

Annie slowed to a stop. "You need to rest after a long day of running and jumping. After you have your nap would you please pack a tote bag for Garth?"

Dorie asked "Where is Garth going Mom?"

"Scrap Iron and other friends of Garth's have asked him and three other boys to spend the long weekend at their father's lake side cabin on Lake Gooie." Lake Gooie was fifteen miles west of Purplehaven. The beach was a large formation of white sand, the water was cool this time of year but swimmable and the boys could shore fish or swim out to an old diving platform and fish from the platform. If the boys decided to fish from the platform they would tie their fishing equipment to a life jacket and one of the boys would tow the fishing gear to the platform. Garth wasn't allowed to take his dad's rod and reel but he was allowed to take his bike.

In the morning Garth left for Scrap Iron's home, but instead Garth rode to Marvel Rock Structure. The boys had misled their mothers. They would ride their bicycles to Gooie then spend the weekend at Mole's father's cabin without parental supervision. The parents of the boys felt Scrap Iron's parents as well as Mole's parents would be at the lake. Garth was the only boy who brought sandwiches and cookies, Mole had one dollar.

At noon the boys arrived at Mole's dad's cabin tired and hungry. To their surprise there was only a bag of puffed wheat in the cupboard. Garth reluctantly pulled out his sandwiches, cookies and thermos of milk. Garth knew among these boys it was share and share alike. It was cool so they didn't go into the water but built sand castles on the beach.

That evening as the boys lay in bed, Scrap Iron said "Let's shore fish in the morning and sell the fish we catch to the tourists so we can buy food for ourselves."

"Great idea!" The boys shouted at Scrap Iron.

Early in the morning the boys shore fished landing several catches. Garth, not having fishing gear was in charge of selling the fish to the tourists. He had the fish in a pail of iced water and with his smile and winning approach to the buyers, soon had all the fish sold plus an extra two dollars from well meaning people who paid fifty cents instead of twenty five cents for a fish.

The boys had enough money to buy them each a hotdog and were able to buy one ice cream cone which they shared. Each of them was allowed to take five small licks then pass it on to the next boy. Garth got to eat the cone part since he collected two extra dollars.

By early afternoon the day became very warm and since none of the boys were good swimmers, they decided to don life jackets and swim to the diving platform to tan and play. After several hours they returned to shore. Mole removed his life jacket and threw it into the lake, but the life jacket sunk. The other boys followed suit, each life jacket sank deeming every one unsafe. Garth said, "I guess we can swim better then we thought."

Scrap Iron replied "It could have turned into a crisis because none of us are strong swimmers. My dad always said 'Scrap Iron, before using any equipment check it out well, unless its an emergency, never take unnecessary chances.' Man was my dad right." After eating the puffed wheat and drinking some cold water the boys had a rest under some trees.

Later in the evening as darkness descended Mole piped up "Let's play Nicky nine doors." The other boys jumped up ready to have some fun but Scrap Iron stopped them. "Wait. Let's discuss this game, make sure we all understand how its played. We don't want anyone screwing up or getting caught. We knock on a cabin door, when the cabin door is opened we all shout 'Nicky nine doors!' and run away quickly."

On the second round of knocking only half the people answered. There was one more cabin at the far end and they would knock on the door for a second time. There was a light on in the cabin but no one had responded to their first knock so the boys would try a second time. Scrap Iron and Garth knocked on the door. With an unexpected quickness the door was opened, a hand reached out and grabbed Scrap Iron by the collar of his shirt, turned him around and gave him a swift kick in his butt causing him to land on his knees in a pile of sand. All the other boys fled. 'Great pals.' thought Scrap Iron. Scrap Iron's and Mole's fathers knew the man that had just kicked Scrap Iron. The kicker had run for government office and was elected. As Scrap Iron retreated he called out "I'll never vote for you Mr. Doug and I hope they kick you out of government!"

Next morning the hungry boys put away the old useless life jackets, locked the cabin door and headed for home. Hunger being the main reason for their early departure, the boys should arrive home by lunch time. Garth was thinking of a large glass of milk and on homecoming Garth looked tired but happy and cheerful. Annie thought he looked more alive and content, and suddenly a large bubble of joy grew in her chest.

Moppet and Dorie were the same age and their birthdays were one day after the other. Dorie's first then Moppet's. This year they would celebrate both on Moppet's birthday. The two girls shared a cake, each year their mothers would wrap money in wax paper and stick it in different parts of the cake then the outside of the cake received a thick coating of icing. Moppet wanted to decorate the cake with wild roses and Alice gave Moppet and Dorie permission to pick the roses and place them on the cake as long as they gently rinsed the flowers with water before placing them on the cake.

On the girls' way home from picking roses they wandered onto a patch of wild mushrooms that their families liked to eat but were rare to find. The mushrooms were dark brown, looked like a partially folded umbrella with a small peak on top. When the mushrooms were fried slightly in butter they tasted luscious, a delightful treat. Dorie folded up her old T-shirt to make a small basket-like holder for them. Soon the two were homeward bound with their treasures. When they arrived home all adult interest focused on the mushrooms. They would be part of the birthday supper. Moppet and Dorie rinsed the roses slightly to wash away bugs, then Moppet placed the roses on the birthday cake while Dorie stood back and watched the enjoyable look on her friend's face, which reminded her of the morning sunshine.

The birthday supper was a great success, even if the mushrooms received the most attention. The parents barely shared the mushrooms with Garth, Moppet and Dorie, giving each of the children a small teaspoon full. While the mushrooms vanished, Dorie hungrily watched, making a vow to find patches of more mushrooms when she had time. Garth found a wrapped fifty cent piece in his slice of cake, running to whisper in his sister's ear "Dorie I'll buy us some bubble gum, jaw breakers and cracker jack." Then went running off while Dorie hoped he wouldn't loose the money. They would have to leave soon as their father wanted to look at a car.

Paul bought an old model T ford which had several levers on the steering wheel and had no top. He was delighted! He looked so happy when he got into his car. Annie called the car 'Dad's Toy' but she was happy, very happy for her husband. She thought 'At long last Paul has received a small pay off for all his hard work and kindness to his family.'

Dorie asked her father how much the car cost and her dad replied "I bought the car for a song and dance." She thought her father had to do a dance and sing a song. She had never heard that expression before. The girl would love to have seen her dad perform.

Tomorrow afternoon Dorie would stay at Moppets, Paul would drive her after school. That night Dorie and her father would pick plants that would be cooked and made into magic healing paste. Her father would make enough paste to last a year. She also hunted and found a patch of Morel mushrooms, much to the delight of her family.

Next afternoon Paul drove Dorie to Moppet's home. While Alice was out tending to the sheep the two girls raced upstairs to jump on the bed. Higher and higher they rose off the bed, their aim was to touch the ceiling. The bed springs almost touched the floor, squeaking with effort. Moppet almost touched the ceiling. Suddenly her mother appeared in the room. "I've asked you girls so many times not to jump on the beds, the mattresses and springs get ruined! Moppet, if you're ever caught jumping on the beds again, you will not be allowed to have friends sleep over.

"Dorie I'm very disappointed to find you jumping on the bed. Can you recall the number of times I've asked you girls not to do that?"

"Yes Mrs. Jake. You told us many times to stay away from the bed. You told Moppet and I 'Beds are to rest on and for sleeping.' I'm very sorry and I promise never to jump on any of your beds again. Please don't make me stay away from your home!" Pleaded Dorie.

Mrs. Jake smiled a little. "Dorie if you keep your promise you'll be most welcome to come to our home anytime. We love you Dorie, and feel you're part of our family."

Mrs. Jake decided to explain the rule. "Our beds are older. Dorie, Moppet, when you jump on the beds, the springs are put under a great deal of stress which eventually causes them to sag. Then the mattress isn't given the proper support. Jumping on beds is not a wise activity. Dorie you have given your promise not to misuse the beds," turning to Moppet Mrs. Jake said "do we have an agreement that you won't jump on the beds?"

"Yes mom you have my word." Moppet replied.

After the wild bed jumping session Dorie felt sharp lower stomach pain. She had had these bouts of abdominal pain on and off for several weeks. The pain usually was a dull nagging pain but at times the discomfort was sharp as it was now. She hadn't told her parents about the pain as it always went away after resting, so she hadn't thought much of it.

The girl went downstairs and lay on the sofa hesitating to tell Mrs. Jake about the pain. When her father came to pick her up the sharp pain was still present in her stomach. Distraught, she went to the kitchen to thank Mrs. Jake for the lovely meals and say goodbye to Moppet. Mrs. Jake thought Dorie felt guilty about being chastised, that's why she walked stooped over with a drawn look on her face. When the girl reached the car, she waited for her dad to appear instead of climbing into her seat. When he came out she quietly asked him to help her into the car. Paul lifted his daughter into the car and after climbing into the drivers side turned to Dorie and asked "What's the matter? Are you okay?"

The girl told her dad she had been getting bouts of stomach pain for weeks, at times the pain was a nagging pain, other times the pain was very sharp as it was now, but always the pain left after resting for a while. "Today the discomfort felt like someone was stabbing me and didn't go away with rest." She concluded.

Paul asked his daughter to point to the sore area. She pointed to the lower right part of her abdomen. Her father's face took on a worried look and he steered the car on to the road to Purplehaven. Dorie looked confused. "Daddy where are we going?"

"I'm taking you to emergency to be checked for appendicitis."

Dorie asked "What is appendicitis Dad?"

Paul replied "Everyone has a small sac called an appendix that's attached to their bowel in the right lower part of their abdomen. If the appendix becomes inflamed it might increase in size and rupture causing the person to feel a lot of pain. When the appendix ruptures it spills toxins throughout the abdomen. Doctors like to remove the appendix before it splits open."

The two arrived at the hospital mid evening, Paul helping his daughter up the steps. She was lifted to an examining table by her father. The nurse then left to phone the doctor.

Soon the doctor arrived, checked Dorie's painful stomach carefully, then ordered a white blood count and urinalysis. It was late evening before the tests results which confirmed appendicitis were given to the doctor.

The doctor met with father and daughter, telling them of the decision to operate on Dorie this evening at ten o'clock. The doctor felt she had a ruptured appendix and it was important to operate as soon as possible. The nurse now would take her to the preparation room. Mr. Kinny bent over and gave his daughter a hug reassuring her he would stay till the surgery was complete and she was back in a hospital room. The nurse then hurried out the room with the girl lying on top of the stretcher.

Paul made a phone call from the nurse's station to Jean who would convey a message to Annie about their daughter's surgery and his not arriving home till the wee hours of the next day.

Dorie felt so frightened, the nurses never talked, just flew past her, running here and there before washing her abdomen, putting a gown on her, covering her hair with a paper cap and putting paper boots on her feet. Not one word was spoken. She wondered how great the pain would be when they cut her stomach open, how large a knife did the doctor use, and then she thought about the blood. 'Oh, if only Daddy was with me, to answer my questions!' Perhaps the nurses couldn't talk, but why didn't they write a note then!? As the fears of the unknown raced through her mind she became restless. Her eyes watched the nurses with nervousness and when they approached her, she flinched fearing the worst. The nurses seemed to have finished their work, opened a side door and pushed Dorie into a strange room with bright lights. People with masks covering most of their face, dressed in green, were standing around. She was moved onto another table with a big machine behind it. She wished someone would talk to her. Slowly a tall man walked over to the big machine, lifted a thick black mask off it, turned a knob then sluggishly lowered the black mask to Dorie's face. The girl became extremely frightened, her heart seemed to stop, her hands shook but the rest of her body seemed paralyzed for a moment, then Dorie with a startling quickness, sat up and slapped the tall monster, feeling she had to escape this bad situation. Suddenly people came from all corners, rushing at her. Someone pushed her down, another person held her arms and then the thick mask descended coming closer and closer to her face. Then all was peaceful.

When Dorie awoke she found herself in a strange bed, high off the floor with metal pieces on the two sides. A gladness filled the girl, a feeling of safety and love when her father softly spoke, "My little brave elf. The doctor told me your appendix had ruptured and you will receive I.V.s and antibiotics for several days plus you must stay in bed for five days. You're in a private room across from the nurse's station, the nurses will be able to monitor you more closely. Now, I must leave for home, your mom and Garth will be worried and anxiously waiting news for your well being." Paul bent down placing a kiss on his daughter's forehead. Leaving the room Paul turned saying, "I'll be back in the morning and I'll bring mom and Garth."

After having a nap Dorie woke up to severe pain in her abdomen and she needed to use the bathroom. Looking around she realized she was in a strange room. She didn't see anyone around, and the last thing the girl wanted to do was wet the bed. "There must be a toilet pail under the bed" she reasoned, knowing she had to find it very soon. Crawling slowly and in great pain she headed for the bottom of the bed which seemed to be the easiest part to climb out of. The pain in her stomach made her feel faint but she would overcome this feeling by stopping for short periods and breathing slowly. Finally she reached the floor but to her horror her I.V. arm tubing had separated and was leaking fluid all over the bed despite this, her main concern was finding the pail under the bed. She searched for the bathroom vessel with no avail. Lying quietly on the floor, wishing the crippling stomach aching to stop Dorie unexpectedly felt a warm wetness beneath her, she knew with a realistic shock she no longer needed to look for her bathroom pail. Tears of shame filled her eyes as she wept in silence and pain thinking she would have to wait until her father came.

When the nurses entered the room they stared at the empty bed, transfixed, wondering if their minds were playing night tricks. Eventually one nurse called out "The appendix girl has vanished and her room is across from our nursing station!" The other nurse, shining her flashlight around noticed the girl under the bed.

The actuality of the seriousness struck the nurses, how could they explain to the doctors and their peers that a child fresh from surgery had climbed out of a side railed bed that was located across from the nurse's station? To complicate the situation further the I.V. line had been disconnected losing an unknown amount of antibiotic fluid and now the nurses noticed moderate amount of fresh blood on the girls dressing.

Placing her back on a remade bed, the nurses reconnected and adjusted the flow of the I.V., then reinforced Dorie's dressing planning on frequent checks.

The girl shrunk back in fear of the nurses knowing they felt a deep anger toward her. Not once did she mention the great pain she was in. Before leaving the room the nurses told her she must not get out of bed or they would have to tie her to it. Dorie remained silent with fear grabbing at her heart not knowing what else these two women might think of. She remained awake happy that going to the bathroom was off her mind but unable to rest due to the discomfort that stayed with her continually.

By morning the two night nurses had labeled Dorie as hyperactive, unmanageable and out in left field who needed almost constant monitoring.

The early morning passed into mid morning and brought the arrival of Dorie's parents. Annie was upset and red in the face and Paul was attempting to calm her when they walked into their daughter's hospital room. After her parents hugged her, Paul said to his daughter, "I would like to ask you some questions about last night. The hospital staff said you were unmanageable, pulled your I.V. apart, climbed out of bed, crawled around on the floor and wouldn't communicate."

"Daddy I'll answer your questions, please first give me an aspirin, my stomach hurt so bad I couldn't sleep all night. Oh Daddy please take my pain away!" Said Dorie with a drawn look to her pale face, with tears in her eyes, and tightly holding her abdomen with her hands. Paul had never seen his beloved child so distressed! Without another word he turned and left the room. Soon he found the head nurse explaining that his daughter was in a great deal of surgical pain and was it possible to give her some pain medicine!? The head nurse on checking Dorie's post op notes found she had received no analgesic since surgery. Finding this unbelievable the head nurse excused herself and went to find a senior nurse to collaborate her findings. The two nurses checked the drug sign out sheets which also showed Dorie had received no pain treatment since her surgery. The head nurse prepared a syringe with pain relief medicine, joined Paul and the two entered Dorie's room to find her still crying, holding on to her abdomen.

The head nurse looked away, hurting internally, distressed to see a child in such agony. The head nurse approached Dorie's bed and said "Dorie may I give you an injection for your pain?"

The girl, without missing a beat replied "Please hurry it hurts like a car has fallen on my stomach!" The first thought the head nurse had was that this child seemed like a bright co-operative child, and she wondered what really happened last night. She had had severe pain yet didn't moan or scream but was contending with the pain as a courageous adult.

Paul sat beside Dorie waiting for the pain medicine to take effect while Annie bathed her daughter's face and hands with a cool wet face cloth stopping now and then to kiss her cheeks and forehead. The injection, the feeling of love and security soon put Dorie into a deep, peaceful sleep. Paul said to his wife "Lets pick up Garth from the waiting room and have lunch at Tom and Molly's while Dorie has a much needed sleep."

George, Molly, and Tom were distressed to hear of Dorie's emergency surgery and having to stay in bed for five days. Molly said to George, "Dorie likes color and pretty things, George you buy flowers, a nice stuffed animal, some books to read and a nice robe and slippers for when she gets up out of bed." Tom turned to Paul and Annie saying, "George's smart he'll pick out nice things. George shops for us, he does our banking and taxes, he is a very smart man."

After a lovely meal with Molly and Tom, Paul, Annie and Garth returned to the hospital. The head nurse met and invited the parents into her office. After offering coffee to them the head nurse went on to say "While you folks were away your daughter woke so I offered to help the other nurses by doing her morning care and while sponging her I learned what happened last night." The head nurse continued saying "When Dorie woke she needed to use the washroom, and was unable to see staff and not aware of the call system, decided to look for a toilet pail under the bed. She crawled over the back of the bed and during this process the IV tubing came apart. Unable to find a pail Dorie urinated on the floor, she felt humiliated that she lost control. Paul, Annie, your daughter is so mature and caring for her age.

"This tragic incident has given me the courage to reorganize my nursing staff, establish new guide lines and procedures for my staff, reward good nursing and have zero tolerance for poor nursing. Poor nursing doesn't belong in this institution."

Paul asked the head nurse "Has Dorie given a reason for striking the Doctor in the operating room?"

"Yes Paul, Dorie struck the doctor out of fear, not one individual spoke to her in the preparation room or the operating room. She had many fears of the unknown, one such fear was that the doctor would cut her open with a big knife when she was awake, and there would be a lot of blood coming out of her. Dorie apologized saying she was frightened, she didn't know what was happening, she felt the mask was being put over her mouth to prevent her screams from being heard.

"Paul, Annie, could you please not discuss the happenings of last night with Dorie or other staff members at this time? If Dorie brings the topic up, listen, as deep hurt is embedded in her mind and talking might ease her stress but don't question her or make remarks until I am able to investigate the nursing care Dorie received last night." The meeting ended with the head nurse saying "This unfortunate occurrence of events that happened to Dorie has given me the courage to alter the emotional and physical approach nurses use toward patients in this hospital."

As Dorie's hospital stay was coming to an end rumors circulated about staff leaving, staff became more helpful and pleasant as witnessed by patients.

The hospital atmosphere brightened, there were more smiles and talk. Then the morning of her discharge arrived with a feeling of sadness as she said good-bye to her new friends. As she was ready to exit the third floor, the third floor staff suddenly appeared singing a special good-bye song to her and then the head nurse presented her with a bag of oranges. Dorie's favorite fruit! She wanted to cry but after a short time span she gained her composure, gave a winning smile and thanked the wonderful staff. The girl thought 'Bad experiences can turn into happiness!'

Her father was taking her home in his car, which he only used to drive to Purplehaven and back home. As her dad drove home he asked his daughter if she would like to learn how to drive the car. She cried out "Oh, yes!" Paul informed her that she mustn't drive the car on her own and they would never drive on the road. "You're twelve Dorie so learning to drive must be done with an adult beside you and in our yard."

Then Paul said he had a surprise for his daughter. The old house that had been given to them would be moved in late September onto the property grandma and grandpa had lived on and who finally moved off after much coaxing. "We probably won't be able to move until early next spring as I need to dig a new well, build a barn and shed, also move the wood and hay bales… I'm looking forward to not having to shovel snow especially since I've learned that Harry and Jean are moving to Purplehaven next spring."

"Yes Daddy Jean told me of their move but assured me Rita and I would see each other. Jean asked mom if Harry could pick me up twice a week. After I had done my chores, then Rita and I would have supper with her family, we would do our homework with Jean's help and after Rita and I played awhile, Harry would drive me home. Oh, daddy I'll still miss Rita, she's my best friend at school but its a year till Rita moves so I won't think about it yet."

CHAPTER EIGHT

Rita was ill and missed school several days and when Rita returned to school she was pale, easily became short of breath and seemed to have very little energy. Mr. Joma let Rita and Dorie stay inside during recess. After school Mr. Joma went out to meet Jean, telling Jean Rita was fairly ill. "Rita found it an effort to stand and was very short of breath on movement. Should I carry Rita out to the car?"

Jean replied "Yes Mr. Joma but please wait while I make the back seat into a simple bed."

As Mr. Joma carried Rita out to the car, Jean had an uneasy feeling when she saw Rita's shortness of breath and the blue tinge to Rita's pale skin. She would take Rita to emergency. Turning to Dorie Jean said "Dorie you'll have to walk home this afternoon as I'm taking Rita to the hospital." Dorie opened the door nearest Rita's head and gave Rita a light kiss on her cheek and her friend raised her hand to pet Dorie's cheek.

That evening Jean visited the Kinny family to tell them Rita was admitted to hospital and placed in an oxygen tent.

Dorie prayed that Rita would soon come home healed. A week passed and then one day after school as Dorie neared her home she noticed Rita's bedroom shade was up, which meant she was home. A joyous feeling passed through Dorie. Running with great haste, she arrived at her friend's home full of happiness. Jean met her at the door and said "Rita told me 'Dorie will know I'm home if my bedroom shade is up.' Come in Dorie, Rita is waiting for you."

Dorie was startled when she saw how frail Rita was and she knew instantly she must put on her invisible mask and smile or she would cry. The girl found it hard to look at Rita's once beautiful soft brown eyes sunk into her head. Her friend was thin, very pale and her breathing was rapid. She hugged the girl and told her school news. She found it ever so difficult not to show her hurting emotions, her friend would get better. She would say two prayers for her tonight.

The middle Kinny missed Rita not being at school. Her friend's activities had been decreased by Dr. Parr. The sick girl not only didn't attend school but spent long hours in bed. Jean had asked Dorie to spend more time with Rita doing art work, playing board games and listening to hymns. Dorie thought her friend came first, Dorie's running and jumping must take second place. Rita needed Dorie's company, she needed to heal and get healthy.

The two girls talked a lot, both girls loved to talk about nature, especially birds and trees. Rita would say 'Birds sing such different songs.' Dorie would say 'Birds are so colorful and lay such beautiful eggs.' Rita would counter by saying 'Birds build such unusual nests and eat such different kinds of food.' Soon both Rita and Dorie were consumed with the study of birds and trees.

Rita's bedroom window looked out on a beautiful marshy meadow with patches of trees and flowers. The meadow always had lots of feathered friends hopping or flying about. On the outside of Rita's bedroom window was a honey suckle bush, oh what fun watching the humming birds feed.

Jean would bring home from the main library bird books and bird song records. Rita being musical soon learned the different bird songs and could sing like a Robin, Wren, Baltimore Oriole and Sandpiper. Rita's breathing was stronger since starting on a new medication thus she was able to practice singing like the birds and Dorie would listen in amazement.

Sunday afternoon Jean would put Rita in a wagon, give Dorie a back pack with some chocolate cookies and iced lemonade and off into the woods went Jean, Rita and Dorie for a fun study of trees and birds.

One evening Paul took Dorie and Garth on a hunt for bird nest building items. Paul, Garth and Dorie soon filled a small box full of string, twine, strong long pieces of grass and small pieces of bark. Dorie would present the box full of bird nest building items to Rita and asked Rita to build a Baltimore Oriole's nest. Rita and Dorie giggled and giggled while building. Jean even allowed the girls to make mud in an old pot in Rita's bedroom. The end result of building the nest was very good, the nest was strong and took on the shape of an Oriole's nest. Now what would a mom Oriole have thought about the nest was the big question.

As the days passed Rita was less able to sit up without the help of pillows, she had started becoming short of breath again and continued to look very pale.

One day on returning home from school Dorie ran to see Rita and was met at the door as usual by Jean. Today Jeans face was red and blotchy like and her eyes were full of tears. Dorie stepped back, paled and finally managed to ask "Is, is Rita... okay?"

Jean looked away tears filling her eyes once again, then abruptly went to Dorie, pulling her in her arms, holding the girl tight for several minutes before saying "Dorie we took Rita to the hospital last night. She was gasping for breath and didn't seem aware of Harry and I so we rushed her to emergency. Going to the hospital Harry had the gas petal to the floor board. You know speeding frightens me but I never thought of the fastness only getting Rita to hospital as quickly as possible." Then Jean bent her head and wept loudly "My child got better and please come home!"

Dorie kissed Jeans hand, patted her head in an awkward way and whispered "Rita will come home, I know she will, I love Rita and I will pray for her." With urgency Dorie said "I want to go to my special place and be alone."

Still sobbing Jean said "Thank you Dorie for making Rita's life so much fun." Words Dorie never heard as she left the house. When Dorie arrived at her special hideout she sat on a wooden box and thought only of Rita until she heard her dad's call, it was time to help with the chores.

Next morning as Dorie was dressing for school, Jean came to ask Annie if she could take Dorie to visit Rita. Jean told Annie "Dr. Parr phoned earlier and told me that Rita had an extremely restless night and kept calling out for Dorie." Jean explained to Dr. Parr that Dorie was Rita's closest friend. Dr. Parr told Jean they very seldom allowed children to visit other children except under dire circumstances and he felt this was one of those times. The doctor felt if Dorie and Rita visited perhaps Rita would be less restless and later get some sleep.

Just then Dorie entered the kitchen. Jean asked the girl "Would you accompany me to the hospital to see Rita? She would like you to visit her and Dr. Parr has given his permission." Jean then walked over to Dorie, took her hand and said in a weak tear-filled voice "Would it be too hard for you to see Rita, your best friend, extremely ill in an oxygen tent?"

Dorie replied "Yes it will be hard to see Rita so ill but perhaps I can help her so she will heal." Dorie turned to her mother asking if she could accompany Jean.

Annie replied "Yes Dorie you may go with Jean."

Reality came to the surface and Dorie said "Mom, Jean, I can't go to the hospital as I must write two year end examinations and Mr. Joma warned all students not to be absent unless they were very ill. Mr. Joma said 'If the students miss writing their examination zeros would be given as a mark and no opportunity would be given to rewrite the examinations.'"

Jean said to Dorie "We'll drive to school and I'll talk to Mr. Joma about you being away from school today." When Jean and Dorie arrived at school, Jean left the car and went to knock on the school door while Dorie stood beside the car. Mr. Joma answered the knock on the school door and listened to Jean's request, Mr. Joma replied that Dorie could write her examinations another day, furthermore Dorie was the only student in her grade.

Then Mr. Joma's eyes fell on Dorie standing beside the car. Dorie looked as if all energy had been zapped from her body, pale as snow, staring into space, so alone. Mr. Joma thought what a brave and caring child, a child hurting terribly, full of tears. Her teacher knew the two girls were closer then twins and he felt that Dorie knew she was going to say her last good-bye to her friend. As Jean and Dorie drove off, suddenly Mr. Joma wanted to sit on the front school step and cry as he had never cried before. Instead after a short while he wearily rose and entered the school.

Dorie was ushered into Rita's room while Jean remained at the nursing station looking lost, her face puffy, and her chin quivering, not wanting to cry, wanting to be strong when she visited Rita, the dear child that had never given Harry and her a minute of difficulty. Rita, the child they loved so deeply, who resembled the most beautiful flower in the garden. She was loving, kind, caring, honest and always smiling, if only they could have seen her graduate, marry and have children. She would have been an ideal mother, full of love and patience.

On entering the hospital room, Dorie's eyes fell upon her best friend's restless pale body lying in a large plastic enclosure that made hissing sounds. As she neared the bed brown eyes opened and made contact with hers, a form of warmth and loving feelings passed between the girls, it seemed as if they had hugged one another.

She ran the last few steps, placing her hands on the oxygen tent saying "Oh Rita I'm so happy to see you, I have so much news to tell you!"

The nurse came up behind the girl saying "I'll open the plastic window so you two can hear one another clearer. You do most of the talking and let Rita be the listener."

When the nurse had left the room, Rita said in-between labored breathing "Dorie I'm being called to heaven. I wanted to tell you what a wonderful friend you were and I wanted to say good-bye."

Dorie Shook her head. "No Rita you'll get better and come home."

Gasping for breath the frail girl said "The angels came to me in a dream telling me it was time to come home. Dorie I love you." And with those words Rita fell back on her pillows, closed her eyes and stopped her heavy breathing .

Before turning to leave, Dorie quietly said "Rita, you look so peaceful, have a good sleep and heal yourself. I love you Rita." With hope and bright eyes Dorie turned and left Rita's room.

The nurse entered Rita's room, closed the plastic window and looked in amazement at how peaceful Rita looked.

The Kinny daughter hoped and wished Rita would come home but deep in her heart Dorie knew Rita would die soon.

That evening after Dorie had done the dishes, she went to sit on her dad's lap to ask him why Rita was so ill. After thinking for several minutes Paul said "Harry told me Rita had contacted rheumatic fever which affected Rita's heart causing the heart to enlarge, work harder and ineffectively. All the stress and extra work placed on the heart causes the heart to tire to the point where it stops.

"I know this is a very difficult time for Harry, Jean, and you. I know you're hurting a lot, Rita is your best friend and I don't know why a wonderful child like her should be removed from this earth. We can ask ourselves and others a thousand times over and never come up with an answer. If you need to talk or need help during this difficult time, mom and I will always be here for you." As Paul held his daughter, she relaxed, lying her head against her dad's chest, while Paul sent a thank you prayer to the Lord for his daughter being safe.

The next evening the sad unwanted news came. Rita had passed on. Paul told his daughter after supper that her friend had gone to heaven. She seemed shocked but expressed no emotion, but Paul sensed underneath this outer shell that she conveyed, that it didn't matter that Rita was gone. Dorie was hurt, angry and failed to understand why her friend had been chosen to die. He knew she needed time to grieve and for the deep wound of separation to heal.

The next morning Dorie did her chores and went to school. She was quiet, not communicating much and after school she went for a long walk, returning from the walk with a tear stained face. Paul heard his daughter crying at night. As much as her weeping caused his heart to ache and bring great distress to his mind, the man was unable to reach out and hold his beloved child. He knew his daughter wanted to be alone, needed to deal with her grief in her own way, to heal herself.

The second evening after Rita had passed on Jean came to visit Dorie. Her face remained puffy, she looked hopeless, her hair in disarray, and her dress soiled. The girl hadn't wanted to talk to her friend's mom until she saw the blank hopeless look in the woman's eyes. Suddenly she felt very guilty. Jean was hurting, her heart aching, Rita's parents had lost a precious child, their only child.

Then Dorie felt Rita was talking to her from heaven, saying "Dorie let Mom be a second mother to you, she needs a child in her life for the present time."

Looking skyward then running and throwing her arms around Jean Dorie said "Will you be a second mother to me? You're so much like Rita and I love you like I loved her."

Jean grabbed and hugged Dorie saying "I would like nothing more." As the two hugged they had a feeling of togetherness, the dark road ahead had a small ray of brightness shining upon it, a new beginning.

Jean had come to visit to ask for some advice and assistance in preparing Rita's funeral. She wanted to talk about what dress Rita should wear and the hymns Rita loved most. Dorie felt Rita would look beautiful in her light blue silk dress. Jean asked her if she should fasten Rita's Baltimore Oriole pin to her dress. "Oh yes Jean the Oriole was Rita's favorite bird and Rita loved that pin! Rita's favorite hymns were 'Just As I Am' and 'You 're My Sunshine.'"

"Dorie, Matty has a beautiful voice, do you think she would sing the hymns?"

Dorie replied "Ask Matty I'm sure she will sing the hymns."

Jean got up to leave, hugging Dorie tightly saying "Thank you my wonderful friend."

"Jean," Dorie said "could I write and read a good-bye poem to Rita?"

"My darling you certainly may!" replied Jean.

On the day of the funeral Dorie asked her mother if she could look for something special in the woods after doing her chores. Annie replied "Yes Dorie you may go but please don't stay long." When she returned from the woods she was holding two lady slipper flowers whose stems she carefully wrapped in damp paper. She asked her dad if she could take the flowers to the funeral and Paul replied "Yes my little elf."

Family, friends, neighbors and most of Rita's classmates attended the service. Dorie sat with her parents and Moppet's family. She sat as straight and still as a steel rod, her face free of emotion, looking straight ahead.

The girl handed her flowers to Moppet when she went to the front of the Church to read her good-bye message to Rita.

"Rita, my dear friend you were kind, loving, helpful like an angel, all good and the best secret keeper ever.

Such a good friend, better then a sister, we talked about our inner wishes, problems and dreams, giggled and had fun.

You never broke a promise.

Rita I know you're surrounded by angels softly singing hymns, beautiful birds, rippling creeks and with stars at your fingertips.

Oh, Rita I love you and shall always miss you."

Looking skyward Dorie finished.

"Rita my secret keeper, someday we'll be together, good-bye for now."

Not a dry eye could be seen, even the pastor shed tears.

After the service the people attending filed out past the open coffin. When Dorie reached the open coffin she bent over and placed the two lady slippers in Rita's hand and left the Church.

On the evening of Rita's funeral, Dorie refused supper after doing her chores. She asked her dad if she could go to her private hideaway for a while.

On entering her personal haven, Dorie sat down and released her pent up grief to her dark surroundings crying out "Rita why did you leave me? You were my special friend and now I have no one to tell my deepest secrets to! Rita when you left you took part of my heart with you!"

After Dorie cried herself into a state of exhaustion she stood up and headed to her home, thinking 'What a sad world without Rita.'

Dorie placed one of her favorite photos of Rita under her night pillow. Jean and Dorie gave each other personal strength and comfort by going on short Sunday afternoon walks and talking about Rita. The two had a common goal, to overcome the loss of Rita.

As time passed Dorie's grief became less, she returned to practicing track and field and started working at building up her endurance - her goal was to run two and a half to three miles this summer. But Dorie refused to have contact with friends and children her age. She would not accept invitations from Moppet or Matty. She declined to go to Belle's birthday party and refused to play games with Garth. Her spirit and eagerness toward life seemed to have vanished.

One sunny evening Mr. Joma drove into the Kinny yard and asked to speak to Dorie. The girl slowly approached her teacher, not sure what to say then opted for "Hello Mr. Joma."

After greeting her, Mr. Joma told her he was in charge of a theater project that would produce several summer family plays to be held in three of the larger cities in Alberta. Mr. Joma asked Dorie if she would like to be one of the actresses.

"The part I have chosen for you is a brave child who has great enthusiasm and zeal for nature, I remember that you studied birds and trees, you know a lot about wild flowers, you're agile, hop around a lot and you're pretty with a clear voice. I think you're ideal for the part, would you consider taking the role?" Dorie made no reply. The man continued to explain. "We will practice twice a week for one hour and the plays would be on Saturday afternoons and early Saturday evening. Nine performances will be given. You and two other students can ride with my wife and I, we would pick you up."

For the first time in weeks Mr. Joma saw a light shine in Dorie's eyes as she said "Mr. Joma I would love to play the role you described and could you talk to Mom and Dad to get their permission?"

Both Paul and Annie gladly gave their consent, perhaps her parents thought this new turn in life would help heal Dorie's soul.

Dorie loved her acting role, she played mother nature's child, enlightening children about the loveliness of birds, trees, flowers and water, telling how nature can arouse pleasure through vision, hearing, smell and feel. The lesson of the play was to appreciate, respect and protect people's surroundings.

Soon Dorie was emitting a sparkle again. Once again she played and worked with Garth. Garth went to Annie and said "Mom the new Dorie has left and old Dorie before Rita died has come back! I'm so happy! Do you think the new Dorie will come back?"

Mrs. Kinny hugged her son saying "Garth I feel the old Dorie is back for good" and then the two danced about with joy.

That evening after supper Paul had gone out with some beaver hunters and neighbors. Yearly, four beaver hunters or better known as the beaver men obtained licenses from the municipal government giving each beaver trapper permission to trap four beavers along an assigned part of Rose Hip Creek which ran through several farmers lands including Paul's.

Beaver pelts were in great demand, they made lovely fur coats and hats.

If the beaver men trapped more than the four allotted beavers they would have to sell the extra pelts on the black market. If each beaver man trapped more then twenty beavers, they each made huge profits and the farmers also benefitted financially for allowing the hunters on their land and keeping their lips sealed. The beaver men would make private oral contracts with each farmer. The hunters and farmers trusted each other, they would shake hands making an honor agreement. If an individual broke an honor contract the untrustworthy person was put on a business black list.

Paul and several other farmers who had Rose Hip Creek running through their land noticed the beaver population was decreasing rapidly. The farmers decided to meet as a group with the beaver men and request that they only trap their allotted quota for three or more years depending on the beaver population. The farmers enjoyed the extra money but their love for nature and animals was stronger.

The beaver men had a secret hideout on each farmers land. The hideouts were used if wardens came along checking for number of traps, more then four dead beavers or pelts and off season hunting. The hunters almost always eluded the wardens and if later approached by a warden, the beaver men would claim a poacher was invading their given territory.

The underground hideout on Paul's land was a large natural cave and the huge entrance was partially closed with rocks leaving a small grass covered lid that was easily raised and allowed a hasty entrance into the cave. Paul had planted some berry plants and shrubs in the area of the cave. Before the size of the entrance was reduced the cave was equipped with a wooden cot, metal box containing two sheets, warm blankets, a pillow, two cans of beans, can opener, two spoons and a cup. Many times when the wardens gave chase the hunters seem to vanish into thin air, this was a big mystery to the wardens, a puzzle they hoped to solve soon.

This evening the beaver men and the farmers where to meet at Mr. Jakes. Paul was traveling with Harry to the Jake's farm.

Shortly after Paul left, Annie's sister Judy, Herb, Judy's husband and their daughter Colly arrived to visit. Annie put the coffee on to boil and started making a light lunch when Uncle Herb suddenly collapsed vomiting bright blood, a big pool had formed on the floor. Uncle continued to vomit blood while mom ran for a catch basin and Auntie in tears bent down to turn Uncles head.

Annie, startled, commented "Dorie can drive, she hasn't driven on the highway or in town but Paul has taught her the city rules. If we give her a couple of pillows to sit on, she should have no problem seeing out the car windows."

Aunt Judy replied with a strong "No" fearing they would end up in the ditch or stopped by the police.

Annie said "If the police pulled us over and noticed we were faced with an emergency, they would help us not penalize us." Colly cried out "Mom we have to take the chance or Daddy will die!" Annie with a quickness called out orders "Dorie remove the coffee pot from the stove, bring two pillows, a warm blanket, two towels and the catch basin. Colly you hold open the house door, and when your mom and I have carried your dad out, Colly run ahead and hold open the rear car door so we can place your dad in the back seat."

The frantic group drove off, Annie looking frightened, instructing Dorie not to speed, Aunt Judy sitting in the back with her hands over her face, Colly keeping an eye on her dad, hastily turned and whispered in Dorie's ear "You're doing a great job."

Dorie smiled and said "Thank you Colly." Annie was grateful the hospital was on the outskirts of Purplehaven.

Before long Dorie drove up to the emergency center and Colly jumped out and ran for help. A doctor and two nurses pushing a stretcher rushed out and took Uncle Herb into the hospital, Aunt Judy and Colly following behind. Dorie said "Mom after I park the car can I go to Tom and Molly's and ask George to drive us home?"

"Dorie its a long way to walk alone at this time of day, lets walk together, we'll be company for each other." Said Dorie's mom.

George drove Annie and Dorie home, but before leaving Purplehaven they stopped at the hospital to see how Uncle Herb was doing and what plans Aunt Judy and Colly had. Uncle Herb was receiving blood transfusions and medications, his bleeding from the stomach had stopped and he was alert. Judy and Colly would stay in the hospital guest room for the night, they wanted to be near Herb.

Seeing that everything was sorted out, the three headed to the Kinny Farm. Paul was happy to see them safe, he had been anxious and mystified by the blood on the floor and a pot of cold coffee.

Next morning after doing his chores Paul drove to Uncle Herb's and did his chores then went to Purplehaven to check on his condition. Judy told Paul "We're lucky Dorie knew how to drive, she seemed so self assured and confident. Could you teach Colly to drive?"

Paul replied "Bring Colly over some August evenings and I'll teach her to drive."

"Herb is still receiving blood transfusions but his condition has stabilized, there's no further bleeding from his stomach ulcer and he's alert. Could you take Colly and I home for the day so we can bathe and change our clothes and do the evening chores?"

It was a big relief to Paul when Herb was discharged from the hospital, now Mr. Kinny could get at his own work building the new barn and digging the new well in between his usual work.

Paul knew he had to take a day off for the country fair. People supported the fair in a big way. Moppet, Dorie and Garth were overcome with excitement as the day of the fair approached, they put many entries into the prize competitions. The two girls loved to enter the grain categories, as fewer people entered the grain division since making grain sheaves was difficult and time consuming. Paul made three separate plots of wheat, rye and barley, while Alice made a plot of oats. Sweet clover growing in the ditch was tall with many blooms and Paul often wondered if the healthy plant growth partially came from the soda pop that ran out of the bottles and cans thrown away by motorists. The other types of clover came from the man's hay patch. Moppet and Dorie also entered vegetables, berries, flowers and baking. Garth did wood work, art and some baking. Dorie loved to walk through the agriculture building after the judging was completed.

Dorie enjoyed seeing a ribbon hanging above her entry, it made her feel warm, a feeling of accomplishment to be one of the winners. If a person works hard, and follows the rules that person can be a winner, maybe not always but that person can be a winner at times.

Dorie had been deep in thought and as late afternoon arrived she knew Moppet would soon arrive to help cut the grain and hay stems. When she arrived, Dorie ran out with the collection boxes which were soon filled. The children and adults made the sheaves taking great care to choose the healthiest well formed heads of grain growing out of strong, straight stems. As the sheaves were completed the bottom ends were placed in water for the night. The vegetables were harvested and washed in the morning then the berries were picked last.

The fair day was here, entries had to be in place in the agriculture building no later then ten a.m. The Jake family and Kinny family watched a lot of the judging at noon. The men brought the picnic baskets to the park, made the coffee over a camp fire while the mothers and children set out the lunch.

After lunch was over the Kinny, Jake and, Matty families along with Harry, and Jean went to watch Moppet race Bell. Moppet had a great cheering section and won second prize to every one's delight. Following the races the children headed for the rides. Dorie didn't like the salt and pepper ride which consisted of two pieces that would rise rapidly then alternately each piece would swing up then down. Dorie would never have gone on the ride if Moppet, Matty and other classmates hadn't made her feel like a coward. It usually took her an hour to recover from the salt and pepper ride, till her dizziness left her. After the rides it was time to play some of the midway games. Paul had lent some money to Dorie and Garth and would collect it after they received their prize money. Dorie won a huge frog. She had pleaded with the carnival worker to give her Lassie, the stuffed dog. The worker told Dorie she looked like a frog and that's why he was giving Dorie the ugly creature. It took all of Dorie's willpower not to cry. Moppet told the carnival worker he was disgusting. Matty told the worker he must have had a louse as a mother since he was so rude.

After visiting the horse barn, watching chicken racing and eating an ice cream cone, Dorie said "We better rush to the park and help our families unpack the food." Garth would be eating with Iron Side's family.

Soon the delicious food; roast chicken, ham, heated ribs, potato salad, cold slaw and raw vegetables were being eaten. Lots of juice and cold water from the pump followed. Chocolate cake and lemon pie would end the delicious meal. Everyone enjoyed the delightful supper, and as they finished the desert, Moppet, Matty and Dorie discussed the mean carnival man. The moms overheard the girls talk and were surprised how they had responded. Alice said "We weren't eavesdropping but just over heard your chatter. How do you think you should have responded to the carnival man?"

Moppet replied "You taught us not to throw verbal rotten eggs back to a person who had bombarded us with verbal rotten eggs. I should have said to the nasty man 'You seem upset, are you having a hard day? I hope the rest of your day turns out better.'"

"You're right, never feed a person's anger, some people actually thrive or receive enjoyment from hurting others."

Matty added "Mrs. Jake you're right, I know how it hurts if I say not nice words to a person and that person walks away, I feel they are the winner." Soon children as well as adults were discussing how best to deal with psychologically troubled individuals that used verbal nastiness.

Moppet, Matty, and Dorie had eaten a huge helping of food but felt they still had room for cotton candy while they toured the fair grounds for a last time before leaving for home. The fair was beautiful, brilliant, with thousands of lights shining this time of evening the layout took on a breathtaking aura of visual excitement which would become in grained in ones mind forever.

Paul and his family headed home since chores needed to be done. He and his wife would do the chores while Dorie and Garth settled for the night. The children were sound asleep as soon as the car started homeward bound. It was a fun day for all the families and in the morning the Kinny family would collect their children's prize winnings from the fair manager.

After berry picking, canning, weeding the large gardens, and bringing the hay into the yard corral, another fun day would soon arrive, the first Saturday in September when they went blueberry picking. Paul had spent a couple of hours making blueberry pickers from small tin cans Molly saved for Paul. He would cut the tops off nails which he then welded to half of the can lip, the second half of the can he cut half way to the base, filing and tapering the rough edges. The cut down part of the can was grasped by the hand of the berry picker. When people used the can picker, a handful of berries could be picked with one swipe.

Dorie had asked her dad if she could keep the money from the sales of her blueberries this year as she needed to save money for a special project she had in mind. She also asked her dad if he allowed her to keep the berry money, would he help her open a bank account. She also told her dad she still had twenty five dollars from her fair winnings hidden under her shoebox Her father said, she could keep the money from the sale of the berries, and yes he would help her open a bank account."

The blueberry picking Saturday arrived. Many pails of blueberries were picked for eating, canning and selling to the grocery store. Harry would take his truck to transport the food and blueberry picking equipment. He also had a small ice box in the back, after all was packed he covered the back of the truck with a tarp, the covering was later used to place their meals on. Paul and his family travelled with the Jakes. The berry picking families had packed extra food to treat the family that was allowing them to pick berries on their land.

The berry pickers arrived at their friend's homes, near a large lake, just in time to have an early lunch. After lunch the women and children packed up while the men readied the horse drawn wagon with pails, pickers, drinks, extra clothes if the woods were cool and a couple of stones in case they met a bear, which was unlikely. Moppet, Dorie and Garth had been instructed about bears, to stay near their parents, be noisy in their talk and movements and stay away from bear cubs.

Soon many pails had been filled with blueberries. Dorie's mom had picked a pail full of high bush cranberries and a small pail of pin cherries promising to share her jelly with Alice and Jean.

Just as the wagon was being reloaded a crashing noise and a growl was heard. The people mulling around the wagon turned to the noise, what the people saw was a scene of horror - a large black bear headed toward Moppet. Paul being the nearest, grasped a piece of wood ran and struck the bear to divert its attention from the girl. The bear turned to the man with a sudden violent movement, snarling and swiping his clawed paw at him, ripping his right arm open. Within seconds the bear was surrounded by angry men with sticks, pails, and rocks. A rock hit it in the forehead, it shook its head, made a strange mean sound and ran off into the woods. Harry had a difficult time restraining the horses. The horses wanted to bolt, they feared bears. When all was quiet many eyes swung to Paul as Dorie ran screaming to her heavy bleeding father. Her father placed his good arm around her telling his daughter he would be fine. Alice, in the meantime, had found the first aid box and headed for her friend. She put two large pads on his arm followed by bandages, then placed a heavy clean towel folded in half over the injury, which Alice then bandaged to secure the bandage. Mr. Kinny sat with a sad withdrawn look. Alice asked Paul if he had pain. To which Paul answered "Yes, but the pain is tolerable, my arm is now a big problem for me. I won't be able to use it for a while and Alice I had planned to start work on the well and barn. I had planned on completing them before the snow fell. Now I'll be lucky to do my late harvesting and Dorie will have to miss several weeks of school. Oh Alice I'm sorry to be going on about my work, it will work out."

"Paul you saved Moppet from severe injury and perhaps death, you have no idea how grateful we are! I don't think she could have handled another severe injury especially deformity. Now lets get you to the hospital" Alice consoled.

Alice told Harry to take Garth and Dorie as she felt Paul needed more room in the car so he could lay back and stretch his arm out on Annie's lap. His wife had been unable to witness the bear attack or look at his injured arm, she had run off into the bush vomiting and retching. Now a very pale woman sat beside her husband holding his hand, while his arm rested in her lap. She was very thankful to have him alive. She loved him a great deal.

By now he was having considerable pain but Alice was afraid to give him an analgesic or water since he would probably need surgery.

When they reached the hospital Annie learned her husband was to be operated on to piece together his mauled right arm at nine that night. The Jakes waited with Annie until Paul was comfortable then they drove his wife home.

Annie arrived home to find Dorie had completed half the chores but was very anxious about her dad's arm. Would the doctors remove his arm? It looked as if parts of it wasn't even there. Annie said, "Dorie your dad is fine, the doctors will do surgery and repair the open areas tonight then the hospital will phone Jean giving her a report that Jean will relay to us."

Shortly after ten Jean knocked on the Kinny's door. The hospital had phoned to say Paul was awake, comfortable and needed one hundred and forty stitches to close the affected arm. Paul would have full usage of his injured arm but must remain in hospital five to six days to monitor for infection and watch the healing process. Finally Dorie was able to settle and sleep. Her dad would be fine.

Next morning Alice took Annie to see Paul and before she left she assured him they would watch over his family. Annie agreed. "Paul don't worry we're managing fine, and even Garth said he would dust away the dust bunnies in the house." That brought a large smile to Paul's face.

What Alice didn't mention to Paul or Annie was her intention to help them in a big way. Early next morning she phoned neighbors, friends, relatives, anyone Alice remotely knew, even Mr. Joma was asked to help after school. She would see that Paul's barn, shed, and well would be completed before the middle of September. The woman even phoned Molly, Tom, and George to request their help in purchasing lumber, paint and other necessary building needs. George asked what day the lumber and paint was needed and could Alice please have one of Paul's friends that had building experience join him when George purchased the lumber and other material? Alice thought about it and agreed. "How about Monday at nine in the morning? We'll meet you at Phil's lumber yard."

What Alice didn't know was how well her plan was gaining momentum, enthusiasm and a desire to help. Molly spoke to Dave and Dave's friend. Dave's friend would bring a truck load of soil and fill the old well in. Mr. Joma had a friend who had well lining experience and the equipment to complete one. Alex's boss heard of the community's effort to help Paul and offered to deliver all needed supplies free of charge. A couple of men offered to build and paint the shed, also put shelves and hooks inside.

Most of the men would work on building and painting the barn. Phil's lumber was donating the lumber and Law's would donate all the paint that was needed. Molly and Tom didn't feel left out as they now decided George could take Annie shopping for bedroom furniture for the house they would move into.

Harry and Mr. Jake who had taken off three days from work would level the land where the older house was to be moved, then bring and place cement squares on the leveled ground. Harry would have Alex's boss bring the cement squares from Purplehaven.

Alice's small project had taken off in a tizzy of confusion evolving into a well organized project. 'The plan has taken off like a whirlwind gaining speed and strength' Alice thought as she looked out the window surrounded by joyful visions. Alice knew for sure this world had to be the most wonderful place to live in, if people just forgot about themselves for a few days and concentrated on others in need. Yes if only people would share and help others in need this truly could be a loving world.

CHAPTER NINE

Alice's project had been completed the day before Paul was discharged.

The day Paul was sent home, Alice and Annie picked Paul up and drove him to the new farm the Kinny family would live on. Paul looked, shook his head in amazement and said "This seems like a fairytale, pinch me, tell me its true, its as perfect as the icing on a cake! The buildings look ideal and they're even painted." Paul then put his head down and wept. Soon Annie and Alice joined the weeping making it sound like a choir. He was full of happiness and now that he was home Mr. Kinny would use his magic healing medicine and his arm would become like new.

A new girl named Vera started school. She was pretty, dressed in beautiful clothes and was in grade six. The first day she started school, her father brought her to school in a huge fancy car. The car was a late model Buick the older boys said. Vera's father brought her into the school, he was wearing a suit, soft shoes and a big white ring that shone and sparkled in the sunlight causing little dancing lights to leap about. At first all the children thought there was something magnetic about her as she soon captivated the students old and young with taking command of most situations whether she was asked or not and the fact that she was elegant and had a great way of using the English language.

Then many changes happened at Elm school with Vera's arrival and not many of them good. Fear of the new girl struck the Elm school students. Students noticed that some of their classmates had facial and arm bruising, one grade four girl had a piece of pencil lead partially buried in her upper ear lobe with blood oozing around the lead, this injured girl had been crying, one boy started to limp after lunch and he had been seen behind the barn with Vera. All students remained silent, no student talked to Mr. Joma or their parents.

A third grader came to Dorie and told her a frightening story about his friend James refusing to do a job for Vera. She had the older male students take James behind the barn, then turn him upside down while she slapped him with a stick. James' friend told Dorie he had witnessed this punishment with his two other friends as they hid in a grove of trees. She was also heard saying 'You do the same to me again and you'll be found beaten and near death in some ditch.'

Matty and Dorie tried to avoid Vera by arriving at school just as the school starting bell rang, and dashing out after dismissal to head for home and playing ball during recess and part of noon hour. Dorie would pitch or take the short stop position. Vera didn't play ball to the students' delight. She said she was afraid of hurting her hands.

During lunch hour one day Vera approached and invited Matty and Dorie to her home after school assuring the two girls that Jeff, Vera's father would pick them up from school and drive them. Both Matty and Dorie declined saying they couldn't socialize after school because of the many chores they had to do. Dorie said "I'll ask my dad and what ever he says I'll follow his instructions."

Matty also responded by saying "I'll check with my parents."

Dorie did talk to her dad about Vera and he said "Dorie please stay away from Vera and her family." He also wrote a note to Vera, thanking her for the invitation and her thoughtfulness but his daughter wouldn't be able to play at fellow classmates' homes after school or weekends as she had numerous chores and other responsibilities to tend to during the light hours of the day.

One of the troubling and strange happenings that occurred in the Elm community was the disappearance of Raymond one of the older boys attending Elm school. Raymond was an only child and dearly loved by his parents who vowed to leave no stone unturned in the search of their son. The police used tracking dogs for days, interviewed numerous neighbors and school children.

Some Elm school children had seen Raymond get into an older blue car, the driver of the blue car was obese with a long black beard. These school children also knew that Raymond went to Vera's home many times and did some kind of work, even Raymond's parents were aware of Raymond's trips to Vera's home. The students kept their lips sealed in case the car belonged to one of Vera's dad's workers and the students felt they might disappear if they talked.

Raymond's parents felt something had happened to their son and hired a private detective, they also offered a fifty thousand dollar reward for information that would lead to their son and each day they took their dog and searched in the woods and anywhere they thought he might have gone. They would never give up their search for their son. The search continued but the more days that went by the less hopeful the family became.

Another startling occurrence noticed by the Elm school students was the change in X-Cee. X-Cee had a new expensive bike and he started wearing expensive clothes. One noon X-Cee showed Dorie a large wad of money that he pulled from his pocket. Dorie gasped and looked away. "X-Cee I hope that money was earned in an honest way?"

"Dorie this money has great meaning to my family, my dad has paid off the back taxes on the family farm, bought an old tractor and ten cows. Mom is pleased with her new stove. Dorie I've never seen mom so happy, she even sings! Before I started working mom felt we would end up on the street when the farm was taken away from us. Dorie I love my family, this job is like a pot of gold!" At that moment Dorie glanced up in time to see Vera hiding behind a tree watching them.

Dorie quietly whispered to X-Cee "Don't do anything illegal," Then in her regular voice "I've got to go X-Cee." and she ran off.

As Dorie approached the school Vera grasped her arm forcefully and demanded "What's up with all this talk between X-Cee and you?"

"Oh, Vera, my father uses a lot of natural medicine and X-Cee wanted to know if dad had some ointment to put on his forehead scar."

Vera pinched Dorie hard before letting go of her arm saying "Dorie don't you ever lie to me."

A ton of fear had settled in Dorie's stomach. Dorie would talk to her dad about the run in she had with Vera and some of the strange happenings at Elm school since the new girl started attending. She knew her dad would know what to do or where to go for help. She also knew it was wrong to lie, she had lied to the girl out of great fear, she would tell her dad about the lie.

That evening Dorie talked to her father for over an hour telling him about the meanness Vera used on the Elm school students, about Raymond going to Vera's home a lot, the rumor of the old blue car and X-Cee going to Vera's to help Vera's father and earning huge amounts of money. No students would talk to Mr. Joma as the students were afraid Mr. Joma would be harmed. "Daddy I'm so afraid, Vera has blue eyes and when she gets angry her eyes look like blue ice."

"Dorie my little elf, I'll talk to my friends on the police force and I'm so glad you came and told me. The information you gave me will be kept secret."

All of Elm school students and families including Mr. Joma and family received a birthday invitation from Vera which was being held in a large hall in Purplehaven. Only three families didn't attend, Mr. Joma's, Matty's and Dorie's. Vera's family was angry about the three families not being present at the party, Jeff was especially cross, no one, just no one slighted him but he also knew he must be careful because of Paul's friendly connections with the police. Jeff encouraged Vera to try extra hard to become Dorie's friend.

Vera did try hard to become Dories friend by offering movie passes, bringing candy, cookies and offering money to her without a take. She told the troublemaker she ate very little sweets wanting to keep fit and she said her parents didn't allow her to go to movies.

Next Vera consulted with the students as to Dorie's likes. All the students knew she loved oranges and seldom got them but not one student passed this information on to the mean girl. Many students weren't close to Dorie but they had respect for her. The Elm school students found Dorie to be kind, helpful, she kept secrets, was honest and never took advantage of others. She seemed to live in a world of her own, was very difficult to get to know as her mind was on track and field, art and nature most of the time. Unknowingly she had the students' respect and protection, the students in their own secret ways would watch over their Dorie.

Paul and Annie decided to visit X-Cee and his family and have a ball game. When Dorie's family arrived at X-Cee's family farm Paul was surprised at the improvements, thinking Dorie was right, this family is receiving a lot of money. Edward, X-Cee's father called his family and soon a fun ball game was under way between the two families.

After the ball game Paul had a chat with Edward. He was interested in what type of work X-Cee did and where the boy worked. "Paul, the bank was going to foreclose on our farm for back taxes!" When X-Cee heard this, he said 'I'm going to work to help us out of this crisis.' Thank goodness for our boy, he saved our farm!" Edward told Paul a new neighbor had moved into the community, they had one daughter, Vera, who attended Elm school. She told X-Cee of the job. I don't exactly know the type of work X-Cee does." Edward replied, then added "When he is asked what sort of work is he required to do, he always replies 'farm work.' Paul," Edward said "I know it's strange that X-Cee should earn hundreds of dollars from doing ordinary farm work but he is kind, honest and hard working and I trust my son."

Paul thanked Edward for the fun ball game and said "We must be on our way home."

That evening Paul was washing his face and hands and Annie was putting the final touches to the evening meal when loud knocking was heard on the kitchen door. Dorie ran to answer. A frantic looking uncle Thomas was standing out side and asked to see Dorie's mom or dad. Paul came rushing to the scene, asking "Thomas what's wrong?"

"Paul, Sally is about to deliver her baby. We are unable to afford hospital fees. We asked my sister, Midge, months ago if she would deliver Sally's baby and Midge said yes. When we stopped at her house a few minutes ago, she declined to do the delivery, as she was frightened and said she didn't have enough knowledge about delivering babies. Paul could you and Annie help us out of this crisis?" pleaded Thomas.

"Dorie get your mom and have her ready the bedroom for delivery, stoke the fire, put kettles and pots of water to boil" said Paul. "Thomas and I will help Sally in."

By the time Sally was helped into the house and had reached the bedroom door Annie had an underlay of plastic covered by a flannelette sheet shielding the top of the bed, with towels, wash basin and gloves still in their packages left over from Garth's dressing change days laying nearby. Annie helped her sister Sally on to the bed, stopping a couple of times while Auntie Sally grabbed her stomach, bent over and moaned. Paul was racing about finding string, scissors and other instruments which he would boil.

Paul instructed Dorie to boil more water, when the water was boiled to set the pot aside to cool, bring water from the well, keep the stove hot, bring another flannelette blanket and towel and monitor supper.

Dorie's mind was racing when suddenly a voice from behind her said "Dorie I'll help you if you give me some directions, tell me what to do, I can boil the water and bring water in if I know which pails to use." She turned to Joyce who looked anxious and ill at ease. Joyce was two years older then her, and Joyce's family lived in another community and socialized mainly with Thomas's family thus not knowing her mother Sally's family.

Before speaking Dorie thought how tall and pretty her cousin was, then she said, "Joyce you boil water in these pots and use these pails to bring water in from the well. Have you drawn up water using a well pulley?"

"Yes I have." Said Joyce. "I really appreciate your help." Within a short period of time the environment suddenly became calm and peaceful.

Paul said, "Dorie, Joyce why don't you girls get supper on the table." Dorie gave tasks to Joyce that didn't require looking for items such as heating the peas, making the salad and mashing the potatoes while Dorie put the Jell-O in bowls, started the coffee brewing and carved the roasted chicken. She had Garth set and put the buns on the table.

Uncle Thomas was sitting in the rocker but when Paul asked him to sit at the table and dine, he got no response. He had to speak twice more to his brother in law as he seemed so deep in thought. Annie came and got a small pot and metal spoon to give to Aunt Sally to summon help should it be needed while she dined.

Thomas spoke saying, "Paul, Annie you have no idea how grateful I am for your help taking us in without notice, your kindness and making us feel at home. I've never seen such unselfish help, my family is totally opposite. What I have seen and felt tonight is caring and love. Thank you Paul,"

"Thomas you're welcome, and you can sit and drink coffee till after the baby is born. Annie feels it will arrive soon."

Dorie screamed "Did you say baby!? A baby is to be born!? Dad can Joyce and I watch the baby being born!?"

Paul replied "No Dorie the bedroom is very small, the space is needed by your mom, the equipment and me should I be required to help."

Paul asked his daughter to clear the table. Joyce said, "Dorie you put the food away and I'll wash the dishes, perhaps Garth will dry some dishes and help me in putting them away."

In the meantime Mr. Kinny was taking items to the bedroom and answering his wife's questions and concerns. He also put another pot of coffee on to brew. Uncle Thomas still seemed to be up in a tree.

The cry came, another cry, then a loud cry summoning Uncle Thomas to the larger bedroom where a baby boy was being placed in a towel then laid across Aunt Sally's stomach. After Annie had made her sister and the baby comfortable and tidied the room, Thomas went to get Joyce, Dorie and Garth to come and see the new baby. Three sets of feet came thundering into the bedroom to see the newborn. Thomas went over to his daughter hugging her and saying to her "Sally and I are so fortunate to have you and this new little boy."

The two girls took short turns holding the baby, Garth declined, then changed his mind and held the baby saying "This feels strange, he's so tiny."

Paul had gone to get his herbal medicine. He would give Sally a tablespoon of plant tonic that he had cooked last week. To make this special tonic you needed four plants, the leaves of a certain plant before it bloomed, the flowers off another plant, seeds of another plant that had bloomed and the roots of a plant that grew in a marshy place. It was difficult to get all the necessary plant parts at the same time so Paul made the rounds each day checking on the needed plants mid to late September. The tonic from the herbs would help Sally gain strength, build up her immune system and was a great relaxant but didn't seem to effect babies through the mother's milk. He also put some herbal paste medicine in a jar to be used around the babies umbilical cord area for rapid healing.

After taking the herbal tonic Aunt Sally fell into a deep sleep till ten o'clock waking up feeling refreshed. Uncle Thomas wanted to take her home, freeing up his sister and brother-in-law's sleeping quarters and getting his wife and new son settled in at home. A neighbor's wife promised to help the woman each day. Annie and Paul used a strong cardboard box lined with soft towels as the baby's transport bed. Thomas and Annie helped Sally out to the car while Joyce hugged Dorie saying "Dorie come and spend a weekend with me and meet Teddy my big St. Bernard." Dorie replied she would try.

Saturday morning came, which was time to bring the cows in from the field for milking. As Dorie was walking near a dense lot of trees she heard someone call her, "Dorie over here, please come." At first she thought it was her imagination, then she realized that someone was actually calling her. The girl turned around and peered into the woods, there stood X-Cee saying quietly "Come here Dorie I need to talk to you." She shooed the cows hoping they would start home on their own then went forward to meet her friend. She wondered why he would be hiding in the woods, he must be in trouble with Jeff and Vera. The middle Kinny child stiffened with fear. What if Jeff and Vera were with X-Cee? She knew she could never outrun Jeff. "Hurry Dorie, I won't harm you!" Called X-Cee. Once again Dorie approached the woods, fear causing her heart to pound, a knot formed in her stomach and her legs felt weak but they still had enough power to let her edge forward. Once reaching the bush he grabbed her arm pulling her into the bush, at this action her heart leapt into her throat, she let out a weak cry and closed her eyes waiting for the worst to happen. X-Cee released her arms and said "Dorie what's wrong? Open your eyes, smarten up, I need your help badly!"

Slowly she opened her eyes still gripped by fear and said "what's wrong X-Cee?" Looking around she didn't see Jeff or Vera but only a pale, edgy, quivering X-Cee. She said, "X-Cee you look cold and sick." and as she said these words she removed her fall jacket and laid it across her friend's shoulders while he attempted to pull the two front halves of the jacket together with no success, thinking 'If only the coat was larger so I could put my arms into the sleeves of this garment.' Dorie was still gripped by fear, would X-Cee try and lure her into a trap if he had been bribed enough? Surely he wouldn't harm her, his friend, that would be selling his soul to the devil.

X-Cee shook his hands, stamped his feet and raising his voice said "Don't play act Dorie, this is serious. I need your help badly." When she heard the urgency and fear in his voice, calm overcame her. The boy continued "Dorie I have no one else to help me, I can't put my family or your family in danger. I have no one else except you that I can trust."

Dorie replied "If I can help, I surely will."

"You knew I was working for Jeff and Vera. Jeff and his elderly mother, Liedie, run a moonshine business."

She interrupted him asking "What is a moonshine business?"

"It's an illegal business where people make homemade liquor which is a very powerful drink. It is sold secretly on the black market, and don't ask me what black market means.

"Jeff's mother who is eighty seven has the equipment and makes the liquor in her secret concealed work shop that is attached to the basement of her house. There is a hidden mystery door behind a basement wall, the wall is pulled back when a large screw is turned exposing Liedie's manufacturing room. Oh, you should see the equipment, big barrels, hoses and bottles!" said the boy. "The police have searched Jeff's home and yard buildings but have never found anything illegal. Jeff has a tunnel that leads from under his coal bin to his mother's secret workshop. Water is piped underground into the processing room. Jeff is seldom seen visiting his mother as Jeff uses the tunnel to visit her.

"This eighty seven year old woman is mixing, fermenting and aging the liquor. Any ingredients or equipment needed is purchased in distant and always different towns and cities by different individuals.

"Who ever would suspect such an old woman? When Liedie answers the door or goes shopping she can barely walk, uses two canes and hobbles along moaning every step of the way. But when in her house the old woman runs about, races down the stairs, carries pots back and forth and pushes barrels around. This woman is a real actress, she should be in Hollywood! This old woman the police would never suspect, a perfect illegal set up."

"What type of work did Jeff have you do?"

"I did general work, bottled liquor, cased it and carried the cases to the delivery truck which was repainted and made to look different many times."

"What put great fear into my heart, was a conversation I overhear between Jeff and his brother Dave, who is in charge of selling the liquor. Jeff said to Dave 'These older Elm School boys are a headache, I have to continually monitor them for mistakes and I have found out these school boys are more apt to talk to friends and family which could bring our operation down. Dave do you know of a tight lipped adult with intelligence? These school boys are turning out to be too much trouble, they know too much about the business.'

"Jeff kept talking to Dave saying 'No one except our close family and a few workers should know about the hidden basement room.' Then suddenly Jeff started to talk about me. Jeff said to Dave 'X-Cee poses a danger, even as tight lipped as he is, if he has a brush in with the law, or questioned by the police about the expensive bike he has or the fancy clothes he wears... Where did the bike and clothes come from when his parents are extremely poor?' He said 'Dave I'm going to tell him he's getting a promotion to enforcer, he can enforce our law by using an iron rod. The kid is strong. People will easily remember him because of his noticeable limp. Then we rid the world of him and the people he harmed will get the blame for his disappearance. We'll be on our own till we can hire the right adult who thinks like we do, I don't want this successful business shut down.'

"I can't harm people even if they're bad, no one should harm others and then Jeff would have me murdered! What really saddens me is that he has turned his daughter at her young age into a criminal. She can inflict pain without batting an eyelid.

"Oh, Dorie!" said X-Cee crying, "I packed a small old suitcase that belonged to my mother and left in the middle of the night, walking through the woods, avoiding all roads to get here. I remember you telling my family when our families played ball that you brought the cows to the barn each morning and evening from their grazing land. I was hoping." said X-Cee "That you still fetched the cows. I'm so terrified, hungry and cold" he said.

Dorie replied "I must take the cows home before my parents start to worry, I'll see you in the morning and bring food and a blanket. We will work at keeping you safe, in the meantime lay low."

Walking home, she glanced back and waved, a frightened X-Cee helplessly leaned against a tree. She felt a great overwhelming sense of fear. If only she was grown up and wise. The girl was engulfed in anxiety and tears came to her eyes as she cried out to Rita's angel "Help me do what's right and guide me on the proper road!"

Dorie would have to rise early as soon as the sky started to loose its dark color in the morning. As soon as the chores and supper were completed, the rest of the family went to help Harry and Jean brand some cattle. Dorie stayed home and packed a bag of lunch for her friend. She packed cheese, cold beef, bread, an apple and a bottle of milk. The girl would hide the lunch and an old blanket behind her cot.

When the sky took on some light, she quickly rose, dressed, grabbed the supplies for her friend and rushed out of the house. X-Cee was waiting for her with her coat still draped around him. Firstly he took the blanket and covered himself. Dorie sat on the ground while X-Cee ate his lunch, not speaking wanting him to eat his lunch slowly and properly.

After finishing, X-Cee said "I can't stay in your house as that would put you and your family at risk and Jeff might put your home under surveillance since our families are friends. It would be very dangerous to stay at your home. Could you keep bringing me food, bring a warm coat and a pair of warm socks till we work out an escape plan? Before I came here I looked through mom's address book and found my Aunt Bess's address and phone number. A year ago she sent us a wedding invitation. Even had we had the money my family wouldn't have gone. My family was scandalized by Aunt Bess years ago and have never forgiven her, and I'm surprised mom didn't burn the invitation. I have no idea what she did as my family never talked about the grim details."

Suddenly a new idea came to Dorie, take X-Cee to the beaver man hideout! Reasonably wonderful, helpful thoughts would just pop into her mind and she didn't feel the new idea's were hers, could Rita's angel be sending these concepts down from heaven through the airwaves?

Yes Dorie would take X-Cee to the beaverman's hideout, the underground room which she and Rita had accidentally found when picking berries from the fruit bushes near the hideout. Dorie had tripped on a grass covered handle. When they attempted to remove the handle from the ground, a door came open and they saw the little room beneath the top earth. She told her dad about the strange underground room they had discovered. Her dad explained the purpose of the hideout and requested that they promise not to tell or show Garth or anyone else this secret place. She kept her promise till this morning feeling very guilty about breaking the vow she made with her dad.

Dorie took X-Cee to the underground room. He was happy to be out of sight and have extra blankets, a pillow and cup which she took to get water from the creek and gave to her friend.

Herding the cows, the girl walked home distraughtly. The worry was beginning to make her sick to her stomach. She couldn't tell her dad it might put her whole family in danger, she must be cautious. When she finally got the cows home, her father was worried and upset, thinking he should search for his daughter. "This is the second time in a row you have been very late in bringing the cows home." Paul said "I've been very worried." Then her dad asked "Are any of the cows being difficult to manage or being rebellious by running off?"

Dorie replied "No Dad the cows are easy to herd, I was distracted, deep in thought and walked in the woods."

"You seem worried and anxious, is there anything I can do to help?"

"No Dad." Dorie fought to keep the nervousness out of her voice. She loved her dad so much, she wanted him safe and would go to great lengths to protect him. "Dad I won't be late again, I promise." said Dorie.

"Vera and her father, Jeff, visited and wondered if we had seen X-Cee. Apparently he didn't come to work this morning." Said Paul. "I told Jeff we hadn't seen him and I hoped he would soon return to work as the money he earned was a big help to his family. Jeff seemed satisfied with my explanation and left but seemed very worried about X-Cee's disappearance. He did request that if we see the boy we are to contact him immediately as his family is worried and he would like to know if X-Cee is coming back to work."

"Thank you for telling me" said Dorie, as her fear grew and she quivered thinking she must get her friend out of the district soon before Jeff's spies came across some clues that pointed to Dorie's family.

Paul noticed his daughter's quiver and asked "Are you ill or just cold? You should be wearing your jacket."

"Yes." Dorie replied. "I'm cold and shall go and get a jacket. Are you going to Purplehaven this afternoon? If so can I come?"

"Yes Dorie I'm going to town as your mother needs flour and I need some thistle spray."

Dorie said "Dad I thought you dried the thistle leaves for arthritis tea?"

"I won't spray the thistles by the fence, there are a couple of smaller patches in the barley field the patches are small but too large to dig out by hand. Hopefully I can find an organic spray, now run along Dorie and get warm and ask your mom if she needs your help this afternoon. If your mom doesn't need your help then you can come along when I go to town." said Paul.

After some time Dorie joined her father who was dehorning cows. In a determined and excited way Dorie said "Dad I can go, mom has no chores for me."

Dorie knew Tom, Molly and George would be able to help X-Cee and keep the help a secret at her request. That afternoon when father and daughter arrived in Purplehaven, Dorie asked her father for permission to see Molly and Tom, adding "Dad I won't ask for treats."

A smile curved Paul's mouth as he thought Dorie and Garth have never had to ask, the treats were always presented with love automatically. He nodded to his daughter. "Go ahead, I'll see you later at the restaurant."

On arriving at the restaurant, Dorie saw Molly, ran up to him saying "I feel as if the world is crashing around me." She spoke with anxiety and fear. "Molly I'm so frightened for my family and a friend." said Dorie with concern on her face while she hopped about. Molly became apprehensive as he had never seen her so full of dismay. He, without meaning to sound stern said, "Dorie sit, you're talking to fast, talk slow, tell me your troubles, is your family safe?

"Yes Molly, at present my family is safe."

The girl sat down and after several minutes managed to calm herself and tell him about X-Cee's fear and dread, her fear for her family and the control and power Jeff had. She told him how one older male student had disappeared and what Jeff had said to his brother Dave about murdering X-Cee. Molly said with a sadness and far away look in his eyes

"Dorie I'll go to the office and talk to Tom and George. No matter what, we will help you. This man Jeff? Very bad, evil, you wait here. I'll come back soon." True to his word he appeared quickly before her with Tom and George in tow. George sat down beside her and asked where X-Cee was now

"Please help X-Cee, he's hiding on our farm and wants to go to his Aunt Bess's home in Ontario if she will allow X-Cee to come."

George said "Do you have Aunt Bess's phone number?"

"Yes I do." And with those words handed him the phone number he requested and her address. "George I don't know how to phone Ontario, but if your show me, I'll ask Jean if I can use her phone."

Molly suddenly became restless and excitable saying, "No no no don't use anyone's phone. Everybody's on a party line, people listen in they just pick up the receiver."

George agreed. "Molly is right. I will go to the office now and call Bess" said George as he hurried away.

Shortly he reappeared and said he had contacted Aunt Bess who was willing to have X-Cee live with her and she would wire money to the restaurant this afternoon for his plane fare. "I have promised to phone Bess as soon as X-Cee leaves Purplehaven.

"The problem is getting X-Cee to the plane and on the plane without Jeff or one of his workers seeing him." George was called to the phone, he listened then said "Thank you Bess." Turning to Molly, George said "Bess said there is a plane leaving Purplehaven at six twenty for Ontario each morning." "This is an excellent time as the criminals should be in bed by four after making their night deliveries and not many workers going to their jobs at five so the possibility of being seen is small at five in the morning but one can't be too careful.

"My big concern is where and when do we pick up X-Cee?" Asked George. "Can you bring X-Cee to the number three highway and get across the road without being seen?" The man began to muse, fading off, suddenly he got an idea. "Would you know someone that lives along highway three that you can completely trust?" George asked.

Dorie replied "My friend's mom and dad, the Jakes' own a gas station and live next to the highway." George became excited, and asked her if they had a green and white banner above their door. "That's my friend's! It's a marvel that we can use their yard." She said.

"Wonderful! It's perfect!" He said his eyes brightening with excitement. "Could you get your friend behind their home by five in the morning?" asked George. "If you're a bit late, that's okay." He added. "There are two things to remember, be on time and don't cross the highway if cars are visible. When no car is in sight then quickly run across the road and head for the rear of the Jake's house. You don't want to be seen crossing the road at five in the morning as it's very unusual to see children out at this time of morning, people would remember and talk. Good luck Dorie, see you in the morning." said George with a wave as he returned to his office.

Molly said "If George's plan doesn't work have X-Cee stay in the under ground hide out and don't visit him except to take food and other necessary items till George can come up with some other method to skirt X-Cee out of Alberta. You're very brave not to put your family in danger like that. We shall keep this secret from your family and all other individuals we know."

Dorie had to wait until it was time to bring the cows home in order to see X-Cee. She had packed and hidden a lunch for him and was anxious to hear his thoughts and feelings about George's escape plan. Also she wondered if X-Cee had a wrist watch she could borrow to keep track of the time, when to get up and when to leave the house as her parents kept the only clock they owned in their bedroom for the night.

"Dad can I get the cows a bit early this evening?"

"Yes you may, what's the rush, thinking of practicing track and field tonight?"

"No Dad I have a big plan I must work on, see you later."

She ran off to collect the hidden lunch, then raced off to the cattle meadow. X-Cee must have been waiting and watching for her as he quietly called out to her from behind a tree. She was cross with him for not staying in the hide out and expressed her angry feelings. Her friend retorted he had to go to the bathroom. When the two friends entered the dugout X-Cee reached for the lunch, he ate while Dorie explained George's escape plan.

Suddenly she noticed his facial expression, which previously was drawn and very gaunt, now was relaxed, his body looked less tense and he had a light in his eyes. She felt he at last had hope he would leave Alberta alive. Dorie noticed X-Cee wore a wrist watch that he had either bought with dirty money or had gotten from Jeff. He handed her the watch when she explained what she wanted it for, but warned her "Don't let anyone see it! Put it in your pocket and keep it there

CHAPTER TEN

Next morning at four thirty Dorie got up and was almost dressed when she heard some movement from her parents bedroom. She froze, what if her father got up? She didn't move waiting for more sounds, ready to dive under her bed covers and pretend she was sleeping. It seemed like an eternity before she realized one of her parents must have turned over, the bed springs always made noise with the littlest movement.

She crept out of the house with the flashlight, making a double check that she had the wrist watch in her pocket. The girl raced through the dark across the field to the hide out, knocking three times on the dugout door. X-Cee came out looking tired and disheveled but smiling. They quickly started toward the creek, running through the woods guided by the first rays of the morning sun which shed their dimness on the path ahead. Reaching the hill they climbed down to the creek, the darkness was deeper in the heavy wooded area near and by the creek so Dorie used her flashlight to find the foot crossing over the creek. Soon they were climbing the hill that would lead them to the railway. They waited on the other side of the railway till the highway was car free, with no car lights seen in a distance in either direction. "Lets go" Dorie whispered. "Move as fast as you can X-Cee" she continued. The two raced across the tracks, down the ditch and over the highway to the back of the Jakes' house just in time, as they turned Dorie and X-Cee saw a car coming down the highway. Now they must keep hidden and wait for George.

X-Cee was shivering and as he went to step on the porch, he missed a step and fell making a large crashing sound.

Soon the porch light went on and Moppet's dad, with his wife close behind, opened the back door. Dorie stood rooted to the ground, wordless, staring at her friend's parents. She felt like kicking X-Cee, hitting him but then she realized she was lucky not to have his lame leg. Suddenly after not receiving any response from the two youngsters Moppet's father said in utter amazement "What are you doing here, this time of day Dorie?" She couldn't answer, she was shocked at being discovered. "Dorie will you please answer me?" Moppet's dad almost shouted. X-Cee was shivering so hard he was shaking.

Dorie said "Could we please come in? X-Cee needs a warm blanket as he's very cold." By this time the shocked Mrs. Jake responded. "What's happening?" Taking one look at the shivering X-Cee she seemed to come to life a little, leaving to get him a quilt. Returning and giving it to the boy, she spoke to her husband. "Dear bring the children in, close the back door, and make a couple of hot chocolates." Mrs. Jake turned back to the two children. "Dorie what are you doing here at this time of day? You should be home in bed!" She paused looking thoughtful. "Has something happened? You're not running away are you?"

"No Mrs. Jake I'm helping my school friend, a ride will soon be here to take him to safety. Mrs. Jake please don't make me talk now, I'm frightened, cold and hungry. It's really a matter of life or death, oh please believe me." The look on Dorie's face was all the convincing Mrs. Jake needed.

"Dorie are we all in danger at this moment?" said Mrs. Jake in a barely audible voice.

Dorie responded "If we're careful there should be very little danger. Please draw the drapes, you have the light on and people can see inside." Mrs. Jake rushed to the drapes pulling the cord and closing off the outside view of the Jake's kitchen. The woman gripping her throat in fear, said "Dorie what have you done?"

Suddenly a soft knock was heard at the back door. No one moved or spoke until a third knock sounded. It was then that Dorie slowly crept to the back door peering through the small glass window. There stood George! Relief flooded through Dorie and she quietly opened the door. He had parked his car at the back porch and now beckoned with both hands saying "Where's the young man I'm to help? We must be on our way!"

"George," Dorie whispered "This is X-Cee." As the boy rose from the chair George took his arm gently and lead him out to the car.

As George put X-Cee in the car Dorie heard him say, "X-Cee get down on the car floor for safety reasons, you won't be seen as easily." Then they drove off into the darkness.

Dorie turned back to the house only to be met by a very angry look from Mrs. Jake who said in a stern voice "Can you give me an explanation for what has happened this morning?" Mrs. Jake guided Dorie to a chair, when she was seated the woman said "When we're involved I need to know what's happening, tell us about the trouble you're in."

Dorie poured out her heart, the great fear she had for her family and the fear if X-Cee stayed in Alberta he would be murdered. "Life is so cheap to these people Mrs. Jake, please don't tell anyone what I have told you not even Moppet." then Dorie burst into uncontrollable sobs.

The girl cried for what seemed forever but finally the tears started to stop and Mrs. Jake handed her a tissue. Dorie stood and said "I must be on my way, get home before my parents miss me by finding my bed empty."

"Please sit Dorie, I'll get some clothes on and drive you home. I promise I won't tell anyone."

Mrs. Jake didn't drive into Dorie's family yard so as not to disrupt the Kinny family she hoped was still sleeping. Dorie thanked Mrs. Jake, ran down the road, up the hill into her yard, hiding the flashlight under the porch. As she entered the house she came face to face with her father. Paul said "Child what are you doing up and dressed?"

"I used the toilet. Since I felt cold I dressed quickly before going out." Paul looked puzzled, thinking perhaps his daughter was getting the flu.

Dorie lay down on her cot turning her head to the wall and cried into her pillow thinking 'I don't like lying, its wrong.' She thought 'I'm so sorry I lied daddy and I wish I could open my heart to you about what happened, but I want to keep you alive.'

Next time Dorie spoke to Molly she learned that X-Cee had phoned George to express his thanks for their help and they were to pass a thank you on to Dorie for all the help she had given him. He said he liked his Aunt and her family. Ontario was a lovely province he said. The boy also would work in his Aunt's window making business, he would earn a salary thus able to save money. Dorie's friend also said he regretted that he wouldn't be able to get in touch with his family at this point, but he would phone George each month.

The Kinny family had moved to the house they were given. The move was slow and long but when completed brought joy to all. Three bedrooms, an alcove, large kitchen and huge living room. Annie loved her big kitchen and pantry.

Dorie felt ecstatic to have her own bedroom with a door which she could leave open, shut, or lock. Her own personal space had a closet, dresser and mirror and a large window with lemon colored drapes, a gift from the Jakes. The room was painted in light yellow, the color of friendship. She no longer needed boxes as she had a closet and dresser.

It was the farm Dorie fell in love with. It consisted of a large pasture area fenced off from the rest of the land, twenty acres of garden land, a huge hill, a wooded area and a rippling creek running between the garden and wooded areas.

The girl loved to sit on the creek bank watching the birds fly about, the small animals scampering along the bank, flowers gone for fall and winter but preparing and resting for their big blooming season next year. Best of all while resting on the bank she liked to listen to the creek that ran near her feet. The creek sounded as if an unseen maestro with a thousand fingers was tapping each pebble and rock giving an end result of a beautiful melody surrounding and enmeshing a person into a deep solitary world blocking out all earthly stimuli. This farm was like a dream world.

Life in general was changing. Since Rita's death Matty and Dorie became closer friends. Moppet had started to date and ran around with a wild crowd. Garth still loved to play pranks, he trained a turkey to dance in a hat which was funny except he taught the same turkey to chase his sister whenever she came out of the house. She wanted her mother to roast the mischievous turkey for Thanksgiving but Annie said "No, its Garths pet, he loves that turkey. Would you like your favorite pet harmed?"

"No mom, you're right no one would want their pet harmed."

"Why don't you find yourself a long narrow light stick and when the turkey comes near you tap it gently on the head, the turkey will soon get the message you're in control."

The girl did find a long thin branch which she kept at her side when venturing out into the yard. The turkey came running at the girl, ready to attack but she gave it a good tap on the head. The turkey retreated and left Dorie alone from then on.

Annie also had a word with Garth about training animals to chase people causing fear and perhaps causing injury. She was hoping her son and his friends would soon mature, take more of an interest in school and plan for the future instead of putting a potato in a farmers car exhaust pipe, painting a neighbor's horse's tail green and exchanging a neighbor's geese with another neighbor's ducks.

Mrs. Kinny was beginning to have back pain but still managed to do a great deal of work on the farm. Paul continued to work hard, looked tired and was taking a lot of aspirin for frequent severe headaches. He asked his daughter if she would help him search in the damp areas for a small plant with pointed leaves and small blue flowers. The plant need not have flowers to identify it as the leaves angled sharply to a very narrow point, from a wide base. The plant could easily be spotted and if boiled slowly for a short period would produce a powerful analgesic. He wanted this powerful herbal medicine for his frequent severe headaches. The two looked all day Saturday for the special plant, finally towards evening when it was time to head home they found two plants they were seeking near the roots of a large tree growing on the creek bank. Paul joyfully called out to the world in general. "These leaves simmered for a short while will take away my headaches. Oh what a happy day! Dorie take note of this place!" Annie kept encouraging her husband to see a doctor but he refused.

The last two years had passed so quickly. During these two years Dorie worked much harder at her academics preparing for grade nine. Mr. Joma was a big help to her. He also had a talk with Garth hoping the boy would take more interest in school and associate less with the rowdy group of boys that were boisterous mischief makers rather than evildoers.

Things slowly began to calm down and just as the daily routine returned to normal Dorie was to start grade nine.

That fall when Dorie started school again she would be bused to the old army barracks near Purplehaven. The van would pick up grade nine and high school students in the Elm school district. She had heard there would be seven students this year, two in grade nine and five in high school.

Matty would be attending high school and Dorie was apprehensive about not knowing any of the students where she was going. She felt the same dread she had when she started grade one.

All too quickly she found herself attending Knotty Woods Junior high school. The grade nine students were dismissed one half hour sooner then the high school students thus Dorie would have a short wait before the van came.

Mrs. White, Dorie's grade nine teacher gave her students several exams in each subject she taught. The test results would help give her the academic level each student was at plus give her an idea of each students weaknesses and strength. The woman soon learned Dorie had little knowledge of the subject English having consistent low marks around 10%. On the fifth day of school Dorie's teacher asked her to remain in the classroom after school dismissal. The girl was full of fear wondering what she had done wrong.

Dorie stayed in the classroom after school was dismissed. Her teacher in a quiet way approached the girl and said she wanted to ask her some English questions and would she mind? Dorie said she didn't mind and explained her former teacher didn't spend much time on English. Her teacher asked her if she could pick out nouns and verbs in a sentence. The girl became fearful, rubbing her leg with her fingers and looking down. Finally she said "Mrs. White I have no idea what a noun or verb is, I'm sorry." Needless to say Mrs. White didn't think Dorie would be able to complete grade twelve with her level of knowledge of English.

"Your knowledge is very good to excellent in your other subjects but English will factor into your other subjects when required to write essays and other written assignments bringing your general average down plus English thirty is a requirement for a high school diploma.

"I am willing to give you a twenty minute English lesson each school day after I dismiss the class, I would also need to give you a lot of English homework."

Dorie replied "Mrs. White I would appreciate the extra help as I very much want to complete grade twelve and attend College!" Dorie thought for a moment then added "Mrs. White I would like to discuss the extra homework with my father, ask him if it will interfere with my farm duties and the time the house lights are put out"

Mrs. White stated "Well young lady, I'll await your answer."

That evening Dorie discussed her lack of knowledge in English and Mrs. Whites offer to help with her father, stressing there would be a lot of homework. "Dad I don't feel I will have the time to do all my homework." Her father knew how important this help was on the farm but he also wanted her to complete high school.

He replied "Dorie, of most importance is your education, for ten months we'll manage. Garth can do more chores, perhaps Alex will help on some of his days off and you can work later in the evening doing your homework and learn to put the gas lights out while we settle. Dorie my little elf go for the extra help, we'll manage."

"Thank you dad." Then Dorie stood on tiptoes to hug her father and kiss his cheek.

Through out the next ten months Dorie worked hard at her extra English homework, always completing her extra work while trying her hardest to help with the farm work. But she was tense and felt guilty about not pulling her weight with the chores, she often lashed out at small irritations.

The family was happy to see the end of the school year. When Dorie brought home her final report card and the family saw a B next to English they felt it was celebration time. Alex treated the family to their first movie. The Kinny family was overwhelmed when they entered the theater and saw the grandness and elegance. The huge screen, the large soft rust screen curtains, the soft plush seats and the aroma of the buttered popcorn. The family comedy brought out peels of laughter frequently from the movie goers. The outing was a fun experience letting all forget their troubles for awhile.

On Dorie's next visit to see George, Molly, and Tom, Molly inquired how she did in English. Dorie smiling said she had passed receiving a B mark. Molly exclaimed "Very good, very good Dorie! Mrs. White is a good teacher, we'll thank Mrs. White and buy her some chocolates and a card."

"Molly I have money for a card and I must pick the card out for her and sign it." said Dorie.

Molly nodded. "I'll take you shopping, you can choose some chocolates and a card and I'll pay."

The girl came back from shopping with a two pound box of chocolates wrapped in yellow wrap with a big white bow and a pretty thank you card.

Dorie's dad drove her to the junior high school so she could present Mrs. White with the gift. The teacher was tutoring students till the end of July so Dorie was able to locate her. She gave Mrs. White a big hug then presented the gift to her. Mrs. White hastily uncovered the chocolates and burst into tears. Dorie lightly put her hand on her teacher's shoulder asking "Are you okay?"

"Yes dear I'm fine and these tears are gratitude tears. Dorie just a thank you card would have been wonderful and conveyed your appreciation. You were so eager to learn and completed all your homework, it was my delight to give you extra help. Hopefully College will become a reality, I'll certainly be praying and pulling for you and if I can be of help please get in touch. Thank you and good luck!"

Dorie felt more confident in grade ten. It was good to have Matty by her side during recess and at lunch time. She adored her math teacher, Mr. Smart, who she felt was an excellent teacher, he kept his students busy and tolerated no silliness. If she had trouble with math she knew he was approachable and he would gladly assist in clearing up her math problems. If she missed a week or more of school he would assign the class a lesson, pull an empty desk up to Dorie's desk and say "Well lassie you've got a bit of catching up to do."

Annie was having back problems, difficulty lifting, bending and walking. She also had gallbladder attacks. The children missed a fair amount of school to help more with the harvest because of their mother's limited ability to do field work.

After Christmas Annie had her gallbladder removed. Paul had sold fire wood and the extra hay in the field to pay for the gallbladder surgery.

During her recovery, Garth needed to do extra chores and help all day Saturday. He got up at five in the morning when his sister did. He got the cows while she packed their lunches, she even made a noon lunch for her father. Paul was cutting down trees and having the horses haul the logs home which were later cut into firewood and piled near the house. He would bring vegetables from the root house to be washed and packaged for the shops in Purplehaven and he needed to throw down hay from the loft into the hay bin. He was kept busy all day and Dorie wished he could rest more.

Garth and Dorie milked the cows, separated the milk, washed up the separator parts, fed the chickens, finished their homework and got ready for school.

After school it was time to do chores, then Dorie cooked a basic meal and Garth washed the dishes. This evening he wanted to talk instead of washing the dishes. He sat down next to his sister and said "Dorie I'm going to work harder at school, I don't want to be a poor farmer. Would you help me catch up with my school work when you've time? So I'll be able to get to my true grade level? You're finishing school so you'll get a better job when you're an adult, aren't you Dorie?"

"Yes Garth, I hope I can graduate and go to college. To be a successful farmer you need lots of land, farm equipment and at times hire workers, seasonal workers are difficult to find. Even if you inherit this farm and work the land you'll always be poor unless you can come up with some creative ideas. Farming is hard work and there are four of us and look how poor we are."

From then on Garth did change his attitude about school, he went out less with his friends and he even asked Mr. Joma to help him catch up with his schooling. The teacher was happy to help Garth and gave him assistance at noon and after school. His sister aided him usually with extra homework on weekends and when she had free time. She was happy to help her brother as he was so receptive to getting help. The girl dug out her grade nine English notes and exercises tutoring her brother when she had time, pleased to think he might go to college and have a better life then they did. Suddenly the youngest Kinny was looking forward to grade nine thinking he had a good future ahead of him.

Paul decided to use his twenty acres of garden land in a totally unique way. He planned on planting five acres of strawberries, one acre of raspberries and fourteen acres of vegetables, planting lots of carrots, peas, beans and potatoes. Then he would place 'you pick your own' signs in Purplehaven and on the roadside near the farm driveway.

In April everyone except for Annie planted strawberries and raspberries. Each weekend they planted rows and rows of berries and after three weeks the task was completed. Then on to vegetable seeding. Paul borrowed money for watering equipment. He was very excited, his excitement aroused his two youngest children who frequently made trips to the vegetable garden to see the little green heads pop through the soil and grow into a plant.

Soon the end of June arrived. Dorie completed grade ten with good marks but Garth passed grade eight with honors.

Paul had planted more grain on the old farm and left the hay field alone. His 'you pick your own' venture was a great success. He also sold cream and eggs thus not having to find buyers in Purplehaven. Annie decided to bake cookies and make home made candy hoping she would make enough money after expenses to pay for her flour, sugar and spices for a year. Her dream was met with much extra money. Paul sold a lot of produce and for the first time he was able to have a bank account that could stay, it wasn't needed to pay off an item or items. The headaches he had vanished with the plant medicine.

The family had worked very hard and it paid off in a big way, less deep were Mr. Kinny's forehead creases, more frequent his smiles, a light shone from his eyes and his walk steps were lighter with a new sense of confidence in them. Next year would be better they would have berries for sale too.

Garth and Dorie helped weed and harvest it and move the hay from the old land to their new barn. Annie looked after the produce sales except on the busy weekends when the whole family helped deal with the many pickers.

The two children had little time for socializing, they spent their time helping their parents. Seeing the happiness in their parents' eyes, in their demeanor, hearing their frequent laughter and seeing the hugs they gave each other meant more to Garth then playing pranks and more to Dorie then eating oranges. This was true happiness they saw.

All too soon, it was time to catch the school van. Dorie had most of the same teachers. This grade eleven school term she would take typing and psychology as her two optional subjects. Her psychology teacher was short, wore a lot of make up, bright flashy clothes and carried a huge handbag that appeared to be half of her size. This teacher had great difficulty controlling the class as the students did a lot of talking, laughing and passing notes.

During one of the students' psychology classes, two boys brought smoke firecrackers. Halfway through the class they distracted the teacher by standing and hopping about while another student lit the smoke firecrackers and quickly placed them under the heating system. Then the mischief makers hollered "Fire, Fire!" as the smoke crackers popped loudly and the smoke billowed out from the heating system. A male voice was heard saying "We're going to have a big fire especially if the system explodes."

The teacher quickly ran out pulled the fire alarm and disappeared down the corridor. She didn't seem to care about the students. The students quickly left the room and headed for the lunch room because of the thick smoke.

The fire team arrived and discovered it was a practical joke. On questioning them none of the students would admit committing the prank and no student would rat on the guilty people. Mr. Odie, the principal, was horror struck by the prank and on questioning the guilty students wouldn't confess and the innocent students wouldn't rat. In frustration Mr. Odie gave the entire psychology class one school week suspension. Dorie was upset as were other students.

The next morning a couple of students went to Mr. Odie and gave him the names of the guilty pranksters. The principle had no compassion for the innocent students as they didn't come forward at the time they were asked who was guilty so they continued to have a school week suspension and the guilty boys now had to remain away from school for two weeks.

On another beautiful hot fall day all the school windows were open and the psychology teacher buzzed in carrying her huge handbag which she plopped on her desk which was situated near a window. "Good morning students we'll be studying egos this morning. Thank you for opening the windows to help cool the classroom." At the exact time the teacher turned to write notes on the blackboard a garbage truck passed slowly with an uncovered collection bin. A student, without giving proper thought, grabbed the teacher's purse, throwing it through the open window and seeing it land in the uncovered bin. It seemed to take only seconds to happen. The students sat glued to their seats in shock as the teacher turned and witnessed her purse being thrown in the bin. The teacher paled, swayed in an unsteady way several times then ran out of the room.

The boy that threw the purse out the window was expelled. The teacher left the high school and never returned. The psychology class was given a stern talk by Mr. Odie on respect for authority which included teachers. "Even if you don't like a person and they have authority over you they deserve your respect unless they bully you, treat you unjustly or attempt to lead you into criminal activity. Students, your fellow classmate's action was reprehensible and you students are blameworthy for not reporting the difficulties occurring in this classroom to me." Mr. Odie said. "Perhaps I could have solved the problems." Before turning Mr. Odie said "I shall teach this class till a replacement can be found." then hastily left the room.

Mr. Odie subbed the psychology class and he was brutal with the numbers of assignments, homework and required text to be read. A form of shame passed over the class, the students could have helped this teacher but most sat back and never even thought of seeking help from the principle.

When they got the new psychology instructor, he also was a very strict man who also gave the students homework each day which he wanted done on a regular basis. He expected passing grades in the students' exams or the disinterested students were to stay out of his class. This incidence seemed to affect the whole school, a certain amount of fear had settled over the students. They talked less during class, worked harder at their school lessons, showed more respect toward their teachers and were aware bad behavior would not be tolerated.

Dorie stopped doing track and field and played volleyball instead but was unable to attend after school practices which kept her off the team. Garth and Dorie were kept busy doing chores and homework which meant that they could do very little socializing. Annie's back was getting worse so Dorie took over some kitchen duties, the heavier types like lifting the cast iron pans and heavier pots on to the stove and off again. She also washed the clothes and hung them outside.

Fall passed and Christmas time neared. Dorie was planning on joining a group of students that would go caroling door to door and make up hampers for needy families in Purplehaven. She also would help Annie plan and prepare Christmas dinner. This year the Jakes, Matty's family, Jean and Harry, Alex and Bubbles, Alec's steady girlfriend, would join the Kinny family for Christmas dinner.

The turkey dinner was tasty and enjoyed by all, then it was time to visit and play games. Out came the checkers, chess, Chinese checkers and snakes and ladders. Garth had finally mastered chess and gave Harry a run for his money.

As Christmas passed away Dorie studied and pre read future lessons in several grade eleven subjects preparing for April when Dorie would stay home to help plant and seed the vegetables. The two children would often study late into the night on Fridays and Saturdays.

June appeared and final examinations were written. Once again Dorie passed with above average marks but Garth passed with honors. The evening when the two brought their report cards home, Paul examined the report marks then said "I must give thanks." walked into the bedroom and closed the door.

Garth looked at Dorie and asked "Now what is all that about?"

Dorie looked thoughtfully at her brother and replied "You are so naive at times Garth."

The 'pick your own' method was a great success and fun especially for Annie who weighted the produce, took the cash and visited with her customers.

Paul, Garth and Dorie weeded, made hay, prepared the vegetables that Annie would can in the evenings. On the weekends the entire Kinny family worked serving customers as that summer strawberries and raspberries were also sold.

Paul and Annie were overcome with their good fortune. Paul was able to see his bank account grow. Annie now could have her back surgery in the big city and there would still be a little money remaining.

The greatest happening in Paul's life would be seeing his children attend college and graduate.

The summer passed quickly. Mr. Joma again was placed in charge of a play festival and he asked Dorie to play Juliet in the play 'Romeo and Juliet'. She hesitated as she felt she wouldn't be able to pre study from Matty's notes and tips on grade twelve work. Also Dorie had a lot of summer work to do on the farm. She wasn't sure she should take off time to memorize lines and act, plus do rehearsals. Her father felt she was young, needed some fun in her life and as she loved acting, he encouraged her to take the acting role telling her they would manage. The girl finally took the role, had a great time plus it also was a learning experience.

Summer ended and Garth and Dorie found themselves back at school. This year Dorie would have to write the government departmental exams that all Alberta grade twelve students wrote in June. She studied late into the night, then closed off the lamp light.

In November the grade twelve students began having great difficulty with math. On visiting the school in December the regional superintendent learned about the math difficulties the students were encountering and the super decided to hold one half hour classes at noon each school day of the week starting in January. The class wasn't compulsory. In January Dorie attended two weeks, then at the beginning of the third week the students were given an exam. Two days later the superintendent returned the marked exam papers. The students that had the highest marks received their exam first. The very last exam paper to be returned was Dories', the instructor approached her desk waving her exam and said, "This person got 15%. I wonder what she is doing in math class". The girl was stunned by the super's grandstanding and of his convergence on her desk and herself. Now every student in the class knew her low mark. Without thinking she stood, frantically ran out of the math class, her eyes blinded by tears. She rushed to her home room desk, sat down laid her head on top of the desk and sobbed in a heartbroken way.

Suddenly she felt a warm hand on her shoulder and heard a gentle voice say "Lassie are you having a school problem, a problem you would like to talk about? Perhaps I can help."

Dorie told Mr. Smart through sobs about the terrible low mark she received in math, how the superintendent waved her math paper around and shouted out her low mark to the entire class and said she shouldn't be in a math class. Mr. Smart didn't talk about the incident, only offering "Dorie, you're fairly strong in math, if you're having a problem I'll set time aside at noon to give you a bit of tutoring. You should definitely write the government exam at the end of the year."

"Mr. Smart," Dorie said "I won't write my government exam."

In disappointment, Mr. Smart bowed his head. "How can you become a success if you don't try? Even if you failed there are many options open it's not the end. You can study during the summer and rewrite in the fall, you can take another year of math while upgrading some of your other subjects but Dorie I don't think you will fail. Don't give up your dreams of college, don't prove him right. Don't give up! I have some excellent work books, I can lend them to you for study purposes, go for it Dorie, put that extra mile in."

CHAPTER ELEVEN

Mr. Smart gave Dorie extra help at noon, her classmates didn't mind or envy her that she was receiving extra help as they too received extra.

As the June finals approached she decided to write the government math exam. The girl was writing the exam due to all the faith Mr. Smart had in her ability to pass the math final and all the help and support he gave so freely. She walked into the exam room determined to do her best.

Dorie felt a great comfort having completed her exams, now to wait for the results which would be mailed out in July. If she failed she would pursue a career in horticulture but if she passed she would take a ten month course in business in which she had enrolled. The Kinny daughter had a job promise in Purplehaven after she completed her ten months course.

Then that dreadful day near the middle of July came. Paul went to Purplehaven and returned with a big white envelope bearing the government stamp. As he stepped out of the car he called "Dorie, this letter is for you!"

His daughter came running realized it was her final marks, stopped short and said "Dad you open the envelope and let me know my mark in math." She turned away from her father afraid to read his face as he read her marks.

Quietness then a loud shout "Dorie you passed and received a B!" Stunned she turned, then stood as if glued to the ground.

Her father was smiling, his heart bursting with happiness when suddenly the young woman realized she would be going to business school. She yelled, ran and flew into her fathers arms crying "Dad I passed."

George had driven Dorie to the large center for her business school interview. She had passed her interview and would be accepted if her math mark was a B or higher. She would start her first semester in Sept. Paul would pay his daughter's tuition. Annie's up coming back surgery and Dorie's tuition would almost wipe out his bank account, but he smiled when he thought for once he could help two of his family members. Yes, Paul felt good about himself.

In early August Paul returned from Purplehaven waving a letter, "Dorie the letter is from Ontario!" His daughter paled, her heart sunk to her toes.

"Dad you should have refused the letter, told the postal people there was a mistake and that they should return the letter. Oh Dad you've made a grave error, you've unknowingly put a lot of lives in danger!" she said, visualizing Jeff's men appearing at the door during the middle of the night, firing guns.

Paul looked at his daughter in a strange way. "Dorie talk to me, tell me what you're afraid of, why does the letter trouble you so much?"

"Dad it probably doesn't make any difference now as there will be a death sentence hanging over our heads"

Dorie told her dad why and how she helped X-Cee escape to Ontario. "No one knew what happened to him, and now he has the stupidity to write a letter endangering his family and our family! Dad what if someone at the post office has a connection with Dave, Jeff or their mother?"

Dorie's father started laughing and couldn't stop for some time. When his laughter stopped silence loomed, then he explained "I think you're the only person in Purplehaven and area that doesn't know that Dave, Jeff, their mother, and whose helpers have gone to trial, found guilty and received long prison sentences. Vera is in a youth prison for two years."

"I'm so glad the gang is in prison! I was terrified you, Mom, Garth, X-Cee and his family might be shot by Jeff's gang!"

"You could have told me sooner, I would have been very careful. Then on the other hand George's plan with your help worked extremely well. I always felt if you had information you would relay it to me.

"One day I encountered Raymond's parents, at first I didn't recognize them, they seemed dazed, almost out of tune with life. They suffered greatly, but still had this uncanny dream they would find their son alive. I felt shattered by the agony of their minds written on their faces showing sadness and emptiness. Often when lying awake in bed, I would visualize the distress of that couple. This vision embittered me, making me angry and filling me with misery. How could such evildoers continue to function in such a small community, why were they not caught? I went to speak to my corporal friend on the police force. The corporal told me they had searched Jeff and Dave's properties not finding any evidence of wrong doing. The police were very puzzled.

"Raymond's parents never gave up hope that he was alive and they would find Raymond one day. In the meantime they couldn't find peace, they always felt unsettled. The story of how he was found was relayed to me by Raymond's father and Whiz when I joined them for coffee in the new coffee house. Every cup perked with love. This is the story.

"Whiz, a former close friend of Raymond, was in a shop and had seen Raymond's parents distraught and sad, still hunting for their only child. He hardly recognized them. They had lost a lot of weight, had haunted sad looks in their eyes, seeming tense and never smiling. He was truly traumatized by seeing the suffering they were going through. While growing up these parents guided and helped him, treated him like their own son. Their home was always full of laughter. He could no longer keep the code of silence and asked them if he could meet with them. They asked him to their home and on entering the house the warm, homey feeling from the past came back and engulfed him. Raymond had loving and caring parents, if only Raymond was alive, why had he let this lovely couple suffer? Why hadn't he come forward sooner? He felt guilty about not approaching them earlier, he felt he would live with that guilt forever.

Sitting at the kitchen table refusing all refreshments, he began to tell Raymond's parents why and how their son disappeared. He told them Raymond was involved with a gang, not a member of the group but worked for them earning extra money. He loved to treat his dates in a special way, taking them to dinner in a special restaurant, then off to a movie, treats during the movie and after the movie dancing at a disco. This part of his social life was costly. Raymond thought his folks were fair with the allowance they gave him each week but he wanted to make a big impression with his dates thus he took the job Jeff offered not realizing it was criminal activity.

"Shortly after he took the job he decided it wasn't the part time employment he wanted so he approached Jeff, promised when he quit he wouldn't talk about Jeff's activity.

"After Raymond quit, Jeff ordered him shot and buried. Jeff's mother who attended all executive meetings was very upset when she heard of Raymond's death sentence and pleaded with Jeff to send Raymond up north to work on her farm which was isolated, had an alarm system, electrical fences and several attack dogs.

"Jeff didn't like the idea but to please his mother he agreed to send the boy up north. Only one man knew he was alive, that man was Dave who transported him to the northerly farm. All other workers were told Raymond had been murdered, this was Jeff's way of keeping his workers in line by instilling fear in their minds, it meant death if they left the organization.

"Jeff's mother packed lunches for Dave and Raymond so they wouldn't use restaurants. If they needed to use a washroom they could stop and enter the woods.

"Whiz said 'The reason I knew about Raymond was because he had written a long letter, wadded the letter up tightly, poked the friendship pin I had given him for his birthday into the wadded letter. He must have thrown the letter out of the car window with a half eaten apple as the apple was lying beside the letter.' Whiz said 'One morning on my way to school I saw something shiny in the ditch, on investigating I found Raymond's pin and letter lying beside a half apple!'

"Whiz said 'I've kept this secret all these months while you folks suffered and while Raymond was isolated. I feel like a lowly louse, I'm as bad as Jeff.' Whiz sat crying, full of remorse while Raymond's mother held him, whispering comforting words.

"Raymond's father said 'We all make mistakes Whiz, we have no hard feelings toward you, let's go to the police and rescue Raymond.' Raymond's mom said 'We are very grateful that you gave us the information you did.' Well Dorie, that's the story," said Paul. "Elm school district will soon hold a welcoming home party for Raymond in Purplehaven town hall."

"Dad what surprises me, no one at high school talked about the arrests." said Dorie.

Paul replied, "Perhaps more parents bought moonshine then suspected and if their children were aware of their parents actions they wouldn't want to discuss the topic."

"Dad we've been talking for an hour and we haven't read X-Cee's letter." She realized, and opened the letter.

"X-Cee's finished his cabinet making course and apprenticeship and Aunt Bess is helping him set up his own business. Aunt Bess will help run the office for awhile. He's met a nice Swedish girl, they are engaged and hoped to marry in a year's time! His family's attitude had softened a lot toward Bess and they invited her and her family to visit. X-Cee's dad is hoping he will help pay off the back taxes which have accumulated once again.

"He ended saying 'I shall never forget your help Dorie, I am alive because of you. When I return I would like to visit. Fondly, X-Cee.'"

Changing the topic, Dorie said "Dad we'll soon be taking that trip I promised you."

Her dad's face softened. "It sounds wondrous."

Next morning Garth asked permission to accompany Iron Side and Howie to the stampede being held in Arrow Woods thirty miles from Purplehaven. Paul felt his son needed a fun break and gave him five dollars from the emergency money box he kept hidden in the house.

When the boys arrived at the stampede, Howie, Iron Side and Garth met a farmer friend who bet Howie ten dollars to ride a small mare into the Laddie Hotel lobby. Howie wanted someone to ride the horse with him. Garth, after some pleading by Howie, agreed to ride the horse if he could sit in front. He didn't think of all the confusion this mare would create when it entered the hotel.

The farmer ran to the double front doors, throwing them open and in rode the boys on the mare. The boys rode once around the lobby, knocking over some furniture while clients ran behind the bar. The farmer ran through the kitchen, opening the back door. As the boys exited the hotel, Garth saw a protruding beam ducked, shouted a warning to Howie who was unable to duck in time. Howie was thrown off the horse, then Garth reached the outside hearing the police sirens he encouraged the mare forward as the farmer ran off in another direction. Garth was stopped by the police one block later, taken back to the hotel to help Howie clean up and rearrange the furniture. The two boys, looking very solemn, apologized to the hotel manager then listened to a lecture given by the police lieutenant. The lieutenant said "This joke could have turned into a grave situation had the horse spooked, trampling people, running over individuals and causing a lot of destruction to the hotel. Because of the seriousness of this hoax you boys will be fined ten dollars to be paid up in three days and don't bother hiring a lawyer."

Howie was angry at his farmer friend. When the police talked to the farmer he kept his mouth shut about the bet and instead lied to the police about the event, telling the police the boys had stolen his horse but he didn't wish to press charges. Howie never did get his ten dollars.

Garth felt ashamed about the mischief he had taken part in, the stunt was really childish and now he would have to ask his father for ten dollars since Howie won't be able to ask his for five. Garth knew Howie would receive a dreadful beating from his father. Howie's body would be covered entirely with bruises having to miss school 'till they disappeared, if his father learned of the prank Howie was involved in and the fine he had to pay.

After arriving home late in the evening Garth decided to approach his father in the morning about his stupidity.

Next morning Garth explained to his father about the silly prank he was involved in and the fine he must pay. He said "Dad I'm so sorry, I can't explain why I did such an idiotic, foolish stunt! It will never happen again."

Paul was angry. "What were you thinking of Garth? I had hoped you had outgrown playing childish stunts. Hotel clients, kitchen staff and others could have been seriously injured had the mare shied and the peopled panicked. Had people been seriously injured you might have been sued and paid damages for a life time!" With a hurt look and a sadness Paul shook his head and retrieved his emergency money box saying "We'll pay the fine this morning and I hope Garth you've learnt your lesson."

"Yes dad I have" he replied

The summer passed quickly with 'pick your own' once again being a great success. The harvest came and went. Garth had gone back to high school and was settling in nicely. George moved Dorie to the business school she would attend.

She found herself surrounded by all new faces, instructors and students where all unknown to her. She felt she was in a foreign land, the huge city was frightening and not knowing a single person was scary. The girl felt she mustn't venture into the city, her main goal was to study and do well. She wanted to learn so she could do justice to the job she had been promised and was waiting for her. As much as she was able, she would stay in her room and study most of the time and go for short walks. Suddenly she felt good she would be fine.

At the school, a study group was formed inviting only students that were totally serious and committed to their studies. Dorie was delighted when asked to join. She liked the group which often went to the park after dinner when the weather was nice to pour over their books. At times they studied individually, at times as a group and always closed their session with questions and answers, helping any students who had difficulty in a particular part of their course.

The group visited and interacted over lunch, discussing world affairs, politics, Canadian business, and money matters. Dorie bought a small radio at the corner store so she could listen to the morning and evening news.

Dorie was very grateful George had given her seventy dollars for personal items and entertainment. Her father had given her ten dollars for spending money. She wrote home once a week telling her parents about the study group, friendships she developed, and the excellent marks she received. The two eagerly awaited her letters, happy about her social adjustment and good marks.

It seemed Christmas had arrived much too quickly. George picked up Dorie and brought her home for the festive season.

Jean invited the Moppet, Matty and Kinny families to the large Christmas Day meal she cooked. It was a fun day catching up on the news, eating and playing games.

With the holidays over Dorie looked forward to returning to school and her new friends. The study group decided to see West Side Story, a movie everyone was talking about. She was so thankful for the money George, Tom, and Molly gave her at the beginning of the school term, allowing her to accompany the study group on occasional outings. She had also received some nice clothes for Christmas from her three Chinese friends. Dorie felt good about being able to dress up occasionally when going out.

As time passed the study group had become more like family, being loyal to each other, showing kindness, patience, a cell of harmony except for little spats but always being there for one another. A lot like brothers and sisters.

The first part of March the study group went to see Fiddler on the Roof. After this play the group settled down to studying for the finals in early April. If the students passed their finals with an eighty per cent or greater average they were given their diplomas and allowed to leave. All other students were given intense classes by the instructors and allowed to rewrite their finals the end of April.

George picked up Dorie on April sixth with her diploma and baggage. She would commence her new job June first.

Molly, Tom and George gave Dorie one thousand dollars as a graduation gift. Paul felt that was too large a gift and wanted her to return nine hundred of it but Molly refused to take the money causing a strife between the men for awhile. Molly kept saying to Paul 'You're my family, Dorie is like my child, I'm proud Dorie finished school. We're proud of Garth, he'll become a doctor one day.' Paul finally relented and took up friendship again with the three men he cared about.

Dorie helped on the farm till May when she heard of a two week temporary employment position in a large home for the elderly situated in Purplehaven and run by two sisters, sister Minnie and sister Martha. Paul took Dorie into Purplehaven to fill out an application and book an interview. The job turned out to be a very responsible job, the individual hired would be answerable for the care of all the residents and the running of the institute for two weeks.

Dorie soon learned she was the successful applicant, little did she realize she was the only individual to apply.

The orientation conducted by sister Minnie made Dorie become edgy and frightened at the responsibility she must shoulder. Sister Minnie had preordered a lot of supplies and made menus up for two weeks. Dorie would give four medications to three individuals each morning, the other residents would be responsible for their own medications as usual. Each morning she would check on all tenants then help with morning care and see that breakfast was on time. After breakfast she was to check with the chef about food supplies and order as necessary. She would have to deal with complaints and frictions between staff and residents, between staff members and listen to family concerns. She would be on duty twenty-four hours being called during the night only for emergencies.

Dorie soon found out she had a lot of support and help from the senior caring staff that had worked at the institution for years, they continually helped her and gave her advice which she accepted graciously. The staff saved Dorie's hide so to speak. The wonderful staff knew what they felt like when they were barely twenty.

Dorie was told by the staff that many of the residents living in the home had made many sacrifices and worked long hours when they came to Canada as pioneers. Then as they became unable to work on their farms or live in their homes they were forced to downsize and ended up having a small room in an institution. They were used to large open spaces, their own home and they were always kept busy, now time passed slowly and they weren't in charge of their lives.

Dorie found the staff caring and kind, going that extra mile to tend to the residents needs and small desires. She was also told if a resident requested purple curtains and a crimson bedspread staff was not to be critical but respect their wish and work with family to make their dream come true.

The elderly were full of wisdom and liked to talk. Dorie was soon caught up in a world of caring and respect. The elderly liked touch; a hug, a touch on their shoulder or taking and holding their hand. They loved music and most of all a cheerful face. The rule, Dorie was told was that the residents wishes were to be filled if possible if their ideas or plans weren't destructive or harmful to others and themselves. Staff were never to argue with the elderly.

'Sisters Minnie and Martha must be extremely wise and loving to have taught their staff the act of caring, giving, respect toward others and how to bring joy into the work place.' The young woman figured.

One old eccentric man lived in the loft. He needed to live alone and away from the other folks, as he didn't interact well with people. He believed he was a scientist and seemed happy when building electronic devices and he felt he eventually would build a mechanism that would be a big service for the world. The man's family took him shopping for metals, wires and batteries, then this elderly scientist worked on his latest new invention. When the elderly gentleman asked to test his creation, he was taken to an empty lot behind the complex. Occasionally his creation would shoot out a few sparks or explode in a small way bringing big smiles to his face and excitement to his body as he jumped up, hopping about and waving his arms thinking he was close to building his masterpiece.

Dorie and Liz the chef became good friends, went for walks after dinner clean up or sat on the terrace talking after the residents had settled.

Sister Martha came back two days early. Martha was cranky, had a tongue like a whip, never smiled and often found fault with the staff's work which most staff ignored but she was always kind and gentle with the residents.

Liz always became tense and edgy when Sister Martha came to the kitchen. On Dorie's last day, Liz was running a bit late for dinner so as a favor she stayed in the kitchen helping by mashing the potatoes, draining and bowling the vegetables and putting three plates of buns out. Liz was placing the cooked fish on the platter when Sister Martha appeared in the kitchen doorway yelling "We're all waiting for the food, what's the holdup!?" She then turned and left.

Liz, in her rush to carry the plate of fish to the dining room slipped, tossing fish in all directions. She looked at Dorie with a fear struck face. "What do I do?" She whispered.

"Liz quick lets pick the fish up!" Said Dorie as she dashed to pick up the platter and reached for the spatula, moving very quickly putting the whole and broken pieces of fish on the dish. She was soon joined by her friend and in record time the fish was off the floor just as Sister Martha reappeared shouting to bring the food to the table, not noticing fish crumbs on the floor or the two friend's red faces. Dorie quickly swept the floor then helped the chef carry the food out to the dining table.

Dorie was sad to leave her care giving job and she would miss Liz's company and the residents. Sister Minnie told her she had done a fine job and everyone seemed pleased with how the care home had been run. Dorie knew the staff had actually run the home and she was very thankful for all their help and support.

After helping her father on the farm for two weeks Dorie started her new job. Her main goals were to do a good job for the company that hired her and to save as much money from her wage as possible after paying her rent and buying a cheap used scooter that would take her to her parents' farm so she could check on them and help them especially on days off.

She bought a scooter from a co-worker for thirty dollars since he had upgraded to a new car. He was happy someone else could use his scooter.

Thursday evening Dorie went to her parents' farm to visit and help. Annie had received a letter from the surgical department requesting that she be admitted Friday and surgery would be performed Monday morning. Paul had been planning to travel to Purplehaven and ask George if he would take his wife to the large city for surgery as he didn't feel he could rely on his car to make that lengthy trip but now he asked Dorie to contact George and ask for his help. If the man was able to take his wife for him, he should phone Jean who would relay the message. Dorie thought how wonderful it would be to see her mom pain free and able to walk properly.

George said he would pick Annie up at ten on Friday, then phoned Jean and asked her to deliver the message to Annie and Paul.

Monday afternoon the big city center hospital phoned Alice and asked her to give Paul a message. She was to say Annie had tolerated her back surgery well, would be in the hospital ten days then sent to a rehabilitation center for three weeks. The woman delivered the message to the two Kinny boys who had anxiously been awaiting post surgery news about Annie. Mr. Kinny was looking forward to his wife being well once again and home.

Near the end of September, Garth left for the baseball series in Arrow Wood. He played baseball for the Purplehaven Badgers. The Badgers were in the semi finals to be played Friday and Saturday. The finals were played on Sunday. Garth was traveling with Iron Side's parents and they would all stay with a relative.

Dorie had visited a travel agent to ask about costs of fares, hotels and meals, she also asked about places of interest in Canada and if she could have some books with interesting places to see and the costs. She then told the agent how much money she had saved. The agent asked her to wait while he went through all his files, eventually telling Dorie she had enough money to travel with her father pretty much anywhere in Canada for at least five days, depending on how far she wanted to go. There was sufficient money for hotels, food and sightseeing. Dorie told the agent she would return after talking to her dad. That evening she checked her bank book to make sure the figures were correct, then looked through the travel booklets. Suddenly a feeling came over her, making her want to shout, jump up and down, sing, she was over come with joy! Paul Kinny would soon go on a trip, this wonderful man who always put everyone first! Tomorrow after work they would talk, make plans. Garth could look after the farm for a few days.

After having a light lunch following work on Sunday, Dorie hopped on to her scooter and headed for the farm. When she drove up to her old home she noticed no movement. Her father was probably bringing the cows home, she would start supper then help with the chores.

On entering the old house through the porch Dorie noticed the kitchen door open. Taking four more steps she could see her father lying on the kitchen floor. She gasped, froze, cried out, fear gripped her as she approached the form on the floor.

CHAPTER TWELVE

Dorie looked down on her dad; she knelt quietly saying "Daddy, Daddy what's wrong?" slowly he opened his eyes, seeming too weak to talk but still reached his hand out to his daughter. She received his hand but it was extremely hot, like an ember. His hand slipped out of hers and fell to the floor, shutting his eyes he moaned. She looked startled, pleading "Daddy talk to me! Tell me what's wrong!" But Paul made no verbal response, just opened his eyes looking dazed and he seemed to have a glazed look to his eyes almost as if a film was pulled over his deep blue eyes. The girl whispered in her father's ear "I'll get help, be right back, I love you and have great news for you."

With tears in her eyes Dorie rushed to her scooter, leaving the yard at a reckless speed, headed for the nearest neighbor, Mr. Cheus. Mr. Cheus and his son Nick came rushing out when she drove into the yard at smash-up speed. When the girl got off her scooter she started to collapse and was caught by Mr. Cheus who held her upright. After several minutes she was able to say "My Dad is very ill, he needs to go to the hospital."

Mr. Cheus said "Come Dorie, we will take your father to the hospital."

When her neighbors had placed Paul in the back seat of the car with a pillow under his head Dorie climbed in the back of the car and sat on the floor so she could watch her dad and hold his hand.

The young woman felt she was in a strange unreal world, surely she was dreaming and would wake up any minute! Then she would look at her barely conscious dad whose hand felt like fire and knew this was reality, no dream.

At the hospital the staff carried Paul into an emergency examining room by stretcher. After some time Dr. Parr approached Dorie with a worried look and told her "Your father is very ill, his temperature is dangerously high, he is delirious. Were you able to get any coherent responses from him?"

"No Doctor. Parr, Dad would open his eyes and look straight ahead when I spoke to him but he never replied."

"We've started IV's and antibiotics, we'll have to work aggressively to bring that high temperature down. At this time I have no idea why your father is ill, it could be viral." Then Doctor Parr rose, and said as he walked away "I'll keep you posted."

Dorie knew she must notify her family but first she wanted to visit her father who had been admitted to a room downstairs. As she arrived at his room she found the nurses very busy with him, she left planning on going to her small suite eight blocks away to make her phone calls.

The landlady let Dorie use her phone, and she would give her the costs when the bill came in.

She phoned her mother at the rehabilitation hospital. Annie seemed very upset and said she would phone her half brother Mefo and have him drive her to Purplehaven, hopefully she would be at the hospital in an hour's time. Next she phoned Alex who said they'd be at the hospital in half an hour and yes he would phone the stadium in Arrow Woods and have Garth come home as soon as possible.

Dorie returned to the hospital and as she walked past the nursing station a nurse jumped up and took her arm. "Dr. Parr is in his office and would like to speak to you."

The young woman turned to the nurse and shook her head. "Please I would like to look in on my dad first."

"Come this way its important you speak to Doctor Parr first."

When she was seated across from the doctor, he spoke in a soft voice. "I'm sorry to tell you your father died twenty minutes ago following a grand mal seizure. We were unable to resuscitate him. Dorie I don't know what to say." Abruptly she placed her head on the desk and sobbed uncontrollably. She wasn't able to fathom her father being dead, she couldn't process the news 'Your father has died.' They were going on a trip, she had enough money! Was she dreaming? Having horrid thoughts? Or had she heard wrong? Anguished sobbing stopped her from talking. She did hear Dr. Parr call a nurse and say "Doesn't this girl have any relatives?"

At that moment Alex appeared, and ran to Dorie's side, holding her and whispering comforting gentle words. Finally he said "Dorie lets go for a walk outside."

As she rose, Garth rushed in and over to his sister crying "Dorie this hurts! My world seems to have fallen apart! Does mom know?"

Alex replied for Dorie. "Yes Garth, mom knows. Lets go outside to the park." The grieving group left the hospital and headed for the park benches where they could watch for their mother's arrival.

When she did arrive, the two boys went to meet their mother while Bubbles, Alex's girlfriend, stayed with Dorie. As the group approached them, she heard her mom say "Its my fault, if I hadn't had back surgery Paul would still be alive, how could I have been so inconsiderate to leave him alone?" Dorie ran to her mother hugging and holding her tightly.

"Mom, its no one's fault and you needed your back surgery, you could hardly walk! Please we mustn't blame ourselves as Dad would say, it's just part of life, and there is no explanation why tragedies happen. I'm going back to my suite."

Garth replied "Come home with us instead!"

"No Garth I need to be alone." And she walked away.

When Dorie entered her suite she fell upon the sofa and cried until she felt exhausted, she called out to her father "Daddy, Daddy why did you leave me, I was all prepared to take you on a trip! Oh daddy now you've left taking a big part of my heart. Daddy I don't have a heart anymore!" Then she collapsed, drifting in and out of sleep.

The funeral came and went, Dorie recalling very little of the day her father was buried. Now the family must decide what to do about the farm.

As the Kinny family grieved broader more complicated issues arose. Annie would not be able to manage the farm alone, with hired help the financial returns would be small. Garth would start grade twelve next year and he really wanted to study, get top grades so he would be assured a place in medical school.

Harry and Jean suggested Annie get a job in Purplehaven, sell the livestock and rent the farm. Jean said "Annie you can clean, you're an excellent cook, you sew and you could clerk, there are many possibilities."

"You're forgetting Garth," She countered. "He's still a boy, he must fit into this picture as well."

"Yes Annie Garth's home should be with you."

Dorie went to the farm on her days off to help her mother. This time when Dorie arrived at the farm on her day off she entered the kitchen grinning widely. She ran to her mother hugging her and saying "Mom we got some good news. My boss' cook-cleaner has moved to New Brunswick to look after her father. Apply for the job Mom it's easy and pays well!"

"Slow down Dorie, tell me more!"

"Mom you would have a two bed room suite, your board is free as well. You cook lunch, dinner and clean four offices, reception room and bathroom in the evening. Mom if you ask the boss, I'm sure Garth can stay with you and you only pay board for him!

"More good news! I visited Molly yesterday after work and he knows a young English couple that will rent the farm, livestock and all else!"

Annie looked up toward the sky and said "We're being helped, isn't it wondrous?" She then broke into tears saying in between sobs "Our family has faced very hard times and always managed with unexpected help and guidance. The help just suddenly appears as the opportunities your news just brought."

Dorie's boss, Elfin, agreed to interview Annie. He needed help very soon and if Annie was like her daughter, an excellent worker, there would be no problem placing her on his pay roll.

Dorie gave her mom money to buy a new dress, shoes and get a haircut. She wanted her to look nice, Annie had good fashion sense and would choose nice clothes.

She looked lovely in her new bright pink wool dress with wide white sash and high white neckline. She wore black pumps and her thick brown hair cut shoulder length shone as the sun's ray's came through the glass panes and landed on the chocolate coloured strands.

As Dorie's boss came through his office doorway, he stood still, his heart thumped, he was at a loss for words as he gazed at the beautiful woman before him. Elfin had never married, there was never a women he wanted to marry, he was happy and content with his business but he felt this was about to change. Was he getting senile? He must be, to think of marriage at sixty. It seemed like ages before he could speak, finally saying "Good morning." and when Annie turned from the window Elfin looked into a startling pair of deep blue eyes, once again he was robbed from words. Finally jolting himself into reality he said in a harsh tone "Have a seat." He hadn't wanted this woman to notice his silliness. "Annie, Dorie told me you would make a good candidate for the open position of house keeper. Do you like to cook and clean?"

"Yes, I enjoy cooking and don't mind cleaning."

"At times we're short staffed when someone calls in sick, would you mind helping out in other areas like answering the phone, place orders I give you or accepting and counting incoming supplies and signing for them?"

"Yes I would be able to assist" Was her reply.

"Well that's final, welcome to our staff. Can you start next Monday?"

"Sir I have a very important question to ask. I have a son in grade eleven who plans on attending medical school. I would like him to stay with me 'till he completes high school, be there for him, help him in anyway I can. I would gladly pay board for him. I won't allow parties and Garth is good he wouldn't bring a lot of friends home. Would you still like me to join your staff?"

Looking at this loving caring mother he knew if he wasn't careful he might sign his business over to her. "Yes Annie Garth can move in, no parties, or acting out in front of the business, or inside by the offices and reception room. Garth and his friends are to stay in the suite at all times. No noisy vehicles around this area and he is to pay twenty five dollars a month for board. Will I see you Monday?"

Annie replied, "Yes I shall be here and thank you!" Elfin nodded.

"I was sorry to hear of your husband's death Annie." Turning, Annie left making no reply.

One evening Elfin approached Annie and asked if she felt Dorie should leave Purplehaven for awhile, the place that reminded her of her father, be with young people, study, learn, going to a higher level of education. Annie thought about it before nodding her head.

"Dorie needs a change, she has some money saved but it would never see her through two or three years of education. I am happy and proud she got one year of business education. It will be extremely difficult to see Garth through medical school but to help Dorie as well would be impossible."

"Would you object if I arrange a free two year business degree for Dorie in a large Quebec city?"

Annie replied "I would be very happy for Dorie but how would this be possible?"

Elfin smiled. "Anz offers a two year free business course, earning a student a business degree. Anz staff is aging and new young staff is needed for replacing retirees. Giving a two year free degree is a way of helping regain some staff as people retire."

"Elfin that would be marvelous!" She exclaimed before returning to her cleaning.

Next day Elfin called Dorie into his office and asked her to be seated. "Each year Anz offers a two year business degree, all expenses paid. The students live in residence, a large twelve bedroom house located near the Anz business. The house also has a small snacking kitchen, living room and four bathrooms. Students eat in the main Anz dining room. You attend business school for four hours and work four hours in the business departments. You're paid a small monthly salary to help purchase personal items.

"Dorie you would love this large city in Quebec, it has a European atmosphere. This opportunity is a plum. I know you need time to think about this chance and talk it over with your family, but could you get back to me in two days?"

"Yes Elfin you will have your answer in two days, it really is a great opportunity to advance myself. Thank you for thinking of me."

Two days later Dorie gave Elfin the news, she gladly accepted Anz's offer. "We'll fill out the necessary forms after lunch and I'll phone the president now to tell him you're an excellent choice and tell him I'll be sending the necessary paperwork today to the head office. If you're accepted could you be ready to leave Thursday and start school on Monday?"

"Oh yes, yes," said Dorie hopping about bringing a twinkle to Elfin's eyes.

"The school is wonderful for the month you missed they will soon help you gain equal footing with your classmates, Dorie I know you'll do well. How does your mother feel about you leaving home?"

"Mom is happy for me, she thinks you're very kind and caring." Elfin suddenly felt weak, giddy like a boy, perhaps one day Annie would grow to care for him.

Elfin knew the president very well, they were good friends. Over the phone the president had said 'Send this young lady to our school, have her there by next Monday. The application papers will be a formality. I trust your judgment Elfin'

Dorie was given the next two days off with pay. She had the money she had saved for traveling with her dad, now she would use that money for her fare to Quebec, buy two suitcases and have spending money for the two years she would be in school.

The day of departure came swiftly it seemed. Harry picked up the suitcases, taking them to the train station to be checked. Dorie had given her mother money to purchase the ticket which she did.

As Dorie approached the platform, tears filled her eyes as she noticed the group that had come to say goodbye. There stood Mom, Garth, Jean, Harry, Matty's family, Moppet's family, Elfin, and her three beloved Chinese friends. They all had come to say good-bye. As her friends gave her parting gifts they were placed in a shopping bag: two books, a book of poetry, a beautiful garnet ring, a beautiful green sweater, a bag of oranges held by an embarrassed George. Dorie hugged George and said "You have made my day! You always know what to buy!" Suddenly George beamed, Dorie was so nice.

The young woman also had two sealed envelopes given to her. Then came hugs and the shout 'all aboard!' Final call. She raced for the entrance steps, suddenly she spun around shouting "I love you all!" blew kisses, spun around and climbed the steps to the conveyance that would take her to a place that held many unknowns.

The train ride was long but the books and two oranges a day took the boredom away. Dorie was met by an Anz worker driving a company car when she made her exit off the train in Quebec.

The van driver carried her luggage up to her room. She would be sharing a room with a girl from Greece who was awaiting her arrival. After exchanging greetings with her roommate Dorie took a quick shower and settled into bed.

Next morning Dorie found herself in class sharing a study table with a young male named Keith. Tables were more convenient then desks for business classes as they had more top room, holding more business tools that the students might use several times a day.

Dorie loved the city and the French Canadian people, they were colorful, had a good sense of humor, and were very helpful. Wherever one looked you spied flower boxes sitting atop balcony railings, interesting shops, breath catching boutiques and restaurants that served unbelievable tasty food. Dorie thought 'Oh how Daddy would have loved this beautiful city!' wiping tears away as memories flooded her mind.

Dorie became friends with Keith and they took to exploring the city in their free time. He wasn't from around there either. Not many people in her class were.

One evening Keith got the news his father had been killed in an automobile accident. He, who was very close to his father, wouldn't be able to go back to New Zealand for the funeral so he grieved deeply. The afternoon he received the news Dorie stayed with him and they talked far into the evening.

On her exploration the young woman had noticed a large flower shop three blocks away. Next day after school she went to the flower shop to buy two yellow roses for Keith; Yellow roses meant friendship.

She waited in line ahead of an attractive young lady. When the flower shop owner called out 'Miss Kinny' both Dorie and the young lady stepped forward. The shop owner looked at the two. "Would Dorie Kinny please place her order?"

She purchased two yellow roses and started to leave when the young lady with the same surname took her arm and said "Please wait for me Dorie."

After the young lady made her purchase she went to meet Dorie near the doorway. "I'm Rose Kinny and I wonder if we're related? There are only four Kinny families in Canada and I knew my dad had relatives in the West, a place called Purplehaven."

Dorie's eyes widened. "That's the name of my home town!"

"Lets go and talk over a cup of coffee, there is a tea and coffee house next door."

When the two young women were seated over steaming cups of coffee, Rose said "I'm very interested in family history especially when it comes to my own. As I researched my family history I discovered I have an Uncle Paul, Aunt Annie, two male and one female cousins living in Purplehaven."

Dorie gasped, looked in total disbelief, then in amazement as she realized she had living relatives other then in and around Purplehaven.

"Dorie you must visit and meet mom, Violet, Lily, and Teddy! My mom loves flowers, so she named all her daughters after blooms. She'll be so happy to have found relatives. We were going to visit Purplehaven next year to meet our relatives. Mom was an only child and both her parents were only children and Dad wasn't interested in renewing ties with kin. Now that Dad has passed on, Mom more then ever wants to connect with family she knows live in Canada. Can you come for dinner tomorrow evening?"

"Rose check with your mother first and if she has other plans call me at this number. I do have a day off tomorrow. I'm delighted I have relatives here and I know I didn't converse much but I'm in a state of shock!"

Rose giggled and said "Mom will throw the questions at you. I must go can't be late for dinner!"

Dorie finished writing the number down and handed it to the other, waving. "Bye Rose, see you soon."

Dorie walked away, thinking how nice to have relatives here and she looked forward to meeting her new found Aunt and cousins.

That evening Rose called and invited Dorie to dinner the next evening. "M is very excited and has the chef in a tizzy, she keeps changing her mind what we should eat! Lily said she overheard the chef saying to the maid 'you'd think the Prime Minister was coming to dinner!'"

Next day as Dorie was dressing for dinner she reflected over the test results she received. Mark wise she placed second, first in her practical exam and work experience. She contributed her high marks to the extra help she received from her instructors, belonging to her former study group, and her work experience with Elfin who was such a good teacher. She felt fortunate for her business background and felt she could slack off her studies for a couple of weeks.

Rose came with the chauffeur to pick Dorie up. The family lived in a mansion on Mount Royal and was very cultured. She suddenly felt out of place. Her cousins had grown up surrounded by wealth and attended private schools and were chauffeured morning and evening. The three girls now worked in the family business, Rose being on holidays at present.

The Kinny family was kind, caring and very welcoming in a pleasant way. Laughter rang out frequently and they loved and protected each other in a strong way. Dorie had a very enjoyable evening, soon overcoming her feelings of being inferior and thought 'What a wonderful world this would be if all people were like my new found relatives!'

The meal was delicious, the chef requested to meet Dorie, this very important person. She was surprised when she looked down at the smallish, pretty, wide eyed girl and the young woman responded by saying "Dinner was delightful I wish you worked for me!" which brought howls of laughter and a big smile from the chef.

Life suddenly was fun and very busy. Rose became part of Dorie's life in a big way. If the two had free time they window shopped, browsed through antique shops, visited the market places and had occasional lunches out. Keith took a shine to Rose and soon a romance blossomed. Regardless of the romance Dorie still saw Rose and her family and developed close ties.

One afternoon Dorie was handed a letter by her resident house mother. The envelope was from her mother and Dorie eagerly tore open the letter. The anticipated joy soon vanished, as she read on Dorie suddenly felt ill, hurt, anguished and betrayed, something she dearly loved was snatched from her. The farm, her dear farm was sold.

Dorie had pleaded with her mother not to sell the farm. After school she would work and save, pay her mother more for the farm then she would receive on the open market. Her dream of owning the farm was gone. Why didn't her mom let her know before she sold it? Perhaps Dorie could have gotten a loan from Molly and paid him back when she stared work! "Oh mom why did you sell the farm?!"

The young woman was crying, she needed to go for a walk, be alone. There was a small park near pine street with a bench, the park would be vacant this time of day. She reached the empty park heading for the park bench, sitting with her head tilted into her arm as she wept. How ironic the last thing she treasured was gone. Dear Garth wrote letters and occasionally phoned, when she was to next speak with Garth she would ask why Annie had sold the farm.

Sitting and crying she didn't hear a person approach until she heard a male voice say "Can I join you on the bench?"

Dorie looked up, wiping at her tears as she said "Yes, please seat yourself." At that point she turned and looked into the most beautiful sky blue eyes she had ever seen. She shook her head and thought 'What lovely eyes!'

"Thank you, I'm Joel. I feel much like you do and need to hash around in my mind the sad news I received this morning."

"I'm Dorie, if you want to talk, I'll listen and later if you'll listen I'll talk." Joel smiled.

"Sounds like a great idea." Joel was an agricultural and research engineer with a lot of chemical experience. The company he worked for promised him a partnership but when an opening at long last was available it was given to the President's young newly graduated son who had no experience. He was told he didn't receive the position as he wasn't fully bilingual. "Dorie I handed in my resignation to the President's dismay, I had worked so hard to build the firm up.

They desperately tried to change my mind but I said no. I was moving on since they had broken a major promise. After packing up my belongings I went to a main rival firm filled out an application form and was asked to wait, then the vice president appeared, bid me into his office and after a short interview hired me as senior engineer of their agricultural engineering department.

"Its a good job, better pay and good hours but I hurt a lot being thrown aside for a wet behind the ears graduate. I'll work twice as hard building up the rival firm and I've signed up for French classes three evenings a week."

When Joel finished talking he asked Dorie to tell her story of sadness. She told him of the dream farm with the musical creek that she wanted to purchase from her mother when she went back to work. Today she had received a letter from her mom telling her the farm was sold. No warning, no time for her to make financial arrangements, take out a loan. The tears began to roll down her cheeks and Joel slid over on the bench, put his arm around her and held her close 'till the tears stopped flowing. They talked till dusk became apparent then he took her out for dinner. A closeness soon developed between the two.

They studied and worked hard but a couple of times a week they took long walks together or talked over coffee but always they did a fun adventure on the weekend. They explored the Laurentian Mountains, a crescent mountain range that ended in the Arctic. They watched beautiful colorful maple leaves red and yellow. They also climbed Mount Royal one weekend, spreading their blankets on the ground, then looked up at the stars while they listened to the orchestra play classical music.

Another weekend, some of Dorie's classmates and some of Joel's friends cooked Shish Kabobs over an open fire pit on St. Helen's island. The skewers had been forgotten so clothes hangers unraveled were used to cook the small pieces of meat and veggies. A student had brought a pot of rice, Joel brought two thermos' of coffee, Dorie had bought two loaves of fresh bread. Rose and Keith came loaded down with paper plates, cups and plastic tools for eating. What a fun afternoon!

One evening while Joel and Dorie were walking in the park he told her he was being sent to Peru for three months to help analyze a new tree disease and plant fungus. He was to help find the cause and come up with a treatment if possible.

Saying goodbye to him was hard. Dorie felt she would be lost without him. At the airport the man said "When I get back, I have an important question to ask you, I hope you'll be able to give me an answer."

"Can't you ask the question now?"

"No Dorie the circumstances need to be special." He chuckled. "See you in three months Dorie, I can hardly wait to get back." Bending, he kissed Dorie's cheek.

As he was about to enter the boarding area she called to him "I'll miss you a lot!" Then Joel blew Dorie a kiss and disappeared.

Dorie remembered the kiss on the cheek but it was the soft sky blue eyes she saw each night before falling asleep. Three months would pass quickly.

CPSIA information can be obtained at www.ICGtesting.com
Printed in the USA
LVOW102345050313

322844LV00031B/2029/P